This book is a work of fiction. Names, characters, businesses, organizations, places, events and incidents are either a product of the author's imagination or are used fictitiously. Any resemblance to actual persons, living or dead, or locales is entirely coincidental.

Published by Griffyn Ink

www.griffynink.com

For ordering information or special discounts for bulk purchases, please contact Griffyn Ink at Mail@GriffynInk.com.

TOUCH OF MAGIC | BOOK TWO

DREAMWALKER

SAVANNAH KADE

CHAPTER 1

Yasmin froze at the sound of the gruff voice, knowing what the man wanted without even having to turn around.

Fear rushed through her, adrenaline kicked in, and that was bad. Fear meant she was out of control. But how was she supposed to overcome fear when she instinctively knew—felt in her bones—that this man wanted to kill her?

Likely he'd hidden in between the cars and jumped up after she walked by, but that wasn't important. What was important was that she hadn't seen him, hadn't been on the lookout. The day was going far too well; she should have been more alert.

Inside her head, his thoughts cut through her own like cars careening down a busy street. His need to kill her fought with his desire to not pull the trigger. The pressure surged like a headache. She could almost feel her own hand shaking like his was.

None of that mattered. What mattered was she could not die like this. She would not get shot down by a man who wouldn't face her. She could not leave this as her legacy. For herself, she would fight.

"Aunt Meeni?" The little voice at her side was exactly why she not only had to fight, she had to win.

Her sister's daughters clung to her, her charges for the week, after their mother dropped them off for a spur-of-the-moment business trip. Yasmin would not get killed in front of them in a grocery store parking lot for a gang initiation. She knew that's exactly what this was. Exactly what everyone in Los Angeles feared most. But she was afraid of something else. She would not leave her sister that way and she would not leave the girls scarred from watching their aunt die.

Squeezing each small hand, she whispered. "It's going to be okay. But you do *not* turn around until I tell you to. Tell me you understand."

The gang kid behind her must have understood what she was doing, and he would have let her do it, too. Instead he was prodded by the second one. Older, harder, practically soulless, she felt him there now as well, along with several other pairs of eyes watching her from various points out in the distance allowed by the parking lot and the street beyond. In her bones, she could almost feel the purr of the getaway car engine.

In her mind, she heard the second voice as he applied pressure, though she was really too far away to catch the sound with her ears. "Do it now. Don't tap out on me, man."

The first one yelled out to her. "Bitch! Turn around!!"

The little hands flinched in her own. She heard Leyla, the seven-year-old say "yes." She understood. In her peripheral vision, Yasmin saw Maryam nod, too.

So Yasmin barked at them, "Get down!" as she jerked around to face her attacker.

Spinning counterclockwise, the universal direction for 'no,' she brought her left arm up, elbow out, palm toward the kid with the gun. With her right first finger she unconsciously drew a circle on the pavement encompassing both herself and, more importantly, the girls.

She was chanting even before she started to move. "In this circle, out of reach, a place where evil cannot breach—"

There was more to it, but the gun cracked as her hand passed in front of her face, blocking her view of the kid, his weapon, his hate, and his own fear.

As she turned, she caught enough of a glimpse to know he was dressed in baggy black clothes with streaks of blue on them. She saw the one standing behind him, whispering in his ear, though she could see neither face. Mostly, she saw the barrel of the gun pointed at her. She'd chanted faster, but clearly not fast enough.

He must have missed, she certainly wasn't dead. The palm of her hand stung, but that wasn't enough to stop her.

More petrified than she'd ever been in her life, and far beyond conscious decision making, Yasmin let her anger flood her. Pure emotion was needed and she had it in spades right now. She bared her teeth and hissed out all her air at him. It was a powerful move, one she had not planned. Now both her hands came up in front of her, palm out as she shoved whatever power she had gathered at the two who threatened her and hers.

In her mind's eye, she saw the gun glowing red and never questioned it as the gang kid screamed and dropped the weapon.

"Bitch!" The second man started to raise another weapon and she directed her focus at that gun.

Her hiss was turning into a yell as she fell into primal instincts, using everything she had to stay alive. She was pushing out another surge of power and praying to all four corners. But his gun didn't heat like the other.

She could see his face clearly as he aimed right for her head.

"Police!"

The new, deep voice cracked through the haze of her fright from off to her left. "Put your weapon down or I will shoot."

A sharp noise registered in the back of her head, high-pitched and long. Something moved to her left, multicolored and leading with a long arm, but she didn't look at it. The threat was still in front of her.

The first gang kid was holding his wrist, and she had the satisfaction of a split second thinking she'd burned that asshole. But losing her focus could mean losing her life here, so she kept her hands up where they were, her vision filled with her own long brown arms, charm bracelets, manicured nails.

She didn't look as powerful as she was. . . . as she was learning that she was.

The gun in front of her wavered, but Yasmin stood her ground.

Beside her, the man who had yelled out he was police crept forward. Once again he implored the criminal to drop his weapon. Once again he was met with no real response except frustration.

The high pitched noise got louder and suddenly the two in front of her broke and ran. They darted between cars and were out of sight before she could register what had really happened.

Keeping her hands up, staying firmly planted, and scanning the scene for further threats, Yasmin fought the confusion pushing in on her from every angle.

She couldn't sense anyone's thoughts now. Beside her, the multicolored man ran into the scene in between her and where the others had stood. Voices raised in a cacophony off to her right and she heard car doors slam shut as the high pitched squeal started up again. This time she identified it as car tires.

Were they leaving?

No one was in front of her any more. She couldn't see any guns, not any aimed at her. Her eyes darted left and right—was it over?

Yasmin didn't move. Unsure what to do, she tried finishing the protection incantation, whispering the words. "In this circle, out of reach, a place where evil cannot breach. Strong as steel my heart has been, my foe without, I'm safe within . . ."

She couldn't remember the third verse.

Yasmin blinked. She *knew* this one. Why couldn't she find the third verse? The circle was not yet complete; she needed to complete the circle! What if they came back?

"Miss?"

I am . . . It started with *I am* . . . Good Goddess! What came next?

"Ma'am?"

A hand waved in front of her eye, breaking her stare and snapping her attention to the man in front of her. The multicolored man. Yasmin frowned at him.

He wore a pale purple, button down shirt, almost but not quite lavender. He had on gray slacks and two cloth grocery bags still slung over his shoulder, each in a different bold color. His teal tie was matched only in brightness by the blue of his eyes and the gold of his hair. Yasmin stared.

He looked concerned. "Ma'am? I'm a police officer."

Only then did she see that he was holding a badge, trying to show her who he was, why he was talking to her. Empirically, she understood that. But he'd put his gun away. Traded it for the silver and gold shield.

She frowned again. "Why didn't you shoot them?"

He ignored her question, but not the conversation. "Are you all right?"

She nodded in response, starting to feel a little fuzzy.

He pointed behind her. "How about your little girls?"

"I don't have any children." As soon as the words left her mouth, she gasped as though the sudden intake of breath would pull them back in. "Leyla! Maryam!"

Dropping to her knees on the harsh pavement, she gathered the small girls into her arms. "Oh, babies!"

They had only begun to move, staying where she had put

them, doing as they were told, until she released them. Now they clung to her like monkeys, like the frightened kids they were. Her voice tumbled out of her mouth, platitudes repeating in a chant of their own. "It's okay now, it's okay now." She rubbed one hand over each of their heads. Their dark hair smooth and silky beneath her fingers.

It was only then that she felt the sting in her left palm. Only then that she realized what she'd done.

She was glad she was facing away from Officer Multicolor. She'd used the craft out in the open. *Oh shit*. What had she done?

Her brain paused, what had her other options been?

That street thug had jumped out at her and her nieces with the sole purpose of achieving his first kill tonight. She'd heard his thoughts as clearly as if he'd spoken them to her. Honestly, she didn't care one shred that he was conflicted about it. He'd held a gun on her and frightened her and the girls. He'd even fired at her.

She didn't have the words.

"Ma'am?"

A hand fell to her shoulder, but quickly lifted when she jumped at the touch.

"Can you tell me if you're okay? If your girls are physically all right?"

The tone was soothing. Just a little low, just a little gravelly. As though he possessed some talent in the craft himself, she found herself wanting to do exactly as he said.

She grabbed one of the girls' hands in each of hers and held on tight. Then she stood up and faced him. She looked him in the eyes and nodded. "Yes, we are physically okay. Just shaken up."

Leyla piped up. "He made us drop our ice cream."

Looking down past her older niece, Yasmin saw the crumpled bag. The puddle of orange juice, the brown of chocolate starting to pool in the L.A. heat. She pushed her lips together to keep the small laughs in her from becoming hysterical.

A mental list started to form in her head. She needed to tell Tristan. She needed to get more ice cream. Needed to find a new grocery store in another neighborhood.

Turning back to Officer Multicolor, Yasmin found him looking her up and down, probably checking to see if the fired bullet made contact and if she was still really upright or just held together by shock.

He must have declared her okay, because he started to reach into his pocket and only then seemed to realize he still had his grocery bags slung over his shoulder. Setting them on the pavement, he looked her in the eye.

"I'm Detective Luke Salzone with the LAPD. I'm going to call this in and get more officers here if you're all right."

He seemed to be waiting for her, so she smiled. "Oh, I'm okay!"

She was looking into the darkening blue of his eyes as the sparkles started crowding the edges of her vision. Her stomach pitched right before everything went black.

He caught her just as she fell. Thank goodness he'd set down his grocery bags.

Luke smiled at the irony. When he'd seen her in the store he'd wondered what it would take to make her swoon for him. Not in his wildest imagination had he envisioned this . . . not her and her two adorable little girls getting shot at in his neighborhood grocery parking lot.

He knelt, one arm around her torso, one cradling her head as he tried to balance her. She sure wasn't putting any effort in; she'd blinked out cold. In an attempt to get her head down on the same level as her heart, he set her on the pavement, her hands listlessly rolling beside her. For a moment, he was thinking he'd just lay her down, it wasn't all that clean, but she was passed out and people could be washed. Then again, if he ever wanted any chance with her, laying her on the blacktop of a grocery store in Los Angeles was a surefire way to guarantee that nothing ever happened. He probably didn't stand a chance anyway as he was now associated with what was most likely the worst memory of her life. Luke certainly hoped she hadn't been through worse.

He looked up at the little girls watching him. As they eyed him sideways, he remembered to smile. "Honey? Can you hand me . . ." he looked frantically around— "that blue bag? Empty the groceries out so I can use it for a pillow."

They did as he asked, albeit warily. The older girl held it out to him, trying to complete the task assigned, but also clearly trying not to make any physical contact with him. Taking the bag, he looked up from where he was frowning at the woman in his arms and smiled again. "Thank you."

He tucked the makeshift pillow under her head and tapped at the side of her face. She didn't come around and he didn't want to tap harder, so he just stood watch over her and scanned the parking lot.

He wanted to pay attention to her and see if he could get those whiskey-colored eyes to open. See if she would smile. He'd seen her light up in the store while she and the girls were picking out pizza fixings and ice cream. But right now there was too much to do.

For whatever reason the Del Sur boys had picked her to be their initiate's kill. It hadn't gone well, and his experience with Del Sur was that they were tenacious. If you screwed with them, you got back tenfold whatever you gave. There was every possibility they were circling the neighborhood, ready to finish the hit. Squealing wheels only meant they were gone right now. They could come back just as fast as they'd left.

Without taking his eyes from the street, he spoke to the girls. "Can you kneel down by your mommy? See if you can get her to wake up?"

They obeyed but still looked scared.

Shit, of course they were scared. There was nothing he could do about it right now.

He had to call this in. Then again, chances were, someone already had. There had been gunshots—and while that wasn't horribly uncommon in L.A. it wasn't common here at the Ralphs' grocery parking lot in Hollywood.

He scanned the area again, listened for wheels, shots, and didn't hear much. Traffic was going by on Melrose as though nothing had happened. No one came forward to help. Maybe because, while it felt like an hour, it had really only been a minute. Anyone who had seen anything was likely still cowering. The sad fact was, anyone who recognized the gang colors wouldn't say anything at all. So he didn't hold out hope for eyewitnesses.

Finally kneeling down next to the girls, he pulled his badge from where he'd automatically clipped it at his waist. He took a chance and showed it to them. "Hey, I showed your mom, I'm a police officer. I'll take care of you guys. Make sure the bad guys don't come back around."

Luke hoped like hell he wasn't lying.

They nodded at him solemnly. "Is she going to wake up?"

A welcome relief, the question showed that they trusted him. It could have gone either way. He'd been in neighborhoods here where the police were the enemy and the locals would just as likely shoot as show their faces. "Yes, she fainted, that's all. She's okay and she'll wake up in just a minute."

Once again, Luke prayed he wasn't lying.

He touched the side of her face. "Ma'am? Can you hear me?"

He would have preferred to call her 'honey' or something equally endearing, but the second he'd seen the gun, he was officially on duty. On duty officers did not call women 'honey,' 'baby,' or anything of the like. And they didn't ask those women out.

Her eyes opened and looked up at him. The color of deep cognac, they slowly focused on him, even if they continued to look confused.

Blinking, her hands came up to her head.

He hoped to hell her head didn't hurt. But now that she was awake there was no putting it off. Pulling out his cell phone, he called into dispatch, rattling off his name and badge number automatically while he stayed focused on her face. As he watched, he told dispatch about the gunfire, the ID on the victim—as he now had to refer to her—and on the perpetrators. He referenced the evidence he'd seen that the perpetrators might be members of the Del Sur gang, even though he didn't think they *might* be. Luke was damn certain.

Her hand reached up and touched the grocery bag he'd wadded up as a pillow. Trying to sit up and pull the bag out from behind her hair, she seemed just as disconcerted that he tried to keep her from doing exactly that. "Stay down."

He was still on the open phone line, but Stacy in dispatch wasn't at all confused by him holding two conversations at the same time. He spoke to her again, giving the address of the parking lot and his location in it.

Speaking to the woman again, he asked. "Are you in any pain? Your girls are right here."

The two girls brought nearly identical dark-haired heads into her field of vision. He watched as her chest rose and fell with a sigh of relief. But there wasn't really time to watch their relief. It all went down fast, and it could again.

Out of information to relay, he disconnected with dispatch knowing all the appropriate responders were on the way. Not that there was much left here to work with. Luke held a hand out to her. "Can you sit up? I can carry you if we need, but I'd like to move us to another spot."

He didn't have to say the words he didn't want to. Alarm instantly flared in her eyes and she started to scramble. She didn't have to do that; she wasn't all together yet. He just didn't want to be waiting in the place the gang boys would look first if they did come back. He wasn't going to let her be a sitting duck.

Along with the girls, he took her around the corner of the store and out of line of sight of the parking lot. Though he kept a hand on her, he kept an eye on the surrounding area, always watchful.

It was another full three minutes until the first patrol showed up. They hadn't been far away, but with traffic eeking along with its usual five pm drudgery, their timing had been slow enough.

Luke stepped out, gun and badge in the air for a moment until the two uniforms got closer and they could all recognize each other. There was a mild interchange of signals and the officers parked the patrol car in the lane as there were no open spots close by.

Once that was settled, he went back around the corner, checking on his charges. The woman still sat against the wall where he'd left her. Only now the littler of the girls was curled into her arms. The older one stood solemnly, clutching the woman's hand. With the other she reached out and grabbed Luke's in a fierce death grip. Startled, he looked down. Her dark eyes let him know she wasn't letting go and she was now counting on him. *No pressure.*

Well, if that was what the kid needed, he wouldn't let go either. He looked her mom in the face, both assessing her state and deciding to start a conversation.

"I'm detective Luke Salzone with the LAPD."

"I remember."

Well, that was probably a good start. He reminded himself to smile. "What's your name?"

"Yasmin Ali."

He rolled the sound around in his brain for a moment like he always did to help him remember names. But he wasn't going to forget hers. "And the girls?"

"Leyla and Maryam Sayeed." He memorized their names, too. The uniforms came around the corner just then; they would take official statements. Although what the girls might contribute, he didn't know. When the shooting started, Yasmin had put them on the ground, facing away, really quick. So they'd likely seen nothing of the scene.

Just as fast as that, the other two officers were talking to her, asking questions and jotting the info down on the ubiquitous little notebooks cops always carried. Since she was in good hands, and safe, Luke decided to do a preliminary check of the area. It wouldn't be his scene, even though he was 'on duty' he wasn't really on duty. Also his involvement meant he wouldn't catch this investigation.

Standing there, holding the little hand still tightly clutched in his, he realized that his initial impressions were still with him and that was more than a little disconcerting.

He started to walk away, but the small grip held him anchored in place. Probably that was a good thing. Because if he went out to check the scene, he wasn't certain he wouldn't find a charred circle on the ground where she'd stood.

CHAPTER 2

Luke was in that parking lot until well after dark. By the time he got home he was too exhausted to think straight. That must be the problem.

Or else today he'd become a liar. For the first time he could remember in his adult life, he'd flat out lied. He hadn't been sparing anyone's feelings, and there was nothing "little" or "white" about these lies. He liked to think he was all altruistic and was protecting Yasmin Ali, but he was well aware that he was protecting himself as well.

He did not want to be sent for a psych eval—which was exactly where he'd go if he reported what he really saw. He didn't truly think he needed to see a shrink, but he wasn't all together convinced he *didn't* either.

If he'd written up the scene exactly as he'd seen it, there would have been a bit too much that would have to be excused as a trick of the light. One optical illusion, he could understand, but as many as he'd seen? *No way*.

In the store, before everything bad happened, Luke had been watching her. He liked the way her eyes lit up when she smiled. He liked that she wasn't one of those moms who was exasperated with her own kids. Of course, that turned out to be because they weren't her own kids, just visiting nieces who got far more out of L.A. than they bargained for. As he understood it, their mom, Yasmin's sister, was already on a flight into town to fetch them back home.

While he'd not outright followed Yasmin down the store aisles—he was no stalker—he'd surreptitiously checked out her left hand and liked it a little too much that her ring finger was bare. It didn't mean anything really. But he'd thought about how to approach her, how to ask her out.

It just turned out that he went out the door just a beat behind her. By then he'd seen the gang guys in the store while he shopped, but they weren't doing anything wrong, just looking seedy. He wasn't in uniform—as a detective, he hadn't been for several years—so he couldn't even give them the stink eye in spite of the fact that they reeked of a gang. Because he'd been right there, he saw the one guy bump her in the parking lot, but Luke couldn't tell if her wallet had been lifted. Later, when the uniforms picked up her purse from where she'd dropped it at the scene, they realized that yes, her wallet was missing.

That was a bothersome fact. Not just that these guys had her things, but that it was a textbook new initiation hit for the Del Surs: take out someone with kids with them. The more kids that witnessed the hit, the more points. It turned his stomach. The kids were never the target, but the idea was to take out the adult with them. Probably gave them nightmares for the rest of their lives.

Yeah, this was exactly what the Del Surs did. Except the Del Surs didn't miss.

Luke had put it in his report that he'd noticed her in the store. He might be a newly minted liar, but he had to admit to that much. He didn't write anything stupid or swoony about her eyes or the bouncy curls with shots of blonde that made his hands itch to see if they were as soft as they looked. Nope. He did not put that part in.

But he had seen the second guy bump her. And he'd seen them take four steps as she turned to her car, putting her back to them after accepting an apology that she hadn't looked him in the eye for. It had been her only mistake. Well, that and not zipping her purse shut. But those small errors were hardly worthy of what she'd gotten.

The thing was, when the thug pulled out the gun and yelled to her, she'd spun around to face them. That took serious guts. The innate kind, because that was a moment when a person didn't think, they just acted. Luke liked that her reaction was to fight back, but he still couldn't describe in any human terms exactly how she'd done it. Or if she'd even done anything at all.

As she'd spun, one arm had pointed low and he thought he'd seen small blue flames spark and burn on the ground around her. Luke blinked, thinking that black tar parking lots didn't burn. The odd vision and his odder thought pattern slowed his reaction, even though he was already reaching for his gun.

When she threw her hands forward, he'd swear he saw the air *compress* in front of her. Except he didn't swear it. He simply left that part out of the report. . . . and he left out the chanting. Her lips had been moving in a rhythmic fashion. She didn't yell, "Get back!" or "Stay away!" She didn't call them names or curse them . . . or maybe she *had* been cursing them. Literally.

The gun left at the scene had nylon melted onto the butt. It was a metal gun. In Luke's memory, the second guy pulled a Glock, which had a plastic grip. The first kid had run off holding his hand as though it were injured. None of it made sense, unless the gun had gotten too hot and burned him.

Burning easily explained the melted nylon—probably a glove —the way the kid gripped his wrist, then dropped the gun. But what explanation was there for the gun getting so hot? There was none. That was the problem. So Luke hadn't voiced his suspicions. The report contained only the facts as he'd seen them. He saw that A-hole drop the gun and grab his wrist. That was all Luke wrote. Well, he didn't write "A-hole" but it was understood.

Before the gun had gotten hot, the bastard shot at her. The idiot didn't hold the gun right. It was an idiosyncrasy of 'being cool' that Luke and every other police officer was grateful for. A sideways grip on the gun was moronic. It nearly guaranteed bad aim. Thought this idiot held it that way, he'd managed to take enough time and line the sight up.

In slow motion, Luke watched as the gang kid's face showed that he was making the decision. Luke watched as the kid pulled the trigger. Convinced she was going to die in front of him, in front of the girls, he felt time crash to a stop. He didn't draw breath. Couldn't pull the trigger of his own well-aimed gun. People were on the street behind the kid. And Luke couldn't stop bullets once they'd left the chamber.

But the gang bullet missed. Even though it didn't look like it missed.

Then she'd yelled, actually *hissed* something, and she'd shoved her hands forward. Suddenly Luke was unfrozen—because she was still alive, still standing—and he ran forward.

That was when he thought he saw her push the air around her. He didn't put that in his report either, but it looked like she was casting some sort of spell.

Yasmin sat on the corner of Tristan's desk. She would have stood in his office, faced him like a big girl, but she was about to crumple. She still had a good case of the shakes.

Her sister, Shori, had shown up to collect the girls at just after eleven p.m. Despite the fact that Leyla had championed

Aunt Meeni, there was nothing to be done about it. Shori's daughters had been involved in a gang attack.

The kicker was that Yasmin had spent so much time convincing Shori to let the girls come to L.A. rather than have Yasmin go to their house outside Portland. She told herself she understood her sister's decision—if it had been her daughters, there would be no way she'd say 'sure, stay in that city. I'll come back in five days as planned.' But the pizza and ice cream dinner was ruined. Her sister's trust was shot to hell. And the fun week with the girls was over too soon, traded for a week of dealing with the police and the aftermath of a gang-style shooting.

The aftermath also included dealing with her boss, Tristan.

"You're still taking the time off, right?" He leaned back in the chair, looking like he was worried about her. Absentmindedly, he flipped his pen, a sign he was deep in thought. Tristan didn't fidget a pen like anyone else. The pen balanced—tip of the pen on the tip of his finger—then he would flick his finger and the pen would rotate once, landing perfectly on the point, dead center of his fingerprint again. Sometimes Yasmin could tell he'd been in his office thinking, because he would have small points of ink on the pad of his finger. From when he forgot to retract the tip of the pen.

Right now, the pen was retracted. It was mesmerizing to watch it flip, but she pulled her eyes away. "I think so. I may come back a little early if I can get the police business cleared up."

"Tell me you protected your credit cards." He shook his head.

With a nod, she tried not to be mad. Of course she had protection spells on her cards, her purse, her wallet. Still she conceded he had a right to ask. Because, even though she'd protected them, something had gone wrong—they'd been stolen hadn't they? That wasn't supposed to happen to a witch of her caliber.

While she wasn't near Tristan's caliber, nor on par with his sister Delilah, she was holding her own. Yasmin did damn fine considering she was 'late' to the craft, having only discovered it in early college. She'd majored in ancient religions and stumbled into the retail job at Blessed Be, thinking it was a good place to clerk until she found the real thing. But the store job had turned out to be the real thing.

Tristan and Delilah elevated her dabbling to an art, and Tristan taught her even more. Born to the craft of a long line of witches, the brother and sister had inherited Blessed Be, the family magick store. Ironically, it was full of real magick. Yasmin first grew her own skills, then started a beginner's class, created an online presence for them, and eventually helped Tristan market all over the world. She now had a regular salary that was sufficient for LA, a place to grow, and a boss she loved.

The problem was she literally loved him.

He was nice enough to her in return, but he needed to open up and really *see* her. She was perfect for him and she knew it even if he didn't.

His expression was kind. Understanding. Friendly.

Too *friend*ly.

"You should go home, you look exhausted."

Gosh, thanks. But he was right. She shrugged. "I haven't slept yet."

"Do you need anything to help you sleep?" He caught the pen this time, his gaze focusing on her.

Yasmin decided it was sweet rather than condescending. "Nope. I've got it covered."

Sure she did. Of course, he worried. She'd been shot at. Her protection spells should have made that nearly impossible. Clearly, they hadn't held up.

She'd taken the week off to be with her nieces. Delilah was all set to substitute for Yasmin's beginner class later that night. Though Yasmin wanted to do it, she was in no shape to be in charge of a bunch of starter witches finding just enough power to throw things out of whack.

While her protection spell hadn't worked, the rest of it seemed to be holding up. She left Blessed Be and climbed into her car—parked in a magically empty spot right in front of the store—and headed home for a much-needed nap.

With a wave of her hand, traffic moved. Some cars just shifted forward a bit, some moved a little sideways, but with her instruction, and a nudge from the universe, they now moved in concert. A space opened letting her onto the packed freeway. Cars let her into the lanes she wanted, then let her over to exit at the right place. With some forethought and a preset spell, the lights were in her favor. And thank the Goddess, because she was about to fall asleep on her steering wheel, which would be really bad since she was driving without her license.

Pulling into her driveway, she glanced up at her place, never happier to be home. The small, brick red stucco house was comforting. Barely a thousand square feet on a barely three thousand square foot lot, it was just the right size for her—the North Hollywood neighborhood bohemian enough for her sensibilities and cheap enough for her salary.

Unlocking the three bolts, she stepped inside, breathed a sigh of relief and closed the door behind her before turning on the lights. Her back to the door, she waved her right hand around the room, from corner to corner, the lights coming up to full brightness. On second thought . . . She brought her hand down and dimmed the lights. It was only mid-morning, but she needed her bed.

The coffee table still held a half-played game of Parcheesi. Through the doorway into the kitchen she could see a small, plastic cup sitting by the sink. Reminders that the girls had been here. And that Shori had come and whisked them home. Shori had arrived from LAX with a rental car and was gone, driving the girls north, all packed up and heading home, before one a.m.

Yasmin sighed. She'd clean up later. Right now, her bed was calling.

Before she hit the hallway though, she stopped.

Turning, she lifted her arms and snapped her fingers. Four candles, set into sconces on the walls, burst into controlled flames. Calling the four corners, the candles were colored red, blue, green and yellow, corresponding to the elements. Protection spells were tantamount now, because her last ones had clearly failed.

The bolts on the front door slid home. As she listened, Yasmin heard the satisfying click as the back door bolt checked itself.

She was going to bed. She didn't need a sleep aid, magical or otherwise. She was about to fall over. As she passed the bookshelves she'd installed in the hallway, she caught sight of the candles and herbs she'd parked there.

She shouldn't have done it. That spell had been a mistake. In fact, it might have just disturbed things enough to have made all this happen. Which was why she hadn't admitted to Tristan that she'd done it.

Well, that was one reason.

She walked down the hall and fell into her bed.

The precinct building was brick on the outside and pretty much white all the way through the inside. Luke thought the work was damning enough, the place ought to have some color, some cheer of its own to fight the negativity that pushed through the doorway every day.

The one time he'd mentioned just the idea of adding color in passing to his chief, the woman had looked at him with a blank face. Just when he thought she wasn't going to respond at all, she said, "Don't you think you bring enough color in here all on your own?"

He'd nodded and walked away, discretion being the better part of valor and all that. Maybe that was why he wore bright things instead of the drab tones the other officers seemed to prefer. Maybe because if he was going to get shot on the job, he wanted to be a good target. He would prefer to get completely taken out over getting maimed or such.

Maybe the place didn't need more color. It wasn't like anyone came in to share their good news. Almost no one ever brought them a fruit basket to thank the cops for helping them get sober, or not letting their kid shoot his brains out with the family gun. Even a "Hey, guess what! I got promoted at work." Nope, there was one girl who'd been taken hostage as a fifteen-year-old and Officer Ramone had talked the kidnapper into surrendering and letting her walk free. She came by the precinct once a month to thank them and see if maybe Ramone had left his wife yet. So even the positive visits were often a bit creepy.

Still, Luke liked his job. Or he had until yesterday.

If he'd been a private citizen yesterday, he would have shot both those fuckers right where they stood. People would have applauded him. As an officer, he had to be aware of the people on the street behind them, the fact that at first, they hadn't fired. Then when one of them did, he almost immediately dropped the gun, and thus dropped Luke's valid reason to drop him.

Yeah, he'd liked his job, until he became part of the worst moment of Yasmin's life. She'd smiled at him—directly at him—once as they were both filling their carts at the store. It hadn't been the "Oh, there you are!" kind of soul recognition he would have been thrilled at, but it did reach her eyes.

As he passed through the maze of work stations, he stopped at Valverde's desk to check up. Luckily he didn't have to try to act casual, he'd pulled his weapon; he was involved. "Any news on the Ali case?"

Valverde shrugged. She was tough, competent, smart and thus she knew there wasn't likely to be much they could do with this one. The Del Sur guys crossed district lines with the shooting—in itself, that wouldn't stop any investigation or prosecution—but they hadn't actually shot anyone. There were no injuries to prosecute.

"The gun is a Sig nine millimeter, the serial number traces back to another shooting five years ago." She sighed. "It's bad enough these guys do this shit, but it really burns that they get weapons we used to have in our possession. That's on us."

Holding up his hands, Luke sighed with her. "Preaching to the choir here, Jess."

"I know." She tapped her pen on the desk, on the paperwork and folders indicating that the Ali case was one of many. "Evidence found melted nylon on the grip, in the shape of a hand. Like it just burned on. That was weird. Ballistics has it now; they're going to fire it and match the rifling to some other crimes no doubt."

A gun like that, Jess was probably right, Luke thought. She was already turning back to her caseload, so he knocked on her desk for her attention. "Grab me if something pops?"

"You bet."

He settled into his chair, trying to follow up on his own cases and not able to keep his concentration anywhere other than where he'd been yesterday. He kept seeing Yasmin, turning and pointing, kept hearing the crack of the gun and seeing her jerk in response. Glad that Valverde hadn't asked him what he thought of the melted nylon on the gun, he tried to ignore his thoughts and at least return emails. He lasted fifteen minutes before Valverde shouted out, "Hey Salzone! You're gonna want to come see this."

As she was pulling on her blazer, Luke did the same. He

didn't even finish the email he'd halfway written. Just logged out as quick as he could and hustled down the hall behind her, the white walls finally opening through the doors into the L.A. sunshine.

He followed her to the grocery store parking lot where two uniforms were once again taking a statement. This time it was from a patron who'd just arrived at the store. It seemed he went to pull into an empty spot but in the parking spot was a wallet. Pretty with orange and bronze designs in paisley, it exactly matched Yasmin's description. Given that it was the same color and manufacturer as her purse had been, there was no doubt it was yesterday's stolen property. Of course, all her cards—credit, gym, grocery club—were pulled from their spots and laid around in a two-foot circle with the wallet. In the center was her driver's license.

Luke could only stare at the silent message. Jessica didn't say anything, just squeezed her eyes shut then joined the uniformed officers in snapping off photos on her PD issued camera.

Luke didn't speak either. But he thought it. *Shit.*

CHAPTER 3

Yasmin had woken from her mid-morning nap refreshed. But the feeling rapidly fled as soon as she remembered all that had happened.

It seemed everything she did that morning, she found something else to remind her of how things had gone wrong. There was only one bathroom in the tiny house, but the yellow duck and blue hippo still in the tub needed to be cleaned up and put away for a future visit that Shori would never let happen now. Yasmin had hoped the girls would be able to come stay with her on a more regular basis. That was disappointment number one.

There were little reminders all over the house. She had cleaning to do, so Yasmin started with herself. She pulled the wide tooth comb through her curls and washed her face and found reminder number two. On her left palm was a dime-sized bruise. Just off center, just big enough to make her wonder. That asshole had shot at her and she'd been pissed as hell, but she wasn't that strong. What had made the bruise?

Ignoring it as best she could—it was on her palm after all and now that she'd found it, it protested each time she used her hand—she went about righting the second bedroom. The girls had slept here on inflatable mattresses which she plugged into the little motor on reverse and folded them as they sucked dry. Two full-size inflatables . . . possibly not to be used again.

The hardwood floors were awesome, but she liked something under her bare feet, and needing to center herself she stuffed the mattresses into the back of the closet and pulled out the rolled canvas floor cover. White with black paint, it was reminder number three.

She'd bought the canvas and the permanent paints and used her fingers rather than a brush. The result was charming rather than professional. She'd stitched a grosgrain ribbon onto the border—it had been soaked in an herb mix then dried. She'd also stitched white salt under the wide ribbon, so she would always have an unbroken salt circle when she worked. She thought it was genius—old world witchcraft meets new world convenience.

She kept it back here in this room because who ever came back here? There would be no mistaking what this was for. A pentagram in black and gray took up the bulk of the center. At each corner, she had traced a circle in the color corresponding to the candle that went there—not that she needed help to remember the colors that went with each element. She'd added the N, S, E & W for the corresponding directions, the signs of the gates, and the name of the element. Given the near perfect alignment of the street north and south, she had to angle the canvas caddy corner to make the four directions work. That this second bedroom was big enough for her spellwork had been a selling point on the house. That and the old trees and the open attitude. There was no mistaking that her floor covering was for anything but witchcraft.

The last time she'd had this out—just before the girls arrived —she'd used it for something she shouldn't have. She'd known better. You just didn't cast love spells, no good could come of it.

Regardless of what she knew, she'd grown tired of waiting. She had the means and the skills. So Yasmin had simply cast the spell the night before she rolled the canvas up. Putting a picture of her and Tristan together in the center of the pentagram, she'd pulled out Paris Nightshade, Juniper, and Mandrake. She posted the candles, stood in the center and called the four corners. She'd cast for her love to see her, truly see her. Then she'd calmly put everything away.

Sure, Tristan was worried about her, but he hadn't asked her out yet. And here she was, getting interviewed repeatedly by the police about a shooting her standard protection spells should have kept her from ever being near in the first place.

It was time to set the balance back. Pulling out her candles, she placed them into the four corners, carefully aligning the colors. From the hall shelf she pulled her Book of Shadows—it was just a leather bound journal for her spells. She didn't have a family Decad like the Goodmans did. Their Decad was a handwritten book of spells passed through more generations than any of them could count. Yasmin would be the first of her line.

Just as she centered herself in the circle, her phone rang.

Delilah. The name skittered through her head. Delilah could do that to her. It was Tristan's sister's way of saying, *Hey, it's me. Pick up.* It had been disconcerting at first. Now it was just the new normal. "Hey Delilah. You know there is this thing called Caller ID."

"So, you sound pretty good then." The other woman laughed. "I'm glad. We were all worried about you."

But was Tristan? Yasmin reined in the thought. Delilah could pick that stuff right out of the air. "I'm holding up fine. I was shot *at* but not shot." She looked at the bruise on her palm again, unsure.

"I want to say 'that's good' but even that's really not. Do you have any idea why your protections failed?"

Wasn't that the million dollar question? Yasmin thought. "No idea."

"Hmmm. Must be preordained then." Delilah hmmm'd again, as though she were going to add more, then a baby cry sounded in the background. "Oh! I have to go. But I wanted to check on you."

"I appreciate it." Just like that the call was over, leaving Yasmin something to think about. It was possible that the shooting was a necessary event, that her protections hadn't really failed her at all. It was also just as possible that she'd screwed up the universe with her love spell. She'd said 'An it harm none' as though the saying of the words in the spell would make it so.

Love spells were always a bad idea. It had screwed up her juju. And Tristan still hadn't looked her in the eyes with anything other than friendly, brotherly concern.

The knock on her front door was the last thing she needed. Standing up from the middle of her pretty pentagram and her musings at how she'd screwed up her own universe, she went to send away whoever was at her door.

Yasmin was just considering not answering it when the pounding started in earnest. With a sigh, she changed her thoughts and went to answer it.

She pulled the door open and was about to say "hello" to Officer Multicolor when she realized his mouth was open. Today his shirt was salmon and his tie a cool yellow. His eyes, however were not the same teal as yesterday. Right now they were whatever shade of blue a person would call 'pissed off.'

Luke hadn't intended to yell at her when she opened the door. But he did it anyway. "This is Los Angeles! Did you learn nothing yesterday?"

The way her head jerked back, as though he had slapped her physically instead of verbally, should have been expected. Even knowing he didn't want to upset her, his mouth kept going. "You don't know who's on the other side of the door! You shouldn't just open it like that. I didn't even hear any bolts!"

"I have bolts." She was calm. More so than she should be with an LAPD detective on her doorstep yelling at her.

"You didn't lock them! I'm a police officer. I listen for those things." Though he really wanted it to, his mouth would not shut up. His hands clenched and only by sheer force of will did he get his brain to override his tongue. He took three deep breaths—far too obviously, if he judged by the look on her face—and then spoke again. "May I come in?"

She didn't answer. Just stood there looking at him.

He looked back.

Yasmin Ali wasn't going to be *the one* for him. Judging from her little nieces, their names, and her sister's married name, Yasmin came from a relatively traditional Middle Eastern background. Her family would not let their daughter get involved with an Italian immigrant police officer. But the softly clinging t-shirts she wore, the jeans, the painted toenails, the shots of silver at her neck and the blond in her hair teased him. Taunted that maybe she wasn't so traditional herself.

Then again, maybe he could just not be an asshole simply for the sake of not being one. "Please."

Staying silent, she stepped back and waved her arm in mock welcome, allowing him into a pretty living room in vivid sky blues and bronzes and yellows. Though the furniture was relatively traditional American, he felt a hint of India in the colors.

She was closing the door behind him when he turned and tried again. "Please use the bolts and check the peephole before opening the door."

"I did check." The words were flat and she looked him dead in the eye.

A sigh escaped him. No, she was not the one for him. She hated him. But he was going to make her stay safe. "Don't lie to a police officer. You didn't look through the peephole."

"I checked." She still stared at him as though he was crazy. And he probably was. They were both aware that he didn't drive up here from Hollywood to check her door etiquette and yell at her.

"It's not like you're magic and you can just tell who's on the other side of the door—" his voice stopped mid-sentence and he looked around the room.

Shelves in deeply stained wood tones displayed rows of old leather books next to new paperbacks. Scarves, candles, and framed pictures held court on several levels. One of the higher shelves had a rack discretely installed under it, and several bundles of various herbs hung there, tied up with ribbons, drying in the L.A. air.

The coat rack held only coats. Her t-shirt had Hello Kitty on it and her jeans had a few well-placed rips. There was nothing suspicious. "Please use the peephole. It's why they're there."

She only nodded, still watching him, still waiting for him to get to the purpose of his visit.

Which he had to do. "I came by to be sure you were safe."

Her eyebrows went up, the side of her mouth quirked. "I'm safe. I have bolts and I just learned the importance of checking before I answer the door."

Nope. This was not going as planned.

Never mind that his plan had involved him showing up on her doorstep and her begging him to keep her safe and probably some nakedness . . . after a reasonable montage of them doing everyday tasks and laughing together, of course.

Luke had not for one second believed it would actually go that way, but a guy could dream, couldn't he? Still, this was worse than even his 'just-the-facts-ma'am' officer scenario. "Yesterday, that was a gang initiation hit."

She nodded, not at all frightened by the fact. He'd wanted to tread lightly on that one, thinking she might fall apart. Her words made it pretty clear he guessed wrong. "I figured as much. That's what it looked like. Any particular gang I have to worry about?"

His mouth opened, but Luke's voice didn't quite work.

"Hit me with it. I can take it."

She was still upright. Besides, he'd come here ready to help out. So he said it. "The Del Surs. The worst of the worst. Up from mid city. They're trying to take out both Jungle gangs."

He didn't like saying it. He'd worked in Vice, in Guns-and-Gangs, and he was with Crimes-Against-Persons now while waiting for a spot to open up with the Narcotics team. It all overlapped a little too much. He knew how awful the Stone Jungles were. And he knew that if the Del Surs were knocking them out, then it was bad. Really bad.

Yasmin Ali didn't seem to get it. "Well, neither I nor any of my family members or friends have ever had any gang involvement. So it can't be personal. I didn't actually get shot. I'll be fine, I'm just shaken up."

Shaken up? This was her *shaken up?*

He couldn't let her be this lax. "Has anyone come to the door besides me?"

"No." She shrugged. "Not today. Well, my sister came last night and took her girls back home."

He nodded as he scanned the room. "Probably a good idea."

She looked like she wanted to protest, but she didn't.

"Can I check out the house?"

Her eyebrows went up. "My house is just fine. I'm in North Hollywood now. The gangs we have here are middle-aged women in peasant blouses trying to impress people into hot yoga or hipsters trying to force you to buy better tech or whole grain breads."

Sighing, he tried again. "I'd just like to be sure that it's secure." He knew better than most that if someone wanted to get to you, they could. There was no such thing as a truly safe house, but the feeling of safety was so important, he didn't want to take that from her. He hoped to make her feel more safe by declaring the windows and the locks solid. He hoped to tell himself she was safe by seeing that she was, in fact, secure. Luke started down the hallway, but her hand out to ward him off stopped him.

Why didn't she want him to check things out?

He was looking at her face, at the frown there, but only for a moment. "Hey! What's this?"

Before he realized he'd manhandled her, he had her fingers cradled in his hand and was outlining the quarter-sized bruise on her palm. The center was dark purple and around that was lighter, bluer coloring.

She tried to yank the hand back from him, but he held firm. When she spoke, she was almost startled. "It's bigger."

Gentling his touch, he traced the edge again, trying not to think what he was thinking. "That means it's relatively new, within the last twenty four hours." He looked up into her startled eyes. "It's from last night, isn't it?"

"Yeah, I guess."

"You don't remember?" Luke didn't know why he asked that, people often didn't remember certain details of traumatic situations.

Her answer made that all the more plausible when she said, "I only noticed it this morning."

"Does it hurt?"

Grinning, she nodded. "Like a bitch."

As gently as before, he turned her hand over and pressed on the back. "How about that?"

"Nope."

"That's good. I'm no doctor, but a sharp pain would indicate a break."

This time she did pull her hand back, closing her fingers over the bruise on her palm. "I'm positive it's not broken."

Nice wasn't going to get him anywhere. In fact, he was pretty certain there was nothing he could do to get anywhere with her. "Please let me check out your house." When she started to protest, he pulled out his cell phone and showed her the picture. "You're going to get a call from Detective Jessica Valverde as soon as they finish processing the scene. But we found this, in the parking spot your car was in."

Yasmin stared at the phone, her pretty whiskey eyes finally shocked and disturbed by the whole situation. "That looks ominous."

All he could do was nod. "It is. The driver's license is in the middle, indicating that it's most important. Since you were a good citizen and your license matches your current address, they can find you here. The Del Surs do not take kindly to people who mess up their plans, and that's exactly what you did."

"By not dying!?"

Luke nodded. It sucked, but it was true. "Precisely. Please let me check the house."

She was too busy shaking her head to say no again, so he started down the hallway and was looking in doors. He'd checked the small bathroom window. It was secure, even though most people didn't pay enough attention to it. His hand was on the knob to one of the back rooms when she suddenly burst out, "No. Don't go in there!"

Luke fought the laugh he felt. "I've seen women's bedrooms before."

"No. . . It's my office and it's a mess." She held her hands out, imploring him not to go in. The bruise on the center of her hand said that she was lucky that's all she got last night, which made him even more determined the bruise was all she'd suffer.

"I've seen messes." He turned the knob, still looking at her while he pushed the door open.

"No!"

But the sound trailed off in his ears as he stared into the room, his eyes processing what he was seeing.

On the ground was a satanic symbol, candles burning in each corner—had they been burning the whole time she was out talking to him? A large leather bound book filled with black ink script lay open in the center. Symbols and letters filled the corners of the room.

What the hell had he stepped into?

Looking back at Yasmin, it was very clear now why she hadn't wanted him to see this. He was opening his mouth to say something when his phone rang. At least he knew what to do with that.

Answering it, he kept his eyes on the beautiful and disturbed Yasmin. "What's going on, Valverde?"

If Jessica said the gangs had embraced Satanism and ritualistic sacrifice, he was pretty sure he would have believed her. But she didn't.

"You told the Ali woman about the DL and such, right?"

"Yeah, I'm here now." He almost rattled off the address, thinking it was suddenly a good idea that someone know exactly where he was and have a last known time of contact as well.

"Cool. Then I won't call her. But get this: the CSIs just called me and found something very weird."

Oh, he just bet it wasn't as weird as what he was looking at. "Do tell."

"There's a bullet from the scene. Only one."

He already knew that, but he was cautiously watching the pretty Yasmin Ali while he had this conversation. He was not turning his back on her again. He made a noise to Valverde that he'd heard her.

"We can't get any rifling on it, because it looks like it was fired into body armor or something. It's flat. We found it last night and collected it because it was part of the scene, but it was obviously old, because . . . Well, because the bullet the banger fired would have hit a car or a tree or a person."

Luke did not like where this was going, but Valverde didn't seem to catch his reticence. She just kept talking.

"But it was shiny, new. Don't know why I didn't notice that last night. Here's the kicker—even though we don't have rifling, the firing pin is a probable match. That squished nine mil slug has to be from the dropped gun with the burned nylon. But how the hell did it get that way?"

Somehow his mouth worked, it made sounds, sounds in English. It said, "I don't know."

But his brain kept thinking about how Yasmin threw her left hand up in front of her when the shot went off, and now she had a round bruise right in the center of her palm . . .

CHAPTER 4

Detective Multicolor was looking at her like she was a freak. He hung up his phone and pocketed it, still standing in the doorway between her and her spell room. The candles burned behind him waiting for a chant, a prayer, or an invocation.

For a moment, Yasmin considered casting a forgetting spell on him, but then she discarded it. Delilah once told Yasmin what she'd done to Brandon when she met him. Her friend had meant it as a warning—because casting those spells had hurt both her and Brandon. Yasmin took it as a different warning. The man Delilah cast her forgetting spells on wound up married to her. Looking Luke Salzone up and down, Yasmin cataloged the suspicious look in his eyes, the badge, the colorful shirt and tie and decided a forgetting spell was not the way to go. She might end up married to him.

Opting for honesty if not enthusiasm, she spoke flatly and clearly. "I'm a Witch."

"Are you a good witch or a bad witch?"

Good Goddess, if she had a dollar for every time she heard that one. "What are you?"

"Catholic." He still looked at her warily, as though he thought she might release some flying monkeys at any moment.

"Are you a good Catholic or a bad Catholic?" She couldn't help it that her arms automatically crossed and her stance was belligerent.

Finally, he relaxed just a little. "There's only one kind. Catholic means good."

Her mouth fell open. It was that or bark out a harsh laugh. "You have to be kidding me! You've never arrested a Catholic? There are no priests who are pedophiles—that's all some weird and nasty rumor with no truth? You can't be that stupid."

This time his mouth worked like a fish.

Good, he didn't have a comeback for that one.

Then he did. "Those aren't Catholic behaviors."

Purposefully and willfully calming herself, Yasmin tried to count to ten. She knew better. She'd had this argument innumerable times in the past and she always stayed serene. People just didn't understand. So why did she want to hit him for his ignorance?

Because she did. That's why.

"Wicca—the religion of witchcraft—is in and of itself good. The basic tenet is: *harm none.* By your definition there's no such thing as a bad Catholic, because when you do something bad, that's not Catholic. The same is true of Wicca—selfish behaviors—harmful ones—aren't Wiccan."

There. Her job here was done.

"What about animal sacrifices? I bet the animals don't think you're following that 'harm none' rule. There's a pentagram on the floor—that's Satanic."

Oh Goddess, save me from ignorant men.

Yasmin wanted to shut the front door in his face. But she couldn't, he was in her hallway and he was in between her and her altar. "Wicca doesn't do animal sacrifice. I think you're confused with Satanism and maybe some Voodoo. There's no animal sacrifice because the original tenet is *harm none*. 'None' includes animals." She bit her tongue and didn't say 'and nosy cops.' She fought to keep the sarcasm out of her voice, but it didn't work. "And that pentagram is *not* Satanic. Upside down pentagrams are associated with Satanism, just like *upside down crosses are.* Don't use your ignorance to accuse me of things I haven't done."

Her arms crossed again. She was pissed as hell. In the past twenty-four hours she'd been shot at, lost this and all future visits with her nieces, and now Officer Multicolor was here accusing her of sacrificing animals.

"So . . ." He drew the word out. "This—" he pointed behind him to the still burning candles, "Is nothing more than a . . . what? And it has nothing to do with last night's shooting?"

Her head came forward and her chin jutted out, a combination of stubbornness and disbelief. She lost the fight and sarcasm now dripped from every word. "Yes, as a witch I decided I needed to be shot at. I thought I'd put my young nieces in jeopardy and get my vacation ended early—with bullets. I desperately wanted to get repeatedly interviewed by ignorant and suspicious police officers. So I *conjured* a gang initiation."

Yasmin didn't care anymore. Had she thought his blue eyes were amazing? Not anymore. Officer Multicolor had just worn out his welcome. She turned and walked away, was even considering grabbing the whiskey she sometimes cooked with and putting the bottle to her lips. Maybe—since she couldn't spell him away—she could drink him away.

She was in the kitchen, slamming the fridge and the cabinets open and shut when she felt him come up behind her. She didn't wait for any more ignorance to come out of his mouth. "You can leave now. Don't worry, I'll hex my own home so the gang members can't to get me. You've warned me, you've insulted me, your job is done."

Pulling a soda out, she almost popped the top, then decided that spraying herself with shaken up cranberry drink in front of the good detective was not a solid idea. She put her hand over the chilly metal and calmed the drink.

"I'm sorry."

Suddenly startled, she didn't answer. Didn't turn to look at him, just popped the top and took a drink. It didn't silence the feelings stirred up in her.

He said it again. "I'm sorry."

"Thank you. You can still go." Staying faced toward the cabinet, she waited to hear him leave. But the sounds didn't come. "Please."

"I don't think you're safe." The words were resigned, tired.

"I told you. I'll put a hex on the house. No one will come in."

Still, he didn't leave. His voice was softer, and for once, his tone didn't sound like there was an underlying *thou shalt not suffer a witch to live.* "I don't mean to be rude, this is a real question. But if your protection spells work so well, why were you shot at last night?"

Yasmin felt her shoulders slump as all the belligerence went out of her. "That is the million dollar question. I've been trying to figure it out all day." She didn't add, *It may be because of a love spell I cast on my boss. It had to be subtle, or Tristan would see it, so it's entirely possible that I screwed it up royally.*

All that stayed in her head and she was suddenly glad Luke Salzone didn't believe in witchcraft, glad he didn't have any skills in that area.

Like a true detective, he didn't give up. "You really have no idea?"

Finally she turned to look at him. His eyes really were a stunning shade of blue, but she ignored it. "If I knew what went wrong, it wouldn't have happened in the first place." She shrugged at him, still trying to think of ways to get him to leave. "You don't have to believe me. You can think I'm a crackpot, that's fine. Just put an officer outside my house and you can be done."

He started laughing.

Yasmin blinked at him.

Detective Salzone laughed even harder. "Wait." He tried to get himself together while she tried to figure out what was so damn funny. She wasn't on her A-game, and honestly she wanted another nap, not another confrontation. This was sapping her, and it seemed it wasn't over yet.

"Give me a second." Taking a few deep breaths, he managed to get himself together. "I'm sorry, but this is Los Angeles. There are no spare officers. We can't keep up with all the crime already perpetrated, let alone get ahead of the crime that hasn't happened yet. Give me a dollar."

He insulted her and laughed at her and he wanted a tip? Her eyebrows raised of their own accord.

"Hire me. Personal protection. I can't just follow you around. That would be illegal and give me no jurisdiction. You have to hire me and pay me. Give me a dollar." As he still chuckled at her, he held out a hand as though he expected that to happen.

"Why don't I hire someone else?" Why would she want *him* around?

"Because no one else will do it for a dollar. They can't."

"But you can?" This day was getting more and more bizarre.

"Look, we can't assign you a patrol officer without a recorded and credible threat. That circle of your stuff isn't enough to issue a full-time guard for your house. If you can afford someone else, that's great, but we don't come cheap."

Yasmin rolled her eyes and considered calling him 'Officer Multicolor' to his face. "I'll put a spell on the house."

His mirth rapidly faded. "I'm not saying you shouldn't do that. Use any means necessary. But I'd feel better if you were also protected by an officer with a gun."

~

Luke felt as much as saw Yasmin's stare, whiskey eyes working some kind of spell even if she wasn't trying to. He honestly had no idea what to do with her. Was she manipulating him? Did witchcraft actually work?

He was more than aware that there were a lot of people with loose bolts in LA. He dealt with them on a regular basis and generally preferred the nuts to the criminal deviants and even the garden variety a-holes.

Luke just hadn't been ready for his dream-girl to turn out to be one of the kooks. And he still wasn't ready to let her fend for herself with just a few candles and a creepy floor mat. Not against the Del Surs.

She took another drink of the soda, some frou-frou organic thing, and eyed him some more. Clearly, she was making a decision. Finally, she set the drink aside and asked, "If I hire an officer, how would it work?"

Good. She'd bitten. Luke started to sell her. "It works how you want it to. Officer outside in the car, inside on the couch, or stalking the property all night. Though that all depends on who you hire and what they are willing to do."

There was a beat, while she thought about it. "What does my dollar get me?"

"Me. Inside the house, probably on the couch—" he wasn't interested in her spare room with the candles and supposedly non-satanic pentagram. "I'm still on shift regularly. So I'll have to sleep, but my being here will be a huge deterrent."

"Why not outside, in the car?"

She really was trying to get rid of him. "Because I have to sleep. And I can't see all four sides of the house from the street, or even the driveway. Besides, if someone broke in, who would let me in the door?"

"And about how much would I pay for another officer?"

That hurt. Knife right to the heart. But he had to remind himself that the point was keeping a citizen safe. He quoted her the average rates for a non-retired, off-duty LAPD officer and watched her choke on her soda.

Once she got it together, she started eyeing him again. "So why are you so cheap?"

He was only cheap for her—probably not a good thing. But he was doing it anyway. He didn't tell her any of that. "Because I was there. Because I was the officer who drew my gun at the scene. And with all the people on the street behind them I couldn't just shoot the fuckers— I'm sorry, pardon my language." He shouldn't have said that. She might be a kook or a witch, but she didn't strike him as that flashy kind of L.A. party girl with a foul mouth.

"Oh, I think 'fuckers' is the right term. It might even be a little tame." Her features pinched. She was pissed. *Good.*

"Then we'll agree on that." He nodded. "I'm in for a dollar because I worked Guns-and-Gangs for a year and I know what the Del Surs will do. I'm in because all any of us can put in the report is the colors they wore and what they actually did. I'm the only one besides you who really saw them. I *know* those guys were Del Sur. I *know* their intent was to kill you in front of your nieces. I don't want them to finish the job."

He was trying not to think about the crazy that went with the beautiful. He was trying not to ramble. He figured he'd given her enough to ponder and paused to let her think for a minute.

When she walked away, he had no idea what she was going to do and he was genuinely surprised when she came back and handed him a dollar.

Luke held his hands up. "I can't take it yet. I have to call in. It has to be official and I have to get it cleared."

Her head tilted. "So you offered me something you're not sure you can deliver?"

"Whoa. Not like that. There's no way they'll say no. That was the Del Surs who took aim at you." He thought that was better than saying he was growing more certain she'd actually been shot. "But it needs to be official and cleared, in case I have to draw my weapon. So first I get it approved, then you pay me. All clean and legal, that's how we get these guys."

She seemed to nod at that and patiently waited, drinking soda while he made several calls. He had to call his own captain, get the assignment. Then he had to check in with the North Hollywood precinct and let them know he was working in their district and exactly what his capacity was.

It took a good twenty minutes, and by the time he was done, she'd wandered off.

This time he looked around, checking out the shelves more closely. The scarves, candles, and herbs could be witchy, he supposed. She didn't seem scary, but he didn't know what to make of it yet. "Yasmin?"

As soon as it left his mouth, he thought better of it and figured he should have asked for "Ms. Ali."

"Back here." She was in the creepy room.

When he came into the doorway, he saw her rolling out something plastic and waited a moment before he realized it wasn't anything supernatural, just an inflatable mattress and plug-in blower.

It wasn't any too quiet and she raised her voice to be heard. "You can sleep in here. This is a full size, it should be better than the couch." The look on his face must have made an impression. "Don't worry, I cleared all the witchcrafty stuff out first."

He debated. The couch looked perfectly comfy for sitting, but it wasn't anywhere near long enough for a guy like him to sleep on. The full size mattress didn't look like it would fit his height either, but at least it had to be better than the couch. If she had any real powers, was he any less susceptible on the couch than he was in here? "Show me."

She pointed at the mattress, then pushed on the surface. "It's almost full. I have some nice enough sheets for it."

That wasn't what he meant. "No. Show me what you can do. If you're a witch and you believe you're strong enough to protect yourself, surely you can do something to show me."

Luke waited for her to offer some excuse. The crackpots always did. “I can't do it on Tuesdays,” or “not when I'm stressed,” or “only when no one watches.”

She didn't disappoint. But she only said. "No."

He had her dollar. They had an agreement, he was going to even write it up tomorrow. So he pushed. "Why?"

She looked away and he waited her out.

"Because people have asked me that in the past, and when I did something, they left. They got scared or mad or *something*. One guy threatened me. He came into the shop for something and asked to see what a real witch could do. Then, when I showed him, he nearly attacked me. My boss had to come in and throw him out."

"You did this at *work*?" He felt his eyebrows rise. Yes, L.A. was apparently full enough of the weirdos that they even worked together.

Her answer surprised him even more. "I work at a magick shop. I teach introductory witchcraft and spellwork."

Well, grab a crayon and color him surprised. "There's a class?" then another thought struck him. "Can I take it?"

"I'd rather you didn't. I try to limit it to the serious. No gawkers allowed." She frowned at him a bit as if he'd just pushed a little too far. He probably had, judging by her next words. "Can I come to your church and play with the things on the altar?"

Oh, no, she didn't. "You can't compare this to Catholicism! It's an age old, organized religion."

Uh-oh. Those had clearly been the wrong words. And he was about to get a beat down. He could see it coming.

Calmly turning off the obnoxious little motor, she stood and looked down her nose at him, a feat she easily managed even though he was a good seven or eight inches taller than her.

"So I can't compare my religion to yours? Mine's not as valuable? Not as sacred?" Her arms crossed again and he deeply regretted his words. Her words kept coming. "Your religion is valuable because it's *old*? Mine's older. At least ten thousand years older. Your religion is *based on mine*."

She kept going, but he'd heard it before, that major holidays were stolen or at least borrowed from the pagan religions. She mocked his Christmas tree and his Easter eggs and finally he held his hands up and surrendered.

Her jaw clenched and those whiskey eyes flared. "Have you studied religion? I have. I have a degree in it. I'll bet you that I know your religion and your Bible better than you do."

Luke didn't doubt her. But he didn't like what she was saying either. "But you don't believe."

Her eyes blinked. There was a sheen of wetness that he instantly regretted putting there. He shouldn't have started this.

Her lips pressed, forfeiting their usual lushness in favor of anger. "I *do* believe. I just don't believe it exactly the same way you do."

He nodded. That he could accept. He couldn't really deal with *what* she believed, but she'd convinced him that she did believe it.

Her voice was soft but quiet. "You know what, this is a bad idea. You should leave."

"No, I shouldn't. The Del Surs are still out there, they're still mad, and they still know exactly where you live." He shouldn't have pushed her. She wasn't safe. He was going to have to learn to keep his mouth shut about her weird ways.

Luke really didn't know why he pushed her. On the job, he'd had one woman say she talked to fairies and he'd only asked her what the fairies said. He'd helped schizophrenics in the middle of psychotic breaks. But he so badly wanted this woman to be sane. That was probably why he was pushing. It was time to let go of the dinner date he'd thought about when he first saw her in the store. Time to forget the punch in the gut he got when she'd looked up from selecting ice cream and smiled at him. He simply had to keep her safe.

She was still mad.

Shit. What could he do?

He opened his mouth and instantly regretted it.

Yasmin picked up a candle from her desktop and snapped her fingers. The candle popped instantly to full flame. Not even a sputter.

It was a cool trick, he could admit that much. But you could buy that one online. He shook his head. If that was her parlor trick, it was pretty clean, but it was just a parlor trick.

Still mad, she lined up a row of the four candles that had been on the floor. "You tell me."

"Green."

It came to life too.

"Turn it off."

She snapped again and it went out.

Luke sighed. She was now trying to run him off. But he wasn't going to be scared. He couldn't run. Because if he did, the Del Surs would show up on her doorstep, or through a window. And lighting a candle wasn't going to scare them away.

"Leave!" Her voice was low but the vehemence was surprising. But she put her hands up, palm out toward him, the way he'd seen her do in the parking lot. She pushed out at him, a sound coming out of her throat that somewhat resembled a growl.

Though he was far beyond the physical reach of her hands, he *felt* them. Luke felt her touch him, shove him, and he stumbled backward.

Holy shit.

She did it again. He stumbled a few steps back. She did it again, until he felt the wall at his back.

He'd been shoved harder in his life. Many times. But he'd never been shoved like that when the person *hadn't even touched him.*

Even angrier at him than she'd been before, she lifted her two hands and started chanting something just under her breath. The air around her shimmered. Or else he was losing it.

It was probably the second one, because he did not believe what he was seeing.

Taking advantage of his shock, Yasmin Ali turned feral eyes on him and said, "I can take care of myself."

Suddenly, he remembered why he was here. Why he was even contemplating sleeping on that inflatable mattress in this weird room for this crazy woman. He pulled his gun and aimed it at the floor in front of her.

The shimmer stopped.

Yasmin gasped, her hands flying up and her feet moving backward. She choked out, "What are you doing?"

Luke put the gun back immediately, snapping the holster down with his right hand, his left up in a wait-a-minute gesture. "I was making a point. The safety was on, you were in no danger, but are you prepared for that? Because that's what the Del Surs are bringing."

Her eyes closed. Yasmin's shoulders slumped and she shook her head, defeated.

Pushing past him, she went into the hallway and shuffled around in the closet. He almost didn't catch the pile of sheets and the blanket she just tossed at him.

Then she turned and stalked off.

He heard her bedroom door slam a moment later and he wondered if she'd pushed it with her hand or if it had just slammed behind her on its own.

CHAPTER 5

Luke hadn't slept well. The mattress was fine, but he had nothing to sleep in, no toothbrush, and no change of clothes. He also had some pretty crazy thoughts ricocheting around his brain.

He'd never seen what she'd done before. He'd seen magic shows—some pretty good ones—but no one had said it wasn't a trick. And he'd never seen anyone take orders from a bystander. She'd lit and snuffed every candle like he asked. She couldn't have known the order he would choose.

Luke considered a remote control of some kind, but she didn't have one. Her hands were empty. He thought about a second person, but who would set that up in their own home and have it ready at all times? He'd barged in on her, showed up unannounced.

And if that hadn't convinced him she at least had the ability to control some small flames, the hands shoving at him had done the trick. He'd never seen a magician *touch* a person without actually laying hands on them. He'd *felt* it—felt her hands on his shoulders though she was several feet away.

Even if she just worked some kind of mojo on him so he

merely *believed* she performed these tricks, that was still her working magic on him, wasn't it?

It went against everything he knew. Everything he was taught. Everything he believed.

Luke was grateful she rolled up the carpet with the pentagram on it and that she stashed the candles out in the hall. The whole idea of sleeping with it nearby creeped him out. When he did fall asleep, he dreamed disturbing images of rituals with him as the sacrifice. Witches in dark robes with pointy hoods surrounded him and plunged wicked looking daggers into his heart or cut it out entirely while he was staked out on the ground.

Thus, he hadn't gotten a wink of good sleep.

It was a damn lot to deal with for a dollar.

He laid there on the air mattress. The sheets didn't fully fit as it was about two feet high. He figured the height was so you weren't sleeping on the floor, but it was hell on the sheets. The corner of the bottom sheet kept popping up, but he was tired of fixing it. It didn't matter anyway since he had to choose having his feet on the mattress or his head on the pillow. He was slightly diagonal and there was still a gap by his feet. Men were routinely over six feet tall these days, why hadn't mattresses kept up? He was only six one, and not all that bulky. Luke didn't envy the guys who were bigger than him.

Of course, they were probably in their own beds, not worried about witches and gangs. When he heard Yasmin around the house, he decided it was time to get up and figure out what to do with the day.

Pulling on his pants and his button down shirt, he tried to ignore the fuzzy taste in his mouth and the fact that he was putting on old clothes. For once, he didn't even bother with the tie.

When he opened the door, she stood at the end of the hallway as though she knew he was coming out. He told himself that it wasn't witchcraft. The girl had ears and was simply listening for a guest.

"Good morning, Officer Salzone." Her tone was shy of pleasant, but he took it.

"Luke. Please."

"Good morning, Luke." Her voice didn't change tone, but she pointed into the bathroom. "There's a toothbrush and toothpaste out for you. What's in there is the guest set, so help yourself." She turned away, not seeing his grateful smile and wondering if she could read his thoughts. He told himself she was simply thoughtful and he couldn't attribute every move to the paranormal.

In the bathroom he found a washcloth and hand towel, along with two fluffy soft, dark blue, bath-sheet sized body towels laid out for him. Tall man towels. He was grateful.

It felt wonderful to be clean, but worse to step back into yesterday's clothes. Still, he came down the hallway, not sure what he'd find, not certain he was ready to apologize or listen to her apologies.

It didn't happen.

She was sitting at the table, playing with her phone or a tablet or something, but she popped right up. "If you want breakfast, I have two kinds of cereal or I can make fried eggs with bacon and toast."

It was more than he'd been expecting, but then her eyes darted to the right, looking suspicious. "What?" he asked, suddenly wary.

"It's all I can make. I can't cook. Really at all."

He wanted to laugh. "You can make bacon."

"No, I can't. I have one of those microwave things."

He did laugh this time. "Why don't you just cast a spell on yourself to be able to cook?"

She gave him a dirty look.

"What? It's an honest question!" He couldn't win, could he?

There was an audible sigh before she responded. "Being able to cook and knowing recipes are two different things. Plus, with skills like that, you have to keep casting the spells. Upkeep. Like you brush your teeth every day. The work required to get me from 'not able to cook at all' to maintaining cooking skills would be too much work. So, cereal or eggs and bacon?"

Her explanation kind of made sense. Luke didn't answer. Instead, he looked in her fridge. Sandwich fixings. A small carton of milk. Eggs. Bacon. Salsa. Mustard. A row of condiments. She wasn't kidding. "May I?"

She shrugged at him, then stepped back.

She answered a few questions about where she kept things, grabbed him a pan and made toast—which she claimed she could do with relative skill. Luke didn't comment on the cheap bread.

Ten minutes later, he turned out the first perfect omelet with tomatoes, spinach, cheese and salsa.

"Wow!" She'd said it several times as he cooked. But then she'd frowned, sniffed him, and patted his head.

Wondering if he was getting sized up for some Wiccan ritual, he leaned away. "What?"

"Are you one of these metrosexuals?"

He barked out a laugh, then quickly reached to save the second omelet. "No."

Her expression showing she didn't quite believe him, Yasmin took her plate and sat at the table, but she didn't drop her accusation. "Are you sure? You wear all those pastels, use cloth grocery bags. You cook. You smell nice. I didn't feel any hair gel, but that could be because you aren't at home."

Sliding the larger omelet onto his own plate, he shook his head. They couldn't connect on anything, could they? "No hair gel. Even at home. You use cloth bags, too. And you can shut up about my wearing colors. I work with some of the best people you will ever meet, but I spend my time interacting with good people in the worst situations of their lives or just truly horrible people. Sometimes the only shot of color in my day is my tie. So stuff it, Miss Witch."

He couldn't believe he'd told her to stuff it.

Apparently, neither could she, because she looked stunned for a moment. Luke was just getting ready to kick himself for not being able to keep his mouth closed when she bust into the most amazing laugh he'd ever heard.

Her voice caught on the air around her and her head tilted back, all those curls in shades of chocolate and gold tumbling around her shoulders. Her eyes glinted with the music of her laughter and he stopped where he stood. Plate and glass in hand, his feet planted in the kitchen, he was mesmerized. He stared. Luke couldn't help it.

He couldn't react over the punch in the gut he suddenly felt. The same one that had hit him when she'd looked up at him in the grocery store. The same one he'd been denying ever since then.

Forcing his feet to move, trying not to give away the visceral attraction he felt for her, Luke calmly set his plate at the table and started quietly eating his breakfast. After a moment, after she calmed down and managed to take a bite—which earned him an appreciative moan—he tried to make normal conversation.

"Did you manage to sleep last night?"

"Yeah." She rolled her eyes as though she didn't want to admit it. "I have to say I slept better knowing there was a cop in the next room."

"Good." That was it. He was out of conversation.

But apparently she wasn't.

"By the way, those weird dreams you had last night? They're mostly wrong." She ate another bite of toast and cut off another piece of omelet as though she hadn't said something truly disturbing.

"What?"

"Yes, covens work in circles, but there are more solitary witches than coven based witches in the U.S."

"Okay." He should have known the conversation would turn weird. And it wasn't even eight a.m. yet.

Tilting her head, she looked at him more closely. "Well, you had it wrong. If the witches were dressed, it would be in street clothes or all white or nothing at all. Not the dark robes and pointy hoods you dreamed about."

He was just digesting his own thought—*how did she know that?*—when she laid another one on him.

"And we sure wouldn't sacrifice a person. That was just ridiculous—some witch chanting in tongues and plunging a dagger into your heart? Not gonna happen. We don't cut hearts out."

She looked at him sideways and shook her head. "We never mess with organs—especially hearts. Human or otherwise."

But he wasn't sure she hadn't already done something to his.

By two o'clock Yasmin was insane enough that she figured her curls should have straightened themselves. Sadly, they hadn't.

Luke, though he had showered at her house, insisted on going to his place and getting clean clothes. As that sounded perfectly reasonable, Yasmin wondered why he'd even suggested it out loud. Then it became clear he wanted her to go with him.

Not realizing it was a straight path to an overwhelming urge for homicide, Yasmin amicably agreed.

After a drive over the hills, at exactly the speed limit regardless of the beautiful day and clear road, they arrived at his place—an apartment in Hollywood. Indoor access, working buzzer on the door. There was a garage gate, which Yasmin checked out as they pulled in and became rapidly convinced she could weasel her way in through the garage quite easily—no witchcraft required.

She checked out his lack of decorating skills while he changed. The building's central courtyard had a fountain and access to a pool out back. It was well kept, pretty, green. But inside his unit was white. With white. And some more white. An IKEA table and chairs stood out in black in one corner and his couch was brown. It would have been called 'taupe' or 'caramel' in any other setting, but against the white wall and speckled white carpeting, it was just brown. Yasmin fought the urge to vomit.

He wore all those colors . . . Why didn't he at least paint the walls?

She didn't get to question it because he came out from the back room in jeans and a long sleeved shirt.

Yasmin learned two things right away. One: Officer Multicolor was also multicolor when he was off duty. And two: the man had a fine set of pecs and guns on him. Somehow she managed to not drool. Then he turned around and she saw his ass. Probably he wore all those colors to keep the ladies from hitting on him.

He was leaning into the fridge, getting some kind of energy drink—had he not just eaten an omelet with her?—when he called out, "Do you mind if we stop by my office? I want to see if Valverde has made any progress."

Yasmin's brain didn't quite catch up.

"Do you wear . . . *that* to the office?" she waved her hand at his teal henley and the gray jeans. It would have been just fine, but his cross trainers were lime green. She shook her head.

He'd just popped the top off the bottle as he looked down at himself. "I'm off duty today. I figured— What?"

She was still shaking her head. She was in a cream and rose

colored top with olive pants in a subtle stripe. "We are going to hurt people's eyes."

Luke Salzone took a hit of his bottled drink then he took offense. "I look fine."

"You do look fine." She withheld alternate definitions of *fine*. "And so do I. But *we* clash like nobody's business." She pointed at her own middle-earth tones then at his brights.

He shrugged and offered her a bottle of what he was having. Pretty sure that she saw blades of grass as part of the logo picture, she refused.

But she didn't say no to going with him.

Which is how she wound up riding around town in his passenger seat to the precinct and meeting everyone he couldn't avoid. She talked to Detective Jessica Valverde and spent far too long giving up all her basic life info.

Operating on the fact that Luke trusted the woman, Yasmin handed over her home address, her education level, her work address, position at the shop and length of time worked there, also her previous address, make and model of her car, age, birth date, and social security number. If the woman asked what valuable electronics were in her home or if she knew the bluebook value of her car, Yasmin was going to put her foot down. But the inquisition stopped just shy of that.

Then Yasmin waited for the other half, the part where she heard what progress was being made on the case.

There was none.

No one had seen the men's faces. So there was no police artist or sketch or even description to work from. Though everyone *knew* these guys were Del Sur, there was no proof. Apparently "Officer Salzone worked Guns and Gangs and recognized the markings" wasn't sufficient for evidence.

As of yet, there were no fingerprints at the scene. Though Officer Valverde *said* she was holding out hope that something would come from some fabric on the butt of a gun left behind, her tone didn't sound as optimistic.

Incredibly disheartened, Yasmin followed Luke from the station and climbed into his passenger seat yet again. "Why aren't you upset?"

"I am." He started the engine and thankfully the air conditioning came out cold right away.

"You don't seem upset." She looked at him as he pulled out of the parking lot. He was checking for traffic, and she was ready to hit something.

"I can't show it. I'm an officer. We can't afford to emotionally invest in everything. But, yeah, I am upset." He sighed. "Right now, unless that gun yields something, there's no case. Not until they come after you. And I hope they don't."

"So they just get away with it?" She couldn't believe it. Did he really care? Because he seemed far too calm. Then again, it wasn't him they were going to come after. Maybe they wouldn't come after her either.

Luke sighed. "American law is a fine mix of punishments, restrictions, and liberties. We have to have proof first and last. We can't just arrest people for being bad, they have to have broken a specific law."

"Isn't shooting at a person in a grocery store parking lot against some specific law?"

He almost smiled as he pulled into traffic. "Yes, it is. But who do we arrest? None of us can accurately identify one person as either the shooter or his friend."

Yasmin sat back into the seat. He was right. She could cast a spell to find the person, but she still couldn't get him into jail. Wreaking her own personal justice was tempting but went against her religion. So she rolled down the window because the L.A. weather was so nice today, and she watched the buildings and people go by, and the palm trees standing tall in the still air.

Her breath caught as Luke turned the car into the parking

lot at the grocery store where she'd been shot at. Unused to the feeling of panic, Yasmin reacted poorly. She stiffened in her seat and ground out the words, "What are we doing here?"

"We both lost our groceries the other night. And I know you didn't replace them because there's nothing in your fridge." He hadn't looked at her as he'd been searching for a parking spot. But when he hit the brake and looked over at her he finally caught on. "Oh shit. I'm sorry."

She didn't know if he was apologizing for swearing or for bringing her here, but he seemed to get the idea.

Using his soothing voice, he talked the whole time. "We're leaving. I'm watching the area; no one is here. You're safe. You're with me."

His jaw was clenched. Yasmin could see that and she focused on his face while she tried to forcibly even out her breathing, but she just couldn't seem to do it. Every drop of her blood had chilled suddenly, and just being here made her afraid.

Even though she knew it was irrational—no one was here, just like Luke said—that didn't stop her from being deathly frightened.

Unfortunately, with the heavy flow of cars in and out of the lot, it took a few minutes to get far enough away that she could start to regulate her heartbeat again. Luke was pulling into an open parking space on the side of the road before she could really get it together.

His hands were warm on her bare arms and he turned her to look at him, his eyes darting back and forth to check her reaction. "I'm so sorry. I didn't think."

With a deep gulp of air, she finally pulled herself together. "It's okay. I'm okay now. I didn't expect that."

She was starting to turn away, embarrassed at what had to have been her first ever panic attack, when his hands came up on either side of her face. Crushing some of her curls to her head, he held her there, just looking at her, teal eyes searching for a moment before he nodded and let her go. "Okay, your color is coming back. You'll be okay."

He sat back into his seat and looked out the front window, finally done scrutinizing her. "That was completely my fault. I don't get those reactions anymore, and I didn't think."

Managing a few short nods, Yasmin finally found her voice. "I'm okay now." But she didn't say anything else.

"Do you still want to get groceries? Or should I take you home? Get you a stiff drink? On me, because that was stupid to take you back there."

A small laugh burbled out of her. "A drink sounds good, but groceries would be better. I just don't know where to go."

"There has to be something closer to your house."

"Prices are higher there. That's why I shop here." Then she tilted her head. "You know, today, I find I don't care." And she gave him directions.

He followed her up and down some of the aisles, then made her spend time in sections she never lingered in. She was pasta and frozen meals, he was apparently gourmet cheeses and fresh breads. It turned out, there was a machine in the bakery that you could roll whole-loaf bread into and it would slice it to whatever thickness you wanted. The man bought fresh herbs while she stared at him and eventually she added an apple to her own cart just so she didn't seem so plebeian.

They unloaded her groceries at her place, then headed into Hollywood again to unload his—which Yasmin thought was simply ridiculous that she had to tag along. She wanted to call her friend Jenn and see if she was available for dinner, but she realized she had to ask Luke first . . . Then he said sure and that he would be coming along.

"Oh no." Yasmin stood in his white living room, her hands out. "You're not coming to dinner with my friend and me." She'd already had him watch her put her groceries away.

"You remember who's after you?" He glared from where he

was arranging his herbs in one of his very neat refrigerator doors.

"They aren't going to follow me to a crowded restaurant! They have my address, not my schedule. They can't have hacked my cell or be reading my texts. What about when I go back to work? You can't follow me there!"

Looking defeated, he rubbed the back of his neck, and conceded. "You're right. I doubt they've hacked your phone. You're probably fine. But what if you aren't?"

Well, she couldn't live like his puppy, tagging around after him, could she? "I'll be fine."

His mouth, normally jovial, thinned. "You got shot. And they came back and left a warning that they know where you live."

"So I'll call you on my way home and you can meet me there. Or I'll give you a key and you can let yourself in when you want."

"Fine. Give me the key." He held his hand out as though she had a spare on her person. No, this was going to require yet another trek across town. "And you don't go anywhere alone."

She huffed out an exasperated sigh. She couldn't help it. "And I wasn't shot. I was shot *at*."

His own sigh was as long suffering as hers was sharp. "I'm not so sure about that."

CHAPTER 6

Luke was sitting at his desk the next day, back on duty but not accomplishing much. Because he wasn't a uniformed officer, he wasn't put on desk duty for having drawn his weapon. But he had become part of the case, which meant his own case load had to be lightened. It wasn't something he wanted, but he had to admit that being involved in Yasmin's shooting was taking time out of his regular workday.

He was worried about her. He told her to stay out of the house all day. She was given strict orders not to go back for anything, and if she had to, wait until he could escort her. The problem was that she protested at every turn and though she finally relented, she didn't seem like the type to follow orders well.

Luke almost laughed remembering his first impression of her as a traditionally raised middle-eastern woman. He'd been most concerned about her dating habits, but had also thought she might be too meek. That had been about the worst character misjudgment he'd ever made.

Only a regular clicking sound and a huff brought him out of

his musings. Valverde had been tapping her pen on the edge of his desk, then finally sat on the corner.

Looking up, Luke decided he didn't like what he saw.

"You want the bad news first, or the bad news?"

"Shit."

Her look shot waves of pity his way. It wasn't something he was used to getting from a colleague. "You on guard duty on that one?"

He nodded. It wasn't a secret or anything.

She nodded back at him. "Is it about a piece of ass or because you feel responsible?"

"The second one." He didn't call her out for suggesting he was after Yasmin. He didn't do that. He never used his job to get in anyone's pants and he abhorred badge bunnies—something Valverde knew. So it was likely she was just asking if he had feelings for Yasmin, but in her own slightly crass way. Because he did, he couldn't take offense. However, those feelings took a far distant second to the need to make up for the fact that he hadn't been able to shoot those mother-f-ers where they stood.

"Well, you can stop. There's never going to be a case."

That got his attention. "Fingerprints on the fabric came back negative?"

"Oh no. It's worse than that. We got two clean full prints and a partial palm. And a witness came forward, got a good look at the whole thing."

"That's amazing! So what's wrong?"

She looked around the office, then back at him. "You need lunch."

"It's ten-thirty." He eyed her askance, knowing he should have just said yes, but he couldn't quite bring himself to do it.

"You *need* an early lunch. Let's hit somewhere we can sit and chat out of the way of anyone hearing." She stood up, checked her watch, and looked back at him. "Let me make a few calls and we'll head out in about ten minutes."

He didn't even get to nod. She just assumed his acquiescence. Ten minutes later he was following her out the door and down the street to the sandwich shop on Fountain Avenue. They found one of the few booths open in the back. Between her calls, walking, ordering, and waiting for the grilled sandwiches and drinks to be handed over, it took nearly thirty minutes from when she told him that there was a clean handprint and a witness and that somehow that was bad.

Without even bothering to unwrap his sandwich, Luke asked, "So?"

Jessica didn't bother with hers either. She'd eat it, but this was clearly about being out of earshot of the others. "The handprint matches to one Homeo Doff. Eighteen, sealed juvenile record. He's likely our shooter."

That made sense. Luke nodded. It wasn't bad yet, so he still didn't understand.

"We think—from what we can gather—that he's running with Doddo's group from the Del Surs. Was that maybe Doddo there as well?"

Luke would have thought he would recognize the new head of the ironically northernmost cluster of the Del Surs. The old leader had been killed recently in a drive by from the Jungle crew. He was glad to be out of guns and gangs, but all he could do was shrug. It might have been Doddo there for all he knew.

"The witness spent some time with the books. He clearly pulled out Homeo as the shooter and Doddo with him. He also correctly identified you and Ms. Ali as present at the scene." Jessica sighed. Loudly. And unwrapped her sandwich, taking a big bite.

Only able to stare, Luke shook his head. It was as though the clouds parted and the angels dropped necessary evidence as well as a credible witness right into their laps. But Valverde was clearly pissed off. "What?"

She chewed her bite, looking as close to forlorn as she ever did. Jessica was a duck; everything rolled off her, except maybe this. Luke consoled himself by unwrapping what he knew to be the best local Philly cheesesteak and taking his own huge bite while it was still hot.

Finally, Jessica spoke again. "This man is crazy credible. Married, accountant, homeowner, father of two. The problem is what else he saw." She sipped the soda as best she could, the drink was too large for her to lift easily with one hand. "He didn't come forward right away because he was shaken up, not only by the fact that someone was shot at right in front of him, but because he saw *blue flames appearing on the ground around the victim as though she traced them there*. His words, not mine."

"Oh." Luke gave his own deep sigh. No one would believe that. All that credibility, right down the drain.

But Jessica gave a crazy grin. "Oh, it gets better. According to Mr. Awesome Witness, Ms. Ali was chanting when she drew flames on the ground. Then he says the shooter *didn't* miss—that Ms. Ali actually *caught* the bullet with her hand and *then*—" she was emphasizing her words with her fist banging softly on the table top. "Then she held her hand out and beamed a red laser at the shooter making his gun turn hot and making him swear and drop it. *Then* she pushed the air around her."

"Is that all?" He wasn't even enjoying the sandwich anymore. Aside from the laser beam, he'd seen all of that himself. He just hadn't put it in the report. How could he?

"Oh no. It gets better." Jessica looked physically pained now. "She works as a clerk and teacher at a shop called *Blessed Be*. I figured, pretty girl like that, Hollywood and Vine address, probably a sweet little lingerie shop."

Luke couldn't help the way his eyes blinked. That had never crossed his mind. Damn, now it did. Luckily, Valverde didn't seem to notice.

"Nope. Not a sex shop. It's a witchcraft store and she claims she's a witch."

Somehow, he felt defensive, even though he'd had the same argument with her just two nights ago. "It's a religion."

"Yeah well, it's a case that will never hold up in court." She consoled herself with another big bite of her sub. "I can't put the time on it."

Luke understood. There were just too many cases for them to work on the ones that would never have merit. There was nothing Jessica could do about it. His heart sank.

"You still gonna stay with her?"

The question caught him off guard. "Don't I have to?"

"No case, no reason for them to come after her." Valverde looked hopeful, but Luke didn't feel it.

"Actually, I think this makes it worse. My hope was to cover her until we got one of them in jail. But now . . . that's not going to happen." He picked up a fry then slapped it back into its boat as though it were to blame for his predicament. "I don't think their message was about the case. The Del Surs finish what they start. I think they're after her because she didn't die the first time."

"That was your experience in Guns and Gangs?"

"All the time. And the Del Surs are the worst. They make the Stone Jungles look tame. That murder is the last step of the Del Sur inner circle initiation and these guys have all the humanity taken from them before they even get to that point. Frankly, I was shocked he didn't just walk up and shoot her. Homeo—if that was him—balked. He gave her a moment."

"Then when he did shoot her, she caught the bullet." Jessica's mouth quirked as though trying to hold something in.

"You believe the witness?" Luke didn't know what to make of that. He was having a hard time reconciling what he'd seen, both at the crime scene and in her house.

"I didn't believe a damn thing. I don't believe in that crap. But I have evidence and I have to tell you to watch your back while you're working with her." This time she looked serious.

"What evidence?" His lunch was getting cold, but he'd figured that was going to be the case even when he walked over here.

"Well, there's the gun with the burned nylon handprint on it. So it got hot while Homeo Doff's hand was in contact with it. Then there's the mild discoloration in the tar on the parking lot where she was standing. It's in a perfect circle around where she was standing and is indicative of high heat. One of the crime scene techs found it even before Mr. Excellent Witness said she lit a blue fire circle. And there's the squashed bullet, which happens to just match that nasty bruise on her palm." She looked him in the eyes. "I can't put it together any way other than the way the witness says it happened. So I have to go back to him and tell him I don't think he's bona fide crazy, but that everyone else will."

"Good lord." Luke's shoulders sagged. There wasn't a good answer here. Maybe if he was lucky Homeo and his gang would find someone else and leave Yasmin alone. Then Luke could move out and know she was safe—or at least as safe as a woman living alone in L.A. could be. But how would he know when that day came? And he had moral problems with wishing the Del Surs would finish the job somewhere else. It would mean another person would die. He couldn't want that.

Valverde was looking at him, scrutinizing. "What do you think? Do you believe she's a witch?"

Wasn't that the million dollar question? "Absolutely. It's a religion, she says she's a practicing witch. That's like asking if you believe I'm a Catholic."

A small nod acknowledged the answer he gave, and Luke could tell she wasn't going to let it drop. "Do you think she did those things at the scene?"

He thought for a moment. "I didn't see any red laser beam making the gun hot." Could he tell her the rest? He'd specifically avoided this because he knew people would think he was completely off his freakin' rocker. But he admitted to part of it. "I saw the circle of fire, it was pale blue."

"Pale blue. That's exactly what this dude said." Valverde sat back, thinking. Absorbing the news. "What about the bullet? Did you see her catch it?"

"I didn't. But I saw the bruise the next day and it was clearly fresh."

"Interesting." She mulled it over. "I just don't think there's a case here."

"Not until the Del Surs come back to finish what they started."

Yasmin was ready to demand her dollar back. Officer Multicolor had taken over her home. When she agreed to protection, it gave her a warm feeling, a sense of security. Now she just felt invaded.

He was there when she woke up. She had to wait for her own shower sometimes. She couldn't cast spells with him in the house and she wasn't allowed to be there by herself. And just the other night he'd woken her up. He was wandering the house and opening all the cabinets . . . She had no idea if he was sleepwalking or what, but for a woman who lived alone it was too much.

The upside was that he cooked. Sure, she'd eaten with Delilah and Brandon a ton, and Delilah was a professional chef. Since she was always feeding Tristan—whom she referred to as her "stray brother"—she was always happy to have Yasmin be another stray at the table. But Luke cooked good Olde World Italian food.

He made the most amazing coffees in the morning and stocked her kitchen with fresh rolls and pastries. He brought crusty breads and simmered tomato sauces while she watched with her face in shock and her stomach rumbling. She wouldn't have been surprised to catch him tossing pizza dough in her kitchen. Every time she asked about his culinary skills he simply looked at her and said, "I'm Italian" as though that explained everything.

She was going to have to cast a spell on herself to keep from gaining weight. Not that she could cast anything with him there. She needed to protect the house—which, of course, she also couldn't do with him there. His bed was in her spell room.

Having thought ahead and knowing she'd have no time for spell work while the girls visited, Yasmin doubled up the week before, but it was going to wear off. Just like she'd told Luke, it was like brushing your teeth or washing your hair, some of it had to be maintained.

She was going back to work the next day, a welcome reprieve from her 'vacation.' But she had to protect the house. She had to get some things in place. The whole reason he was here was because it was likely she was already a target for murder. The thought alone made her shudder.

When they sat down for dinner, she decided to make conversation and bring it around to the fact that she was going to have to cast tonight. Yasmin started easy. "This soup is amazing."

"Thank you." He'd already said he learned all of it from his mother.

"Your mother must be a fantastic cook."

"She is." He smiled.

Trying to keep the conversation flowing, Yasmin stuck to the safe topic of food. "You'd like my friend Delilah, she's a professional chef. And she's amazing."

He nodded. "Is she a witch, too?"

Okay. Conversation not so safe. "Yes. She's my boss's sister and half owner of Blessed Be."

"Is she as good as you?"

That startled her. He thought she was 'good' . . . Though she didn't think he meant it that she was a good person, just skilled. Then Yasmin laughed. "I'm a junior witch! Delilah and Tristan were born to it. She makes me look like a rank amateur."

That stopped him cold.

Uh-oh. She really should have thought it through before she said that. He was wary enough of her small skill set. If he thought too hard about Delilah and Tristan and what they were capable of, he just might run screaming into the night.

When the silence became awkward, he filled it with a change of topic. "Listen, if I'm still here next Sunday, our family has a big dinner. I can skip it if I have to, or you can find someone else to spend a few hours with?"

"Sure!" That wouldn't be a problem. He'd worry about her and not go if she didn't have somewhere to be. She'd have to figure something out. Maybe Jenn and Lissa could come over . . .

Her interrupted her thoughts. "Or you could come with me. I have eight siblings, a handful of nieces and nephews and even a new great-niece. My mother would be glad to have the extra."

Her mouth was open. The invitation was a surprise. She knew she frightened him just a bit. But eight siblings?

His grin was infectious. "I know you have just the one sister."

She nodded. "Typical nuclear Middle-Eastern-American family. My parents want to help choose my husband, my career, and my breeding schedule."

"Ouch."

"Yours don't?"

He laughed. "My mother wants me to be happy. She has a definite plan for how I should go about making that happen and she's not shy about sharing it. But if I push back hard enough, she figures I either know what I'm talking about or I'm too stubborn to change, so she accepts it."

The knot in her chest indicated she was jealous. "My parents have a plan for me. And when I don't follow it, I'm not just ungrateful, I'm . . . I don't know how to put it. They think they made me. They picked my schools, paid for private education, took me to mosque. They molded me, and to them I have no right to break that mold. They would never say it—because it wouldn't be right—but they act like they own me. The thought that I can get away with all these ideas of my own is simply insulting to them."

"But you're good with your sister, right?" His food was rapidly disappearing and she couldn't figure out why he didn't weigh three thousand pounds.

"Yes. She feels the same way I do, but she hasn't taken any heat for it. Her natural choices are more in alignment with my parents' beliefs. So, ironically, they're much freer with her. She brought her fiancé home and because they liked what he was, they agreed to let her pick him. She would have picked him anyway, but she had their support." Yasmin shrugged as though it didn't hurt as much as it did. She'd tried to live that life for a long time, to be good in their eyes. She found she just couldn't do it.

Clearly, she had Luke's sympathy even if he'd never lived that life. All those brothers and sisters. He must be northern Italian with those blue eyes and that gold hair. She tried to imagine a family of Lukes and all she could picture were the Italian families she'd seen in the movies. So different from her own subdued upbringing.

While Yasmin would love to go and at least observe his big family dinner, she wasn't sure he wouldn't decide she couldn't come after tonight. She broached the topic. "Look, I have to do some spellwork tonight."

The bite of chicken stopped halfway to his mouth; his eyebrows went up. "Spellwork? Casting spells?"

She nodded.

The poor guy was clearly at a loss. He wasn't going to tell her what she could and couldn't do in her own home, but he was clearly uncomfortable.

Trying to allay his fears, Yasmin started explaining . . . or maybe just babbling. "Look, I'll do it out here in the living room. You can stay in your room and never know what's happening. I usually don't work with an audience anyway."

"So the whole coven isn't coming over?"

"No. I'm a solitary witch. Just me. On the other end of the house."

He still looked wary. "The house won't shake?"

"Well, if there's an earthquake it will, but not from me." She shook her head and tried to resume eating her meal as though their conversation resembled anything normal.

"What will you be doing?"

His concern rolled off him in waves. Though if that was from his proximity to the spells or what, she couldn't tell. Yasmin also thought he was asking for details—lighting candles, chanting, burning herbs. But she avoided that. "Protecting the house, me. You?" She let that one hang.

He nodded, clearly digesting her words. "Not sure I need it. I have a gun."

Nodding back, Yasmin let him have that idea. That was the protection he wanted, and she didn't cast on those who didn't ask for it.

"So what do you actually do?"

Well, shit. She didn't want to answer that. "Protection spells. I'll try to hide the house from anyone who wishes me harm."

This time a frown met her in response. He'd all but quit eating. "They have your address. How could you possibly hide that? Could you make them all lose the information?"

She nodded. "I think so, but that's a very specific thing to do —it takes a lot of energy and is more likely to fail . . . or go awry." Yasmin thought back on that love spell she'd cast before all this started. It may have gone wrong, may have brought all this to her doorstep. She'd decided to stick to more broad spells, even if that love spell hadn't been all that specific itself.

When she looked up, he was sitting back in his chair, his arms crossed. The look on his face was troubled. Already pretty sure she didn't want the answer, Yasmin asked anyway. "What?"

"I just—" he stopped himself, clearly biting off his own words. Then he gulped in air and went for it. "I just don't believe it works."

She nodded at him. She'd been doing that a lot. It was a good answer that didn't involve yelling or being hurt. She could scream at him, that he was an idiot not to believe after all he'd seen in the last handful of days. But she didn't yell. He had a right to believe what he did. It took a moment to be able to answer calmly, but she managed. "That's okay. You don't have to believe in it to make it real. Lots of people were convinced the earth was flat for a long time, but that didn't make it any less round."

"Sure, but that was ignorance."

She just raised one eyebrow at him and forced herself to go back to the meal, wishing she could enjoy it more, it was truly wonderful. Only the conversation was getting in the way.

"Okay. I set myself up for that one."

At least the man could concede gracefully.

He just couldn't drop it and let her be. "So what exactly do you do?"

Thinking for a moment, she pondered how to best put it. Just laying out the steps of a spell wouldn't mean anything to him and would probably just make her sound as kooky as he already thought she was. She tried another tack. "When you're Catholic, you pray and light candles. I've heard of people burying Saints medallions or throwing them into fountains or rivers and saying certain prayers. It's like that."

"It's nothing like that."

So, comparing witchcraft to his own religion didn't go over

well. That didn't make the comparison any less valid. "Sure it is. I have candles, prayers, sacred objects, and certain ways those go together to ask for forgiveness or for something I want to make happen."

He couldn't refute that, but he tried. "Your sacred objects are . . ."

"What? Because counting to ten on a string of beads, or painting a picture of a woman on a candle and calling it the Virgin Mary makes your prayer that much more potent?"

"It does!"

"Exactly!" She smacked her fork down on the table, "Mine does, too. Mine are just the sun and the moon—things that any one of us can see exist on a daily basis. Just because you don't understand it doesn't make it any less valid."

Now he was just as worked up as she was. "There's no church, no altar, no priest."

Her anger fled. She picked up the fork and toyed with a bite. Chewing, she simply ignored the question. This was the big difference. So much was similar through all religions, but this was big.

"What? Why won't you answer that?" He was moving his head, trying to catch her gaze.

Realizing he wasn't going to drop it, she gave up and gave in. "My church is everywhere. We worship nature and all things alive. Putting up a building would only separate us from that which we revere. It's the one thing I really dislike about L.A. My backyard has a privacy fence, but I have only what I grow . . . I should be out in the woods. And I'm often in my house."

He thought on that for a while. "A priest?"

"Don't need one. Many religions believe that we are each our own best path to God."

"Catholics each have a direct relationship to God!"

This was devolving. "But you have a Pope and priests and cardinals, all telling you *how* you should get to God. What if that's not the right path for you?" Picking up her plate, she stood and headed for the kitchen. Carefully saving the remainder of her dinner, because it was really wonderful and didn't deserve to be argued on top of, she tried to show that the conversation was over.

Luke also stood, though his plate was empty. "Look, I think bullets are what's coming. And I'm just not certain you can protect yourself against that."

She held up her left hand, mostly to ward him off, to make him stop. But when his eyes went to the bruise there, she changed her mind. "Maybe I can."

He conceded. But only a little. "Is 'maybe' good enough? Show me what you can do."

CHAPTER 7

"Fine. You want to see? Watch and learn." Yasmin was tired of it. She thought his religion was a bit kooky herself, but she didn't say it. She thought her own religion—the one she'd grown up with—was a little off, too. Wicca spoke to her soul. It made sense and it gave her power in a situation that required her to nearly shed her family because they didn't approve. But she was in no shape to burst into a chorus of "I gotta be me." No, she was mad.

She pushed her furniture back and rolled up the paisley floor rug. Then she hauled her pentagram mat out of the back closet, begrudgingly noting that Luke had made the inflatable bed as neatly as a person could.

Though he might be neat, and he might—in general—be a gentleman, he didn't offer to help her with the mat. Just to test him, she tugged the front end of if toward him and withheld a smirk as he stepped deftly back. Yup, big, bad cop was afraid of her floor canvas. *Ha*.

Unfurling the rug into the space she made, Yasmin took a moment to stop and breathe. She had to align the corners on a straight north/south line. When she first started training, she'd needed a compass, now she could just feel the direction. Then she pulled down candles and placed the colored pillars at the corners. She hauled out her book and flipped the pages finding what she needed.

There was more, small crackled glasses—a gift from Delilah for her birthday last year, handed down through the family, but unused in the last generation. Delilah said she wanted someone to use them. Yasmin had been humbled.

Two orbs—one crystal, one onyx—her ceremonial knife and a handful of found objects that were sacred to her alone. She wished she had something that belonged to the shooter; that would bind the spell better, make the direction clearer. Then again, it would also bind them together more than they already were. Maybe she wasn't so unhappy to not have it. Yasmin headed into the kitchen for a handful of rock salt.

Luke had seated himself cross-legged in the hallway. Though he wasn't writing anything down, she had no doubt that he was taking notes. He raised his eyebrow at the salt.

"Yes, you've been cooking with my spell salt."

He sighed.

She wondered if he thought that would cast some sort of pall on him, as if it might turn him into a toad.

Well, sometimes—like right now—she thought he was already a toad.

She didn't say it. Instead, she held her tongue and ducked into her room to change. When she emerged, she found he hadn't moved from where he sat and she had to high-step over him again. There was something about the way he was watching that made her think perhaps she should offer him some popcorn for the show.

He looked her up and down and couldn't seem to not comment. "Does this mean you're a white witch?"

"That's a silly term." She was in white drawstring pants and a white t-shirt. But her toenails were still teal. "It's all cotton. We worship nature. Rayon and spandex fibers don't really fit with that." Actually it wasn't all cotton. Her undies—white, too—were silk. But they were natural fibers and this wasn't the place to mention that.

The whole thing was weird enough as it was. Occasionally, she'd cast with Delilah and Tristan. And she'd cast with her students all the time. But . . . never before with someone watching and not participating.

Oh well, here went nothing.

Everything was set out. There was no more room to stall, to wish that he would just get up and decide it wasn't interesting.

Yasmin positioned herself in the middle of the pentagram and began by calling the four corners. When all the candles were lit and the circle complete, she started her usual prayer. She didn't look at Luke, just raised her hands and felt the power surge through her.

"This circle is bound with power all around. Between the worlds I stand with protection at hand." Around her, the air pulsed. As she continued speaking, the flames of the pillar candles stretched higher and she felt the energy she called surge through her. It was a heady feeling, but one she had grown accustomed to. "I am of the trees and of the fields, I am of the woods and of the springs, the streams and the hills. I am of thee and thee of me."

Her eyes were closed, and she was trying not to wonder what Luke thought of all this. She was supposed to concentrate and forget that she had an observer. But she felt something snap into place between them.

Shit.

Had she just bound herself to Luke? It must be different when the others were practicing with her, when they were part of the circle.

Cautiously opening her eyes, she found him sitting in front of her, mouth open. Yasmin could almost see it and she could definitely feel it—the air almost shimmered in a bridge between them, crossing the boundary of the circle.

Well, that was an error. She had not intended to bind them together. What she chose to do was ignore it.

She raised her hands up, closed her eyes and started again. This time she began the protection spell. "I need protection for my home, Grass and floor and roof and bone. Wrap us in the heavenly mire, Protect us Earth, Wind, Water, Fire."

The candles flared and flickered. Though she didn't open her eyes, Yasmin could feel them burning hotter, the flames turning blue. "Elements here wise and strong, surround us fully wide and long. Love is the will and love is the bond. So mote it be."

As she opened her eyes, a small circle of blue flame appeared on her floor, flaring for just a moment and dying. Luke still stared—gawked really—and she felt like she was on display. Which she was. But she settled her hands loosely at her sides and turned clockwise three times, raising her hands as she went. When she hit the end of her turns, Yasmin tipped her head back, mouth open to the sky and spoke again.

"Stone of earth, stone of shade into thee this spell be made. That no eye may notice this place, the address gone, the light posthaste. Another home shall they see, any conjured other than me. As I will so mote it be."

Again the energy in the room pulsed around her. This time when she opened her eyes, she looked at Luke on purpose. "I'm going to protect myself. Can I protect you, too?"

Very rapidly, he shook his head. It was a tiny, tight movement as he was clearly disturbed and didn't understand what he was seeing. Though she wished she could do it, it went against her faith to work against another person's wishes. He wasn't her child; she couldn't just protect him. Well, he was protected in the house.

So Yasmin worked a spell on herself, having protected the

house, it was as important that she was as safe as she could be when she wasn't in it.

When she finished, she was exhausted and sat down in the middle of her pentagram, head in hands. She was so powerful when she was casting, but so drained afterward.

Though she couldn't lift her head to look, she saw Luke's feet as he rushed to grab her. Hands shooting out to stall him, she pushed him back before he crossed the line. "Don't break my circle. I'm not done."

He stumbled as though he had bounced off something, but when he reached out and didn't encounter anything but air, he frowned. Only a nod let her know that he understood.

From her seated position, Yasmin tipped her head back again, and released the four corners, ending the circle and leaving her protections in place.

Then, more drained than she had ever been, she laid back and let the blackness take her.

~

Leaping up, Luke didn't make the decision, but he heard the words in his head. *Screw the circle.*

He hoped she was finished, but that wasn't his primary concern.

Ignoring the fact that he'd felt compelled to watch her, and even linked to her during the ceremony, his only objective now was to take care of her.

Part impartial law officer and part frightened friend, he knelt over her and checked first for a pulse, then that she was breathing. Both seemed to be in fine working order. His next concern was to get her conscious, then lucid. Those were proving to be a bit of a problem.

He grabbed her shoulders and gave her just a little shake. But nothing happened. He tapped at her cheek but again she didn't respond.

Starting to get very worried, Luke looked around for something that would have caused this. Really, she had just raised her arms and spun around a few times—not even enough to get dizzy. Then she'd carefully sat down, less than carefully laid back, and now she was unrousable.

His brain scrambled for something to hold onto. Maybe she was like this each time she cast a spell? She had passed out in the parking lot after the shooting. If that was the case then he could just wait a second and she'd be fine.

The other option was that something had gone horribly wrong. Maybe she mis-cast something—if that was even a possibility. Could she have actually hurt herself? It just didn't seem she'd done anything that could cause a real injury.

Just as he was mulling those possibilities over, her eyes began to blink, the deep color pulling his focus to the exclusion of all else. Her gaze flitted one way then another, as though she couldn't process what she was seeing. Then, finally, it landed on him. She mumbled something that sounded like "multicolor," but that didn't make sense. "Yasmin?"

"Officer Salzone?"

Her voice was a bit thready but her enunciation clear if her choice of words wasn't. He did what he was trained to do and stated to her what had happened to see if it brought her back to her surroundings. "Yasmin, you cast a spell then you passed out."

"Ah, crap." This time she pushed at the hand he still cupped her face with. She pushed against the floor, hauling herself upright but he drew the line when she tried to get right to her feet.

"Just sit for a moment."

"Nah, this happens sometimes. You get a really big surge of energy and when the spell is done . . . I guess the difference is a bit hard to handle and you pass out for just a moment." She waved away his concern.

"This has happened before?" He was trying to look into her eyes, make sure she was clear and that she wasn't trying to get away with something. For a moment he wondered if maybe she had a disease that caused this and she was trying to cover something up.

But she looked him in the eye, held his gaze while she answered. "Well, I've read about it, and I saw Delilah do it once. She sent this huge surge out and then closed the circle, calm as could be, then passed right out. And I've had it happen once before."

"In the parking lot, after the shooting?"

Her intake of breath was audible. "Okay, twice before."

"This was big?" He clarified, because he could understand why the spell that stopped a bullet would be a big deal. In fact, even before he'd understood any of it—not that he understood it now—he hadn't been surprised she'd passed out then. It was reasonable that anyone crashing off that adrenaline cliff would just lose their marbles for a minute. But . . .

This time she looked away. As though she was about to lie. And Luke knew liars. He spent his days talking to them and sorting them from the truth-tellers. "Tell me."

She looked at him again—truthful this time. "You don't want me to say it."

"Yes, I do."

"No, you don't." She practically glared at him.

Maybe she thought he should be afraid of that cold stare. He was pretty certain he should be. He didn't know how she did what she did, but he could see it. He was still convinced it was a lot of smoke and mirrors, but he still thought she was capable of some serious injury. Only he really wasn't afraid of her at all. His teeth were clenched together, but he spoke through it. "Tell me."

"It was normal spellwork, but you connected in somehow and that made it bigger." She tipped her head, raised her eyebrows and flattened her mouth as though to say "are you happy now?"

No, he wasn't.

He'd thought that was some weird feeling he conjured up himself from watching her. It was quite the show.

As a rational thinker, Luke knew you couldn't see the wind. But he'd swear on a Bible that he saw the air move around her when she worked. And it wasn't just in the candle flames; during most of it, the flames went one direction and the air another. The feeling that he'd somehow linked into the spell was something his mind created.

At least that's what he told himself.

Yasmin was right; he didn't want to hear that it was something real or even something she saw, too.

There was something in the way she was looking at him now that told him she knew he wasn't prepared to hear that it had actually happened. And he didn't like the idea that it might have hurt her in some way. He tried denying it. "That didn't happen."

A tight nod accompanied her words. "Sure it didn't. That's why it took you so long to answer."

"Fine. You're right." Then he changed the topic with no grace whatsoever. "Are you okay?"

"Hunky dorey."

This time she did stand up, leaving him there on the floor. He only watched for a second. She did seem all right. She didn't waver or sway. Her words were clear with no slurring and her conversational skills were normal, maybe even a bit sharp.

After a moment's deliberation, and acknowledging that he wasn't going to get anywhere, Luke stood up too. "So what spells did you cast?"

"I hid the house."

It was almost as though the words flew right past him he had so much trouble grasping them. "You *hid* it? How does a person hide a house?"

She laughed. It burbled up from somewhere inside her and lit her face up. Luke wanted to enjoy it, but it was at his expense, so he really couldn't. "You watched me do it. Any more 'how' and you'll be able to do it yourself."

He didn't respond. He watched her turn in circles and speak in rhymes. He even saw the pages of her book flip on their own while she worked. He could easily attribute that to the wind, but what could he attribute the wind to?

Watching him carefully, Yasmin looked like she could almost tell what he was thinking. For a moment he panicked and wondered if she actually could.

But she didn't say anything that hinted of it. "If you really want to know what hiding a house does . . ."

"Okay." He'd bite.

She started cleaning up. Gathering candles while she talked and putting them back on shelves, where they would appear to be innocuous decorations. "Well, you said the gang had my address. If they drive by, they won't be able to find it. Oh, shit!"

"What?" Suddenly alarmed, he took the book from her hands before even thinking he did not want to touch that book.

"I'm gonna have a bitch of a time getting my mail! Crap!"

This time he laughed. She really seemed to think she'd hidden the house. And that she'd hidden it so well the mailman —who had come to this address every day for god-knew-how-long—wouldn't see it.

Frowning, she snatched the book back out of his grasp.

Damn! It had occurred to him while he held it that he should inspect it for wires, magnets, any kind of trick set-ups. But her words cut through his thoughts.

"You want to see how well my house is hidden? Go! Drive around the block and come back."

He shook his head. He wasn't supposed to leave her and the whole thing was ludicrous anyway.

"Do it. Drive out of sight of my house then turn right around and come back. You won't be able to find it! Call me when you give up."

This time he spoke it. "I shouldn't leave you here by yourself."

"Oh please. Twenty minutes isn't going to be the magic window where the gang appears." She crossed her arms, clearly daring him. "Do it."

"It won't even be twenty minutes."

"Yes, it will. It will be twenty minutes and you'll call me on the phone. Desperate to find the house." She looked so certain.

They argued for another five minutes before he gave in and took her silly dare. It was possibly the stupidest thing he'd ever done.

He drove away, keeping the house in the rearview mirror as he thought about what kind of ruse this might be. She could be rigging the house for another show, another "spell." She could be using the time to call her friends to help set him up for another trick.

Luke turned right out of the driveway and took a right on Collins, then another on Farmdale. Two more turns and he was back on her street wondering what kind of idiot he was to leave her alone for even just these few minutes.

He was calling himself all kinds of fool when he realized he was already at Collins Street again—past her house. He pulled an illegal U. He was a cop, dammit. This time he counted down the numbers. He saw 5639 and then 5631 . . . But no 5637.

Luke squinted. *Shit.* He must have mis-memorized the address. Driving the street again, this time he ignored the address—figuring he had it wrong anyway—and looked for the cute reddish stucco bungalow.

He didn't see it.

Passing a second time and a third, he saw nothing.

In his head, his swearing was getting louder. He was obviously on the wrong block. He tried Camelia between Miranda and Collins, then south of Burbank Boulevard.

Fifteen minutes later, he panicked and called her. He shouldn't have left her alone that long. Screw her stupid games. He was supposed to protect her. What if something happened while he was out here getting his sorry ass lost? He'd never forgive himself.

Relief crashed through him at the sound of her voice on the phone. Then, almost as fast, he was pissed off.

She didn't even say hello. "I saw you drive by about four times. Where are you now?"

That was bullshit. He'd have seen the house. But he had to get back. He knew his job and it wasn't to drive around playing silly mind games. "Collins Street."

He rattled off the cross street and she had him turn down Camelia on the same damned block he'd been on before. Now she was just messing with him. He drove down the block as angry as he'd probably ever been. "Come on, Yasmin. I'm supposed to be there with you."

"You just passed me."

"Bull. Shit." His head swiveled. He knew he was being a terrible driver. He was on the phone, looking at house numbers on all the mailboxes. This was a residential neighborhood, he was in danger of hitting a kid. So he trained his eyes forward.

"I just came out of the house. Now I'm on the sidewalk, waving at you."

This time, he only looked into his rearview mirror, but there she was. Same white top and pants, probably same bare feet and blue toenails.

Keeping her squarely in his sight, he executed a sweet three-point turn.

Her voice came through the phone in dulcet tones belying

the absurd and probably dangerous game she was playing with him—and therefore with herself, too.

"I see you." He answered back. Luke was pissed. This had been an exercise in futility.

But he didn't take his eyes off her as she walked down the street toward him. Hanging up the phone, she motioned him to stop and when he did, she jumped into the passenger seat. "Go slowly."

He sighed. Deeply. Audibly.

She ignored it but gave him another command. "Stop. Now look to the right, do you see the driveway?"

He did.

Luke frowned. It was an empty lot. What was she—

She interrupted his thoughts. "Don't look for the house. Just look at the driveway. Turn into it."

He wanted to tell her to go to hell, but she probably didn't believe in it. He wanted to tell her to stuff it, but that was unprofessional. And he was trying so hard to be a professional here, even though it was so difficult on so many levels.

Luke kept his mouth shut and turned into the driveway. He was looking at how it kept getting longer when he saw the garage at the end. In reddish stucco. "Holy shit."

Yasmin grinned. Impish and full of satisfaction, she shrugged. "Look around."

He was at her house. Sitting in her driveway. "Holy shit. I drove right by here."

"I know." She almost managed to keep the smug out of her tone. Almost. "I watched you drive by a handful of times. I told you. I hid the house."

"How the hell did you do that? I thought I was lost!" He couldn't breathe. Couldn't process.

Luke had a rational mind. He understood that a person could perform a trick to make the pages of a book turn. He might not know if it was strings or magnets, but he believed in a rational explanation. Even the candles lighting and going out, even the flames jumping several feet into the air—it was no more or less than what those close-up, street magicians did. So he didn't really let it bother him.

But hiding a house? How did a person do that?

Sure, Vegas acts had done much the same thing, but she was a lone person and this wasn't a soundstage. He climbed out of the car, walked up the front walk and pushed open the door—just to check that it was real.

Finally he conjured up a few words. "How did you do that? I didn't see it at all!"

She was right behind him, closing the door and locking the three bolts just as he'd made her promise. Her voice said things that didn't answer his question. "I told you, I hid the house. I cast a spell on it and I hid it."

"That doesn't explain it."

Her head shook back and forth and she faced him, her expression almost sad. "I don't know how to explain it to a non-believer."

"But, I'm Catholic. I believe in so many things."

Yasmin seemed to grasp on to that. "Then you believe in miracles. Think of this as a small one."

Luke shook his head and looked around the house. It was the same house. The candles were even in the same order she'd put them back in, which was a different order than the one they'd been in before she'd cast the spell.

He wanted to look at all of it, touch it, be certain it was real. But instead he grabbed for her left hand and smoothed her fingers with his own, leaving the circular bruise there clear. "I'm beginning to believe."

He just didn't know if he was changing his life or declaring himself a fool.

CHAPTER 8

He couldn't sleep. Tossing and turning, Luke tried to shut down his brain but found it to be an impossible task.

Surely there was an explanation for how he hadn't been able to find the house. He'd simply gotten lost. He was mistaken about driving up and down her street; he must have been on a different road. He'd probably misread the signs. Also, he was agitated before the whole 'experiment' started, so he was susceptible to careless error.

It could all be explained away with a little hypnosis, or maybe even simpler suggestions, and a few errors. All of it could.

What Luke couldn't rationalize was the bulk of evidence he was accumulating. Sure, the lost house was one thing. The pages turning in the book by themselves: that was another. The candle flames a third . . . And a fourth and fifth thing—if he were counting all the times he'd seen her supposedly manipulate fire.

The shooting was another problem all together.

Not only had he seen something bizarre, but he was unable to completely write it off. There was a perfectly reasonable explanation there too: people saw weird things when they were in a traumatic situation. But Valverde had a witness who claimed to see the same things Luke had seen. Even Valverde's recitation of the witness's story held some important details that matched too closely to what Luke himself remembered.

The last thing was the most troubling. It was the one he hadn't wanted to admit to himself, but he was now hard pressed to hold back any longer. And it was why he was having such a hard time getting to sleep.

The first night he'd stayed over, he'd dreamed he walked around her house. He'd woken ill-rested, as though he had actually been up prowling the house the whole night. But the next day he saw that the books on her shelf were in the same order he remembered from the dream. The pillows on the couch in the exact same way. Though it was disturbing, Luke consoled himself with the reminder that he had an excellent memory. He'd solved more than one case in the past by calling up something he'd seen in passing, some clue that made the witness a liar, or incriminated someone. He'd brushed off the strange feeling to a strange room, strange bed, strange roommate.

But last night . . . In his dreams he'd not only prowled the house, he'd opened cupboards, shifted the magazines on the table, and opened a book on the shelf that had a bookmark stuck out of the top.

Though he'd hidden his shock from Yasmin, he'd barely been able to stuff it far enough back in his head. The cupboards—ones he never opened before—were arranged exactly as they had been in his dreams. He even lifted an out of place ceramic pie dish to see the sticker on the bottom. It had never been used, just as he had known from his dream. The cool touch of the red and cream glaze was exactly as it had been while he slept.

He almost cracked the dish, he set it back down so fast.

The magazines he had shifted in his dream were now in the new order on the coffee table. What were the odds that Yasmin had gotten up between going to sleep last night (though not slamming her door nearly as loud as the first night) and this morning and had arranged the magazines *exactly* as he had done in his sleep. He checked—alphabetical—just like he'd decided.

The kicker was the bookmark. When Yasmin was brushing her teeth, he pulled the book from the shelf, telling himself that the bookmark was clearly dark from the part sticking up but that it didn't fade to purple and didn't feature a teal cartoon unicorn with pink hooves. That idea was ridiculous anyway—it was so out of character for Yasmin. She might be a witch, but a teal and pink unicorn?

The sharp twist of his stomach had stopped him cold. He didn't know how long he stood there, looking at it, staring.

Yasmin had come out of the bathroom and grinned at him. "Ignore that. My niece Leyla got that for me. I can't get rid of it even though it makes me want to hurl."

He simply nodded in return and made them breakfast, trying not to be as disturbed as he was that he knew where everything was.

Now he was afraid.

What if he did it again?

It doesn't matter. And what did it matter? If he saw the cupboards? If he touched some magazines? Looked at a bookmark?

But even he was smart enough to admit that it wasn't about what he did—it was that he *could* do it. Could he only do it here? What about at home? How would he even test that while he was protecting Ms. Ali?

His mind turned to more nefarious means: had she cast a spell on him?

He couldn't figure out what end there was to having him walk around the house and move her stuff when he thought he was asleep. Then he sighed.

He was sleepwalking . . . Some kind of lucid sleepwalking.

Everything he'd heard about it was that sleepwalkers didn't remember anything afterward, even if their eyes were open. But he must have had open eyes. Must have been mentally asleep and dreaming but actually up and walking around and looking at things. He was just a sleepwalker with a memory.

With a sharp flick of his wrist he threw back the covers, stalked to the door and locked it. The older house had flimsy push-button locks that clicked right open when turned from the inside. It wouldn't stop a sleepwalking baby.

Looking around, he found a doorstop, not an uncommon find in old homes and he shoved it under from his side. He had laid back down, feeling better but not completely secure, when he popped back up. In his bag he found a pencil and he added a small mark to the paint, exactly at the left edge of the doorstop. That way he would know if he moved it in the middle of the night.

Even as he made the mark, he felt the tension drain from his shoulders. He might sleepwalk, but he would have proof. He didn't really care if he moved some magazines. She was only paying him a dollar anyway. And he didn't want to be here.

Luke wanted to be in his own home. He wanted there to never be a shooting. And he still wanted to ask Yasmin Ali out on a date.

Eventually he'd get back to his own place and sleep in his own bed. But the rest was not going to come to pass. She was a witness, a victim, and he was an officer. He almost added "and a gentleman" in his head, but refrained.

Exhausted, and finally convinced he could sleep safely in the mysterious disappearing house, he dropped into sleep like a rock into a pond.

The blackness of sleep had come around him like a fog and it peeled back just as cleanly. When he looked at the clock it read 2am, but the numbers were fuzzy, the time unclear, and he knew then that he was dreaming. In the haze of his sleep his wants became clear, no longer obscured by logic and reason.

He wanted Yasmin.

His body wanted her.

His heart tugged in her direction, repeatedly. Her smile lured him in, her laugh captured him, and the few times she showed fear shackled him to her as surely as chains.

Though his brain was confused by what she showed him and often afraid of what she might just be capable of, he was enamored with her easy conversation on all other topics. She didn't hold back, told him what she thought—even when she thought he was wrong. And she did it without being mean.

Though there was no logical way to overcome his desire for her, the desire itself seemed very logical. And in his sleep-fogged brain it was clear that if he was dreaming there were no consequences. So he reached for the doorknob and pulled the door open.

His bare feet padded across the hallway. The runner carpet appeared less vibrant in his dream than the deep blues and greens it had in reality. Luke only briefly made note of this as he looked around, realizing that everything seemed to be in black and white.

The shadows of the hallway drew long lines that reached out to him from their epicenter at the small nightlight plugged right into a stray outlet.

Her doorknob was different than his, shiny faux-crystal, it seemed appropriate as the entry to her bedroom.

He turned the knob and pushed the door open to see her lying there, hair tumbled around her, deep sleep easing the dark shadows that had grown under her eyes in the past days.

On the high, antique bed, she was in vibrant full color against creamy, yellow sheets. Her chest rose and fell in accordance to her heavy breathing and he realized she was exhausted.

Leading with his heart, and unable to not follow it, he stepped into the room, his feet sinking into the plush carpet. It was looped, soft cotton that made him want to wiggle his bare toes into it and become a tactile creature.

Her whole room was tactile. The coverlet was cottony soft, begging his fingers to stroke it. She slept in some camisole top that hugged her as surely as he wanted to. Even her skin beckoned him.

Unable to resist, Luke reached out and ran his finger down the soft inside of her arm. He breathed in the sigh she released at his touch.

~

Luke found himself sitting at his desk, once again frustrated with the state of things on many levels.

Jessica was inches from declaring the "Ali shooting" unsolvable and closing the case. She told him what he already knew—they could always re-open it if new evidence came to light. But given that the victim was a self-proclaimed witch who said she cast a protection spell while she was being shot at and *both* witnesses saw a circle of blue fire there was little chance of the case surviving a trial even with more solid evidence.

Just like him, she had a desk full of other cases and priority had to be assigned where she could accomplish the most good.

One of his many problems was that closing the case didn't stop the problem. His bosses had already allowed for his private security detail and that wouldn't change. If Ms. Ali was willing to pay him, he had permission to protect her.

But without an open case, there would be no active investigation into the Del Surs and what they were planning. If there was an ongoing plot to finish the job on Ms. Ali, no one would be looking for it. He could certainly look—on his own time. But his own time was dedicated to keeping Yasmin from getting murdered so some gangbanger could become a full-fledged member of one of the dirtiest clans in L.A.

He wanted to have someone tailing her around the clock. He knew she had a clerk and teaching job at Blessed Be. But he'd seen her house, and he had a hard time imagining how that job would pay for a house in Los Angeles, let alone full-time trained security personnel. He hoped she was independently wealthy and she could afford someone other than him.

The way her jaw had dropped when he quoted standard pricing to him said she wasn't. Not at all.

One of his other problems was his sanity. He was dreaming about her now. Often. In his dreams she hadn't roused at his touch and he'd walked away. Gone back to his room and lay back down on the air mattress. Fallen back in to his standard vague and odd dream-state.

Luke woke this morning in a rush of sense memory. The feel of the plush carpet, the sight of Yasmin reposed like some modern-day Sleeping Beauty on the high bed, the feel of the downy comforter brushing against his bare chest as he'd stood there looking at her. Before he could figure out what he was doing, he'd rushed to the door of his own room and was on his knees, then sitting on his ass, breathing heavily.

When he checked, the pencil mark was right at the edge of the door stopper. He hadn't moved it—hadn't left the room last night. Even though he could swear he'd seen her, stood over her, touched her and heard her murmur in her sleep, he had not. He'd been solidly under, dreaming here in his own uncomfortable air mattress bed.

The breath he'd been holding fled his body and he checked the mark one last time before pulling the door stop from where he'd wedged it.

Knowing it was only a dream was a comfort, but it didn't leave him better rested now at work. It didn't leave him less concerned about Yasmin out during the day with no one watching her. The Del Surs definitively had her home address so Luke wasn't leaving her unguarded at the house. But he couldn't watch her all the time. So she was on her own outside the home.

His comfort was that she was relatively hard to find on the web. There was plenty of information about her. About her degree, her senior project—which he flagged to read later—and a little about her family. But she was a smart girl and her address and work and other common stalker-tells were hidden. He'd checked the website and associated information about Blessed Be. Though her first name and her smiling picture were part of the website, a person would have to know to look for her there. The information didn't link back to Yasmin Ali, or her address. Not until he got into police files. So Luke felt relatively safe about that.

He also figured he had to feel a little better about her "protection spells" after going through his own missing house scenario the night before. It still freaked him out just thinking about it. The problem was: would it work on anyone? Did it work at all, or was he just a moron who fell prey to some cheap ruse? And lastly, if it all worked so well, why had she gotten targeted and shot at in the first place?

There was a good possibility that he would never sleep a full night again.

He'd followed her into town this morning. Over the hill, in stop-and-go traffic, until he was certain no one was following her. Then he'd waved and peeled off to the right while she went left, him heading to the precinct, her to the shop.

The store didn't open yet; she was heading out early because he needed to, but she didn't make a fuss about it. Yasmin simply said she'd made an early appointment and off she went.

The good news was that there was no evidence as of yet that the Del Surs were actually coming after her. It had been four days since the shooting and nothing more had happened. Well, the contents of her stolen wallet had turned up in an ominous looking circle in the same spot where she'd been standing when she was shot at, but nothing had happened to her.

No one had followed her. No one had turned up at the house. No one threatening had showed up at her work. At least not that he knew of. Luke had checked and double-checked all these things. He searched for footprints around the house, watched for suspicious cars on her street. He talked to Tristan—Magic Box owner and Yasmin's boss—and asked questions, told him what to look for.

Luke didn't know what to make of Tristan Goodman. He seemed perfectly friendly toward Yasmin, his employee—more so than most bosses would be. Some acted disturbed that the hired help would bring this to their doorstep. Tristan only seemed to want to help. But by the same token he was highly dismissive of Luke and the help offered. Tristan seemed to think as Yasmin did—that the shooting was just a glitch in the universe and that a few candles and incantations would protect her from bullets.

Having no past opportunities to hone his skills with such beliefs, Luke hadn't been able to form a good argument while he was talking to the man. So he'd informed Mr. Goodman what to look out for and given him strong guidelines on what to call in and when. Luke had left both his work and personal numbers and hung up. Only then did he realize the argument: the bruise on Yasmin's hand. It said that the spells and candles both *could* and *couldn't* protect her.

Trying to keep his focus on the job at hand was a much more difficult task than usual. He was grateful for the phone call he received an hour later. Yasmin's voice let him know that she was safely at the shop, she was not alone, and her tone let him know she was more than a little annoyed at having to check in on a regular schedule. Luke didn't care. After he hung up, he was finally able to get some of his regular caseload work done.

~

Yasmin heard the door to Tristan's office open behind her. She felt his presence even though she didn't turn to see him. She didn't have to.

This morning when she came in he asked again about the shooting and how she was holding up. While Delilah had called and checked in on her, Tristan hadn't. But this morning, he commented that he hadn't been worried—he'd known she could take care of herself. He even checked her palm and told her that the bruise there—probably a la bullet—was pretty cool. Unable to hold back her grin, Yasmin had silently congratulated herself.

That love spell she'd cast maybe would have some effect after all. It damn well should; it seemed to have cost her a good amount by way of the shooting and now having live-in protection and possibly a target on her back.

Tristan was far too skilled of a witch for Yasmin to cast anything directly at him. He'd detect the spell instantly—he'd probably just *feel* it. And if that didn't happen he'd see it when he did his standard cleansing ritual every few days. He'd probably do one even sooner if he felt out-of-sorts or thought he was acting oddly.

So she'd cast that general Universe-bring-my-love-to-me spell just before the girls had arrived. Though it had screwed up everything—she really did blame it for getting her protection mojo out of whack—it had worked. Yasmin had *felt* the power as she'd closed that circle. She almost jerked with the cosmic *click* of the energy she'd raised reaching out and grabbing what she sent it for.

While she hadn't passed out after that one, she'd come close. Now, Tristan had a week without her to miss her and realize the feelings he'd always had.

Yasmin had a week away—except for that one visit to the shop—to gear up for getting this thing together finally. She hadn't lied to Luke this morning. She did have an early appointment, but it was for her hair.

Blown out straight, it hit her lower back where the tips still clung to the slightest amount of curl. The blond streaks showed more in the milk chocolate color of her hair and she looked less like the mixed-middle-eastern girl she was born as and more like the L.A. girl she was in her heart.

The fact that Tristan knew she was capable was icing on the cake. He was in his office most of the day, again trusting her ability to run the shop. Her heart rolled over as he came out now while the shop was empty.

Was he going to finally ask her out? Really flirt with her? Yasmin got the conversational ball started.

"So what did you do without me last week?" She grinned. She was essential here and she knew it.

A return smile and a laugh tugged at her feelings. "Barely scraped by. I got nothing done in the office . . . and you know it."

She was stepping closer when the bell at the front door chimed. Customers. Already missing her conversation with Tristan, Yasmin turned to help. She could put them off, but as the owner Tristan valued taking care of the people who came through the door as a top priority. The shop had belonged to his parents and it was a legacy he took as seriously as the craft itself.

She was partway into her standard conversation of sussing out what the customer wanted and where in the store that might be when the door chime went off again.

This time—as Tristan stepped forward to be helpful—Yasmin worked to keep the smile steady on her face. Tristan hadn't come out to talk to her. If he had done that, it would have been when there weren't customers coming in. He'd come out because he'd sensed they were about to get busy—he didn't like people to have to wait for service, even if that meant that the boss came out from his office and his numbers and dealt face-to-face with people in the store.

Just as she was ringing up her first customers, two women who asked about starter tools, the door chimed again. Whoever it was went down the aisle, checking out the other side of the store and Yasmin didn't worry. Whoever it was wasn't upset about not being greeted right away and seemed more curious than in need of help. After a few more questions, she felt the women were a good fit for her beginner's class and she signed them into the remaining spots for the next week.

They left happy and she went to help the man wandering the aisles as the door chimed again. Tristan would get that person, and the other clerk, Libby, would be here in a moment. Yasmin checked the back of her brain; they were busy just a little earlier than usual today and Libby was just a little late, still parking.

Coming up behind the man, Yasmin almost sighed. His slacks were gray with a tinge of blue to them and his shirt was green with a gold thread shot through it so that it caught the light when it folded certain ways. She didn't even have to wait for him to turn around, she'd seen that bright blue patterned tie when he'd put it on this morning. Giving up on holding it in, she did sigh. He was here checking up on her, and she didn't need it. It was enough that he was in her house every moment she was home.

"Hi Luke. Why are you wearing a tie that has naked women on it?"

"What?" He turned suddenly, the glass gazing orb still in his grip from where he'd picked it up. Tristan had cast on it so people could touch it but not break it. Luke held it like a baseball. "There are no naked women on my tie! It's a design."

"They call it abstract," She pointed to the curves in the colors, the dots that represented navels, nipples. Wavy hair-in blue of course—covered more revealing bits in abstract lines and shades. "But those are definitely naked ladies."

Luke pushed her finger away, no longer looking at her, but holding the tie up to his face for closer inspection. "They are not! . . . Oh shit. They are!"

While Yasmin laughed, Luke began tugging at the tie as though it burned. "Why did no one tell me this? I never saw that!"

"Sure you didn't." She frowned at him, mocking his panic.

"I didn't! I wear this tie to work!" With a slick zipping sound, he yanked the tie through his collar and then stuffed it into his pocket. "I can't believe I—"

He suddenly stood stock still and stared at her. Then he frowned again, but this time it was at her. "What happened to your hair?"

CHAPTER 9

Luke consoled himself that she was safe and everything was okay. Sure he'd gone out the door this morning wearing a tie with naked women on it. He had to wonder how many people besides Yasmin had noticed that. Had they looked at him—acting as though he were a serious officer—while he questioned victims about cases, thinking that he was completely irreverent and disrespectful?

But Yasmin was here and everything seemed all right. She was just her usual self, still a little irritated that he was following her around and checking on her. Well, too bad. He worried about her.

Finishing up with a customer, her boss came over. He offered only a nod as they'd met just briefly before, but Luke knew quite a bit about the guy.

Yasmin however wrapped her hands around witch-man's bicep and smiled. "Tristan, this is Officer Salzone—he's working the case from my shooting." Then she turned to Luke, "This is Tristan Goodman, my boss."

And holy shit, it was clear from her gooey smile that she wanted this guy to be a hell of a lot more than her boss.

Luke looked back and forth between the two faces, trying to quell the churn in his stomach. He told himself it didn't matter what she felt for the guy, because she couldn't be with Luke. She couldn't be anything other than a case to him. But apparently she wasn't what she wanted to be to this Tristan guy either.

Though Yasmin held onto him and smiled, Tristan kept his hands to himself. Luke tried to objectively assess what he saw, but he was finding it harder and harder to be objective about any part of this case. Still, it looked to him like this Tristan guy was completely oblivious to Yasmin's feelings. Luke immediately decided the guy was a moron.

Though he should have said, "We already met," words didn't actually come out of his mouth. Stupid words came out of Tristan's.

Tristan looked at Yasmin, checking her clinically, "What's wrong with her hair?"

So he'd heard that, had he? And he still didn't see. Luke addressed his answer to Yasmin. "It's straight! All the curls are gone."

She was beaming. "I know. Do you like it?"

Why did she have to ask him that?

Why would anyone like that? There were straight-haired girls everywhere, but where else could a man find curls like hers? For days he'd been fighting the deep urge to bury his fingers in her hair just to feel it and dipshit here didn't even notice. Luke refused to think of Tristan as anything other than a rank idiot, now that he knew Yasmin had a thing for him and this fool didn't even notice. Or maybe he did and he was just a jerk, too.

Yasmin was looking at him, waiting. So Luke answered. "No, I don't like it."

She blinked.

Oooops.

Tristan patted her hand where it rested on his arm. "It looks fine." But he didn't even look at her, just kept his eyes on Luke as though he were the fool here.

Given the way Yasmin was now looking at him, and honestly assessing his own feelings for her, Luke was becoming inclined to agree. Maybe he and Tristan should be friends. Clearly they were both running low in the brains department where it came to Yasmin.

Her equilibrium restored by Tristan's less-than-a-compliment, Yasmin finally let go and narrowed her scope to Luke alone. He would have been glad for the attention, but for the words.

"Why are you here?"

Apparently, he had not lost the capacity to shrug at her. "I was worried about you. I just wanted to be sure everything is okay."

"Clearly it is. That should also have been clear from the text messages I have been sending you, exactly on the schedule you demanded." She crossed her arms and her straight, straight hair slid over her shoulder. "Each of those messages said I was fine and that I hadn't seen anything suspicious."

He'd just needed to see her. She still didn't seem to have a real context for what she was up against. Yasmin seemed more upset by the restrictions he was desperately trying to place on her than by what the Del Surs would do if they got to her. "Can you come down to the station when you get off work today?"

"You going to babysit me there? Can I just wander around away from the house, maybe get some dinner until you get there?" She didn't uncross her arms, but her hip jutted out as she got more impatient with him. She obviously wanted to get back to flirting with the guy who didn't even notice anything about her except that she was there.

"Not babysitting. Something about the case."

At least she loosened up a bit. "Fine. I assume I can drive myself?"

"Of course." He wanted to say 'no' but he couldn't be there all the time. And there was no evidence whatsoever that any of the gang members had followed her here and they sure wouldn't come to the precinct. Then he had another thought. "Where are you parked?"

The attitude popped back into place and he almost understood it. He'd invaded her space—first her house, and now her last bastion of independence.

"I'm right out back. There are reserved spots for us." She must have seen that he wanted to check it out because she made a countermove before he could even say anything. "I'm perfectly fine there. Tristan will walk me out."

Luke supposed it was better than not so he forced out an agreement. "Good. But if you don't get a spot right in front of the station, call me and I'll come walk you in."

It would be just like the Del Surs to score points by killing her in front of his office. Still Yasmin didn't seem to get that. Her mouth opened and Luke tried to make a valid argument but she stopped him. "I have great parking karma. I won't call—I'll have a spot right in front. No worries. So I'll just walk in and find you at your desk?"

Parking Karma? But he could only agree. "That's fine. Just please call when you leave here."

It was an uneasy truce they reached before he left her there in her shop. Before he walked away having given firm instructions for Tristan not to have her walking the streets alone and to accompany her to lunch if she left the building. It grated that he had to say it and it grated more that he had to endure her smile at the command to eat lunch with her crush. Tristan had readily agreed to watch out for 'his girl' and Luke rescinded his thought that they should be friends. He pretty much hated Tristan Goodman.

So it was that he returned to his desk that afternoon in a bad mood. He should be doing knock-and-talks on several of his open cases but they were going to have to wait until tomorrow. It was about as late as he could put them off but he was no good today. Today he would only reinforce people's preconceived ideas of the cops as heartless a-holes. LAPD was really working to change that image and Luke wouldn't help the cause today.

He'd grabbed a burger on his way back from Blessed Be and eaten it at his desk, not even realizing he'd finished the meal until he looked down and realized he had to move the empty papers to clear his desk for the next assignment he'd given himself.

Pulling up a map on screen, Luke then pulled his old cases from Guns and Gangs. He marked each of the spots where there was a gang initiation that he knew of. Then he used another color to mark other killings associated with the Del Surs. There was a lot of overlap with other gangs—particularly the Stone Jungles.

The Jungle Crew was known to take out Del Sur targets just to piss off the guys trying to take over their territory. It was exactly the kind of thing that gangs were known for, even though most weren't this bad. Just your standard turf war that Yasmin Ali had gotten herself in the middle of with her borrowed children and bad timing.

Luke's stomach turned as he thought about the possibility of the Jungle Crew finding out about her and taking her out just to get a point up on the Del Surs. He was going to get an ulcer over this one and Tristan Goodman was going to get the girl even though he had no appreciation for her. What man wouldn't take that if offered?

Getting his head back on the task at hand, Luke checked his watch. He needed this out for Yasmin to see before she arrived. Just then a tone came over his phone—a nice respectful tone that wouldn't offend anyone if he was dealing with a bereaved family when he got a text or something like that. Yasmin was on her way. With traffic and parking she would likely be about twenty minutes. He pulled and printed picture after gruesome picture. He gathered articles about the violence the Del Surs were known for. And he hoped it would be enough to stop her from being so blasé about her own safety.

He knew he wasn't going to get the girl. And he sure didn't want her boss to get the girl either. But the girl had to still be alive and safe at the end of his story. He knew that above all else.

~

Yasmin pulled up in front of the Los Angeles Hollywood Police Station just after six-thirty. She'd left Blessed Be at just after six, finishing up her day and trading out with Angela on the evening shift. Traffic had been a bitch, but that was expected. Since she wasn't all that anxious to get babysat at the police station, Yasmin just literally rolled with it.

Putting the window down she inhaled the fumes and the heat. It was one of those days when you could smell the sunshine. The palm trees were evenly spaced along the street and she recalled Delilah once saying it looked to her like someone had planted party toothpicks all down the line.

The precinct was tucked back off the main road ironically amid black door clubs that probably trafficked cocaine to the celebrities who came there. It wasn't too far from the Viper Room, where River Phoenix had died years ago.

Snapping her fingers, Yasmin invoked her parking karma and, sure enough, as she pulled up a driver pulled out of the frontmost spot allowing her to sail right in. There was even another hour left on the meter. At least that she could smile about.

With her purse tugged higher on her shoulder, she forced herself up the steps, into the building and checked in. She almost referred to Luke as "Officer Multicolor" to the uniformed man behind the front desk and she had no doubt the man would know exactly who she was talking about. She'd been in here several times now and hadn't seen one single other person wearing anything further from grays and browns than a good, solid navy.

"You told him about the tie, huh?" Jessica Valverde called to her as she passed.

Veering over to say hello to someone friendly—even if she was dropping the case—Yasmin stopped in front of the desk and nodded. Then she caught on. "You knew? You didn't tell him?"

Valverde shrugged. "I have a small wicked streak. It seemed harmless."

Able to see his desk if she looked over her shoulder, Yasmin did just that. "He seemed a little freaked out by it. I thought he knew."

"Nope. He's had that thing for over a year."

Yasmin almost let her mouth fall open. Valverde had let him wear it repeatedly?

Clearly a keen observer, the woman shook her head, "He didn't wear it much and I talked him out of interviewing the parents of a murder victim the last time he wore it. I got my jollies, but I'm not that insensitive."

Well, Yasmin could understand. She could even make him forget what she'd told him about the tie; he could put it back on and not be any the wiser. Valverde could continue to have her fun. But there would be no real way to explain to the woman what she'd done.

Who knew what Luke had already told her?

Then there he was, flagging her down, motioning her toward his desk. Good thing she brought a book with her. Time to get babysat.

It turned out she was wrong.

Luke Salzone had no intention of babysitting her. He had evidence. Maps and articles he made her read. Her stomach was turning before he showed her the pictures. "I'm good, Luke. I don't need to look."

Though her hands were up and she was backing away from his desk, he didn't relent. Grabbing her wrist, he held her there. "I think you do."

"I get the message." She stared him in the face. Her religion worshiped life in all its forms, showing her pictures of murder victims wasn't anything she could take.

"I don't know that you do." He sighed, his hands on his hips now that he let go of her. "These guys will kill you. And they'll do it viciously. They'll stake you out and shoot you point blank on the steps of the precinct just to get back at me."

Taking shallow breaths Yasmin absorbed that for a moment. "Then maybe you aren't the best person to protect me. I mean, if there's a possibility they'll do this to get at you. Or is it any cop?"

"It's both." He shook his head as though there were no way out of this, then his words confirmed that. "You can get someone else, but the Del Surs know me—along with a handful of other cops. I just came off the Guns and Gangs unit. I arrested as many of these guys as I could. But the revenge on me will be because I happened to be on scene. Because one of the guys there may have recognized me." His body language was all over the place: his hands almost waved around randomly, his shoulders shrugged, he paced a tight circle beside his desk. "I don't know that they did place me, but I don't know that they didn't either. If you want someone else and can afford it, that's fine. As long as it's someone and you stay safe."

Yasmin nodded. She couldn't afford anyone else. Her gasp the first time he'd told her the going rate wasn't just because it was an arm and a leg, it was because the cost was way out of her possible range. She admitted as such. "Aside from refinancing my house and pulling all the equity out—which is stupid in this market—there's no way I can come close to affording it."

She was babbling.

He didn't notice.

"I've got you covered. I don't want these guys to win." He finally stopped pacing, but he was now standing over her, hands planted on his desk, staring her in the eyes. "I need you to help me here. I know it sucks not to go anywhere alone, to lose all your real privacy, have someone invade your house. But you do not want to wind up in their hands. It was bad luck, but you have to deal with it."

Nodding, Yasmin thought to herself that maybe it was bad luck she'd conjured up herself. And to what gain? She had lunch with Tristan and he was fun, polite, all the things she loved about him . . . But he didn't seem all that interested in her.

She had *felt* her love spell work. It would bring her true love to her, but Tristan hadn't changed at all. She'd asked him if he wanted to go out for lunch. She bought, he said thank you. If anything, he held back—as though he knew she had feelings for him and didn't want to encourage her.

Telling herself it all sucked, she looked up at Luke, still towering over her, but she didn't—couldn't—speak.

His voice was soft, calming. "Are you ready to go?"

She nodded and he pulled back, standing now, gathering his papers. He'd pulled back psychically, too, she could feel. That sharp gaze was no longer on her, no longer testing her to see if she'd comply with her own safety.

He'd won. She was on board, including following him down the hall. Though he hadn't shoved those pictures in her face, she'd seen them more than clearly enough. She worshiped all life, but she was having a hard time extending that to the life forms that called themselves the Del Surs. She was not willing to simply become part of their life cycle.

If Luke was going to stick to her like glue for however long this took, then she could at least be friendly. He was after all working for the single dollar required to make the whole thing a legal police matter. "What do you want for dinner?"

It earned her a smile. "Nothing fast. I eat crap for lunch almost every day. If you're up for pasta, I can cook."

Her agreement came almost too fast. Subjecting him to her cooking was punishment on top of her bad attitude. "I'll buy the ingredients, you just tell me what."

For a moment he looked like he was going to refuse, but then he simply said, "Thank you." Then he tipped his head to the side. "I'll go to the store with you. I'll even push the cart."

They didn't discuss that they weren't going to the store near the precinct. And Yasmin didn't mention that her heart rate had sped up at just the thought of going to that place by herself—even though she would be surrounded by other shoppers. The grocery store had never been her friend but she was now bordering on panic attacks at the thought.

Luke followed her out of the station and admired her parking spot before following some elaborate maneuvering to get him into his car without once letting her out of sight.

Last night she would have balked. Now—after seeing the pictures and thinking about the shooting again—she felt better about it.

He followed her over the canyon, not letting another car get between them even once. It was as alone as she was going to get until she curled into her bed tonight. Though she didn't sob, she couldn't help the tears that silently tracked down her face.

She'd done everything she could. She'd cast a major spell she shouldn't have. A vicious gang was hoping to murder her to finish something as insipid as an initiation. She'd lost all her freedom. And for what? Tristan didn't feel that way about her at all. Not the way she felt about him.

In the rest of her life, the love spell had changed everything.

But where Tristan was concerned it had changed exactly nothing.

~

Sleep had come easier this time. Luke felt it rocking him into darkness as he lay down on the air mattress. It pulled at him and he welcomed it easily. The only thing that gave him pause—the only reason he didn't voluntarily instantly succumb—was that he wanted to know why it was better tonight. He wanted to do it again tomorrow.

Maybe it was because Yasmin had been so agreeable tonight. She hadn't complained about him sticking to her like glue and had even seemed to be glad he was there. Luke let himself enjoy the feeling although he knew it was a false one. She stuck to him because she was afraid, because he'd made her so. Her softer feelings were all aimed toward Tristan Goodman too. That dipshit didn't even see her. Sure he probably looked—what man wouldn't?—but he didn't see. She had tried to impress him by changing something that was uniquely Yasmin and he hadn't even noticed or cared.

That was all levels of honked up, but Luke couldn't get involved in that one.

Maybe he was finally at his rope's end. He'd been awake, nervous, on edge for nearly five days. It was entirely possible that he'd simply used up whatever store he had and his body was tapping out with or without his approval.

He'd heard Yasmin go into her room and when he'd come out from brushing his teeth he'd seen a soft light under her door. He assumed she was reading or something. Since both rooms were at the back of the house, she was as safe as she could be right now. Luke was confident that—no matter how tired he was—he would come right awake the moment anything happened. Usually before. He had a good sense about these things, as though he could hear someone sneaking around the house.

Then again, maybe it was the pasta. Maybe he just needed to carbo-load and fall into a food coma each night. Perhaps pasta was the answer he needed to fight his anxiety. He sure didn't want to take any medications. His anxiety would be a good thing if something went wrong.

He started making plans for the next night. He would have pasta again, with crusty bread. Yasmin had enjoyed it and Luke wondered how many nights he could feed it to her before she complained. He was hoping to count on her compliance to his program for a few more days before she got antsy again. But he couldn't duplicate his sheer exhaustion tomorrow. At least he really hoped he couldn't.

Finally giving up and giving in, Luke calculated how many days he needed to keep her on lockdown before they could call off the dogs and assume that the Del Surs weren't coming after her, when he fell asleep.

For a while he rolled aimlessly through his dreams, one person morphing into another, one idea trailing to a second then a third until all vestiges of the original thought were long gone.

Then, in a moment of clarity, he recognized where he was. As he realized this, he felt as though all the energy around him coalesced into his form—as though he had suddenly become real. The feeling was so odd it could only be a dream, so he paused for a moment to feel the cool weight of the crystalline doorknob in his grasp then pushed Yasmin's door open.

Once again, she was asleep, spread out on soft sheets, cream colored in the low light. Her hair wound its way around the pillows, long and straight, the shots of caramel more obvious without the curls he loved.

For a moment he just looked at her, sooty eyelashes resting on her cheeks, her arms out as though to embrace the world, her chest rising and falling beneath a camisole that was too thin to stop his imagination.

Even in his dreams his body reacted to her and knowing he was asleep he made a decision he would never had made in the daylight. Grabbing the corner of the covers, he pulled it back and slid in beside her.

Truly his dream-girl, she fluttered her eyes and looked back at him, heat warring with surprise. She slid away from him, stuttering his heartbeat for a moment, but then he saw that it was just to make room for him in the bed with her. When she rolled, she rolled toward him, pressing her nearly bare body against his length.

It wasn't real, so he didn't bother with finesse, with worry, with charm. He tugged at the straps of her cotton top and pushed at the tiny buttons with no concern for their survival as he exposed her breasts to his gaze then quickly to his mouth. The sounds she made fueled him, and in a moment he felt her fingers in his hair, holding him against her.

He didn't ask permission but figured she would tell him no if she wanted. Luke prayed it was a good dream and she would only say yes. She said no such thing.

He slid his fingers under the cotton of her insubstantial underwear and found her ready for him. Her hips rose, pressing against his hand and his already pounding heartbeat rose as well.

His dream Yasmin didn't say yes or no or any words that he recognized, but she gave him sighs and breathy gasps telling him what words could not. Her hands roamed his chest and back. Her head tipped back and her eyes fell shut as she reveled in his touch and he reveled in the feel of her against his fingertips.

He wrestled with the clothing in his way and when he pushed into her, he found her eyes wide and staring deep into his own. For a moment he had to stop, his labored breathing reflected in her own. Then—almost of their own accord—their mouths fused and he began moving again, as did she. Luke could feel her reaching to him, trying to bring them closer still, her body straining with his until they both came in a rush.

Later, when he was beside her and she was falling asleep against him, Luke wondered if it would ever be that way in his waking life. Then for a moment he questioned how he could fall asleep inside a dream.

CHAPTER 10

Yasmin woke to sunlight and an empty bed.

Blinking hard, she thought to herself, of course it was just her in the bed. She lived alone and she slept alone. But her muscles told her that her dream had been vivid and for a moment she was grateful no one had stood over her while she slept. She must have squirmed and probably moaned a bit.

It was almost embarrassing and she worried for a bit that she would have to face Luke this morning. But he would have no idea that she'd dreamed about him—or *what* she'd dreamed about him. As long as she could keep her face from turning beet red when she looked at him, she would be fine. And she had a little while to lie here and think since she'd woken up well before her alarm.

There was no reason for Luke Salzone to suspect she'd had such a hot and bothersome dream about him. When he'd come by the store at lunch he was much faster at picking up on her feelings for Tristan than even Tristan. Since he knew how she felt about her boss, he'd have no reason to suspect she was going full-erotica on him in her dreams.

With that thought, her recent days came crashing back around her. Amid the rubble, she found some hard truths.

Had Tristan been shot at, had he been under police guard, she would have been all over him. Worried. Afraid. Helping.

That was the big thing. Tristan had said he trusted her—which was wonderful and heartwarming—but it wasn't helpful. It also kept Tristan from having to step up and do anything. He left that to the LAPD and to Officer Salzone.

It was becoming clear that Tristan either didn't notice her feelings at all or else he did and was keeping a cool distance while still trying to be a friendly boss. Either way it didn't add up to him having any romantic feelings for her.

Yasmin put her hand to her head, briefly startled by the feeling of her straightened hair. It would last today and tomorrow, then she would have to wash it and the curls would spring right back.

She had done it in part because every woman she noticed Tristan flirting with had straight hair. They were all standard beauties with relatively large breasts and straight hair. There was nothing shy of surgery to be done for the American melting-pot looks or breast size he favored. Apparently the hair wasn't enough to get him to look her way.

If she was being honest with herself, the hair was a stupid move. If getting shot at and being considered the murder target of an L.A. gang didn't make the man step up, then a change in hairstyle wouldn't do the trick either.

The dream from last night came back to her and Yasmin pushed the details away lest she break out in a sweat or have to catch her breath at just the memory. Perhaps that dream about Luke had been a nudge from the back of her brain pointing out that it hadn't been Tristan who noticed what she'd done, but Luke. In fact, he'd looked at her like she was stupid—as though he wondered why any woman wouldn't want those amazing curls. The ones she hated with an almost daily passion.

Words from her college roommate, Eileen, came back as Yasmin decided to get out of bed and found that she was even more twisted in the covers than she'd first realized. Eileen had told her that it didn't matter what body type you had or what your physical issues were, there was a man out there who thought that thing was the best ever.

Yasmin had to admit Eileen had certainly never wanted for male attention and had reveled in the size of her backside. Yasmin's own curls and dark skin were something Eileen simply snorted at. Some man would love it, she said. The right man.

As her feet hit the carpet, her brain hit the off switch. That man was not Tristan Goodman. If he came back, proclaiming his love for her, she might consider his suit, but it was time to let go. Her dream guy needed a new face and for a moment Luke's too-blue eyes and surfer-gold hair swam through her thoughts but she pushed the idea away. Latching onto Luke Salzone would be the same mistake latching onto Tristan had been.

Her memory fought back.

Her heart rate stuttered as she remembered dream Luke softly tracing her dark eyebrows and down the bridge of her nose. He'd run his hand along the inside of her arm as though he'd never felt anything like it and she'd wondered if he was looking at the differences in their skin color like she was.

But those thoughts were as damaging as the ones she'd had about Tristan. They all belonged to men she'd made up. Just because she'd attached the ideas to the face and body of a real man didn't mean the man in her head existed.

Surely her version of Tristan never had. While she'd been waiting for him to notice her, he'd noticed—and probably slept with—half the pretty women who came into the store.

All the arguments she'd given herself in the past for his behavior—he didn't want to ruin their friendship; he didn't date employees; he didn't date his own kind—fell away like crumbling dust. Though any was reasonably valid, if he actually really wanted her he would have found a way around it. Just like she would have.

She had a personal policy about not dating at work, but her feelings for Tristan had led her around it. His had not. And any buildup of Luke Salzone as a Tristan replacement would be just as stupid. So what if Dream-Luke could play her like a piano?

Enough of this. She should get up and get dressed. Luke had to go into the station at his regular time, even if she wasn't due for work until three. He wanted her out of the house and though she didn't like it, she did like staying alive.

Luke had easily won her compliance yesterday with those pictures and the map of the Del Surs' activity. They had run hits north of here before. West of here. Though their territory, as Luke had defined it, was south of Hollywood there was no reason to think they wouldn't come over the hill to get her. She was well within their strike zone.

To her right, her alarm went off and she slapped at it, shaking away the last of her deep musings. She had errands to run today. A lot of them.

She was standing in front of her 1940s sized closet, picking out clothing, when she realized the buttons on her sleep cami were open. The top gaped, nearly allowing her to see right down her own shirt, and for a flash of a moment she could see Luke kissing her there, sucking, licking. Her whole body flashed hot at the thought and as she grabbed at the closet door to steady herself, glad that this happened now and not while Luke was standing in front of her wondering what the hell was wrong with her.

Before she could gather her far-flung memories back together from that searing image, a knock came at her door. She used her free hand to tug together the loose placket of her top and turned to where she faced the door. There was nothing she could do about the string bikini underwear she slept in and she stood there like a startled deer, watching the door handle, waiting for it to turn. But it didn't.

His voice came through the heavy wood, clear as day.

"I'm making English muffins with eggs. Do you want one?"

"Sure!" She nearly shouted it despite the fact that she didn't think she could eat anything. His voice had triggered another flash through her system even though he hadn't said anything in her dream. Fighting against her own reaction, Yasmin dialed up a tone that she thought was correct for being offered breakfast and tried to implement it. "I'm getting dressed. I'll be out in a minute."

He mumbled some kind of acquiescence and she heard him walk away from her down the hall. It took another minute before she could calm her thoughts enough to get to her day.

She checked out the window and found she was looking at another sunny L.A. day. For a few moments she contemplated whether she wanted to wear that relatively short skirt to show Luke her legs, then she decided that she was giving far too much credit to a dream and pulled on the skirt over clean underwear. She added a simple white top with raglan sleeves in blue then hit the restroom to wash up and add sunscreen, a necklace and her usual small amount of makeup.

There was comfort in the ritual of her morning. As she tied on espadrilles she thought, *Screw Tristan Goodman*. If he didn't notice her, he didn't. His loss. And she would open her eyes and find someone who did appreciate her rather than pining for someone who still didn't see her after all the time they'd spent in each other's company.

She was coming down the hall, slipping in dangling earrings to match the necklace, when she realized that Luke was standing at the small dining table waiting for her.

Was he that much of a gentleman? Was he waiting for her to be seated? She hadn't noticed him doing that before and she spoke up. "Don't wait for me. I was going to pour myself some of that amazing coffee that I smell."

She smiled at him and hoped it wasn't overly reminiscent of last night. Just a friendly thank-you-for-making-me-breakfast grin, then she tried not to think too hard about context on that one either.

"It's on the table already, and . . . you look really nice." He sat before she did and dove into the food.

Poor man.

He couldn't help but notice her unrequited attraction for Tristan. Yesterday she would have called it "love" but today her view was clearer. And Luke was trying to make up for the fact that he also noticed that Tristan did not feel the same way. She almost sighed at him.

But she didn't get a chance; he was eying her oddly. "Will your hair ever go back the way it was?"

She laughed, grateful that the tension was broken, even if she was the only one who felt it. "Tomorrow night."

His fork was still paused, halfway to his mouth, "What happens then?"

"I wash it."

This time he frowned. "And it curls right back up?" As though the mysteries of hair care were well beyond his scope.

Then she glanced at his short blond swirls again and wondered why she'd ever accused him of hair gel. It just went that way apparently. "Yes, this was done with a little hair balm, a dryer, and some time. It will go right back when it hits water."

"Good." The word popped out, followed by a sheepish look as he realized he'd just insulted the hair she'd paid good money for.

Yasmin laughed at him again.

~

Despite the fact that she spent her morning trying not to burst into flames at the memory of her hot sex dream from the night before, and despite the fact that she had let go of a fantasy man she'd held onto far too long, Yasmin had a good morning.

She'd learned when she first arrived in California to enjoy the sunshine. Though her parents had quit calling on a daily or even weekly schedule to tell her how silly it was to move here, she still felt as though she should enjoy each day for the weather if nothing else. That turned out to be what got her through the first nine months here. Luckily her parents had stopped their routine calls before she had learned that 'winter' in L.A. didn't just mean calling your out of state relations and mocking them for their cold climes.

In L.A., the Holiday season was beautiful and in January the rains came. They lasted days on end and not only doused everything but created floods in some of the valley streets two to four feet deep at times. The currents could bring to mind man-vs-river movies and kept Yasmin inside when she could avoid the weather.

The rains were necessary to get any water at all into the city for the rest of the year. So Yasmin enjoyed it just a little more.

Shori had called the night before to check up on her and for some reason, Yasmin had lied. She wasn't one much for holding back from her sister, but she'd done it this time.

This time she said she was fine. That the shooting had blown over and of course she had a few nightmares but mostly things were okay.

Luke had looked at her like she was out of her freakin' mind. Clearly things were not okay. And she hadn't once mentioned live-in security. But he was smart enough not to butt in while she was talking. That would not have gone well.

She'd had to explain that her mother would have showed up and shooed Luke out of the house. It was bad enough that Yasmin lived by herself—her parents considered themselves fully born into the new age that they came around to the thought that it was acceptable for Yasmin to live in a house with other single women. But live by herself? It was shameful. It reflected badly, that she didn't have friends or wasn't able to keep a roommate. Who would want her?

Her continued unmarried state only bore out their dire predictions.

That Luke was staying here? Well, her mother might have had a heart attack.

Yasmin's police protection would have been shoved out the door and his soul prayed for. Then she wouldn't have been able to cast any protection spells because her mother wouldn't let her go anywhere alone—including work. In fact, her mother wouldn't let her work. They would have been praying to Allah for the souls of the gang members and for Yasmin's safety.

Yasmin had no doubt that her mother would take a bullet for her. But that wasn't at all what she wanted. And having her mother here would only make things worse. So she told them all she was fine. Which meant lying to Shori because Shori was such a bad liar that even just telling her sister would mean that her mother would turn up, prayer mat and a spare rolled and ready, armed with a bedrock belief that Allah would save her daughter.

Luke nodded and responded that there was a lot of that in his mother, too. Though apparently his had grown to accept his decisions and his belief that bullets stopped gang members maybe a little better than prayer.

Yasmin was grateful for his acceptance and even ended up defending her mother. "I believe in prayer. But I don't want her ways forced on me. I know she believes that I'm a lost soul in need of pressure to rejoin the herd, but I'm not."

There was something in the way he looked at her, the way he absorbed what she said—that made her think he understood on some fundamental level.

It was a good start to a good day. Now she soaked up the sunshine, safe behind her SPF, and picked up her dry cleaning, visited the library for an audiobook—hoping she might get the chance to go running one day again. At each stop, she let people move in line in front of her. She was in no hurry, just filling up her morning.

She could go to the shop and get ready for her class, but there would be plenty of time for that even after lunch. Given the big breakfast Luke had made her, she wasn't anywhere near hungry yet.

Traffic was as non-existent as it could be in L.A. and she had three hours to kill. She hit Target for supplies and before she knew it she was sitting outside the Humane Society building wondering if she was actually going to do this.

When she considered it, Yasmin had to admit that—though she could still back out and no one would be the wiser—she'd just spent too much money on a litter box, a collar, food, treats and too much paraphernalia. The decision was really already made.

She walked out an hour and a half later with her wallet lighter and her arms full of two small, black kittens, mewing at her and squirming.

"Babies! You have to go in the box."

The unnamed kittens did not agree. No wonder. They'd previously been neutered and gone home with someone only to be returned. As small as they were, Yasmin had to wonder at the center's policy that no animal went out the door without first being fixed. She understood it, but these guys were far too young.

It turned out that stuffing kittens into a box—even a box designed to hold much larger cats—was as hard as everyone said it was.

The woman at the shelter had expressed concern that these two wouldn't get adopted and Yasmin's heart had cracked. She not only now had a kitten, she had two of them. Somehow, in the process she'd become borderline late for work.

Driving through a burger place turned out to be harder when you had kittens caterwauling in the seat beside you. But she made it into her parking space and hauled her stuff inside ten minutes before she was due.

Libby looked up from a sale she was ringing and her mouth dropped into a perfect "Awwwww" at the sound and the sight of the house-shaped box with regular holes punched in the side.

Grinning, Yasmin set down both the bag with her lunch and the box and waited for the customers to leave before she released her new little sidekicks. But the customers waited for her, and Yasmin opened the box to much oooooh-ing and ahhhhh-ing over her new pets.

Even Tristan wandered out and checked out the scene. Kittens were climbing all over the customers in his store. Where Yasmin had been sure even fifteen minutes ago that he wouldn't mind—many L.A. stores had resident animals—she wasn't so certain now.

It turned out as long as the customers were happy, Tristan was fine with it and he went back into his office only coming out just before they got busy.

By the time six p.m. rolled around, Yasmin was wondering whether the kittens would even know to come home with her. They were handled by so many people that day how would they even know she was their "forever home"? She still had to teach her class and she was beginning to wonder if she'd need to hire a kitten-sitter or—God forbid—try to keep them in the box during class. Focus was the primary concern of new witches and focus would not be possible with her two adorable little distractors around.

She wasn't surprised by the nearly constant chime of the door as her students showed up. Many came relatively early and shopped a bit. While traffic and parking were always a concern, she taught them tricks early on and valued promptness. It became almost a weekly challenge to get the good parking spots in front of the shop.

Yasmin smelled him first. He was standing behind her and she was surprised that he was in her store. She turned, trying to find something to say and cataloging that it wasn't a cologne or anything specific, just a blend of all things Luke—a smell her brain had filed away some time before and pulled out last night in her dream. Forcing a smile, she tried to find words.

Her expression alone must have worked because he said, "I'm here to take the beginner's class."

Startled, she blurted, "Really?" Had he signed up? She vaguely remembered him commenting on it. Hadn't she told him no? But when she looked at the clipboard in her hand and the list that Libby had printed up from in-store and website sign-ins there was the name Luke Salzone at number seven. She couldn't very well turn him down so she said, "Yes you are" and marked him present.

Then she had her hands full with students checking in and trying to play with her kittens. It was seven-thirty before she gave up trying to wrangle people and animals. She wasn't sure which was making more noise: the mewing kittens, the cooing students, or the few who were grumbling that they wanted to get started.

It was Luke who stepped up and said he'd take care of them. It took only seconds for him to leave his spot in the class and scoop a tiny kitten into each big hand and head out the door. While they had been crawling all over everyone and everything and begging for attention, they were disturbingly docile in Luke's grip. She wasn't sure if they were feeling safe or resigned, but they went quietly with him and she taught the class until fifteen minutes after time to make up for the late start.

It took another fifteen minutes to say goodnight and answer all the questions. Libby stayed, even though they officially closed at nine, ringing up sales. Yasmin knew that the extra sales showing after nine p.m. would make Tristan happy and she waited for her heart to twist at the thought.

It didn't—which only further solidified her theory that she was an idiot. She'd been in love with an idea with Tristan's face. The real Tristan was someone she wouldn't know what to do with.

Searching the store for Luke, she finally heard a tiny mew and followed the noise around behind the counter. She'd expected to find a wayward kitten having escaped from its box, instead she found Luke, sitting on the floor, nice work slacks covered in black hair. One kitten slept on his shoulder, head burrowed into his neck. The other rested on its back in his hand, Luke's other hand was giving the tiny kitten a belly rub.

Yasmin clamped down on her heart where it wanted to roll over in her chest. No, she was not falling for another guy that she didn't really know. A few nice facts and she stitched together a make-believe perfect man. Not again.

"Luke, thank you. It's time to go though."

"Okay." He looked up at her and smiled, his eyes bloodshot. He looked like he'd been on a three-day bender until he scrambled suddenly.

Yasmin was too late putting it all together. He'd grabbed a tissue he stashed at his side and sneezed.

"Oh Luke!" What a fool she'd been. "You're allergic."

"Just a touch."

CHAPTER 11

Luke's dreams had wandered into Yasmin's bedroom the night before for a second time. He'd had stable, steady relationships before and he had to admit he liked the camaraderie that went with it. He liked watching TV together and talking about anything and everything. Except he hadn't quite found a real 'anything and everything' yet.

Nicole hadn't liked anything he liked. Except in bed. And Reese had been completely compatible in everything and too competitive at all of it. She applied to be a police officer because he was and lorded every test score she beat him at and fumed or sulked when she didn't. Those had been his longest term relationships.

Though he and Yasmin had started out on shaky ground, they were settling into a rhythm. He was becoming much more at ease with the witchcraft and she was becoming more at ease talking to him about it. He figured it had just taken a handful of days for him to be confident that she wasn't going to give him a tail or turn him into a toad. Though he wasn't at the point where he would lay money on her ability to actually turn him into something else, he wouldn't lay money against it either.

She listened to him when he talked. She took it to heart when he'd scared her about the Del Surs and he felt bad about that still, but staying alive was more important than ignorant bliss.

Her apologies last night about bringing home animals he was allergic to were incredibly sincere. She even volunteered to take them back to the shelter and berated herself for being thoughtless.

He'd grabbed her by her upper arms when she'd about worked herself into tears and made her face him. "It's your house, you can bring in any animals you want. They make medicine for this. I'll just take something."

"I have Benadryl."

He was already grinning but too late he had to fight off another sneeze. Good thing he knew he wasn't going to get anywhere with her—this was not manly. "Can't take it, my job is to be alert."

"I'm so sorry, Luke." Her shoulders sagged and so did her smile.

"I'll be fine by morning." Had she been his girlfriend he would have held her. Kissed her to reassure her. Had she been his girlfriend she probably would have known that he was allergic. So he settled for helping her find a place for the cat litter—the laundry room—and training the cats where it was—not as simple as he would have thought.

Then he sat on the living room rug and played with them regardless of how much his eyes watered.

Yasmin was grinning at him. "You like cats?"

"I like the ones that are friendly. I think if you get them little you can kindof make them that way. Then they're good pets."

She nodded before saying what she'd clearly been thinking. "I figured you for a dog guy. Aren't dogs manlier?"

"Real men don't like cats?"

She nodded. And he reminded himself that she was not his

girlfriend, despite the way he'd touched her in his dreams. Despite the way he wanted her even when he was awake.

"Would you rather I ignored them? They're small creatures." He shrugged. "Any creature that needs help defending itself should have someone watching out for it."

As he watched, she seemed to absorb the words. "Like a woman who has a gang after her?"

He couldn't fight the sigh. "Yes. But one day it might be me. Maybe you'll have to make a forcefield around me and stop a bullet. But while I have the opportunity, I try to stand up where I can." He held the kitten in front of him. It dangled there, looking him in the eyes but not looking uncomfortable.

"That's why you're a cop."

He nodded but changed the subject quickly. "I didn't see this coming. Two kittens. What prompted it?"

She laughed. "I had to stay out of the house this morning. And it was something I always toyed with. You know, 'one day when I get a cat'—that kind of thing." She stroked the silky fur of the still unnamed kitten in her lap. "Then I got there and these two had been returned. They said they didn't know in this case but it happened a lot because someone turned out to be allergic." She looked sheepish at the thought.

"I'll be fine tomorrow." He waved her off. "You don't think it's because they're black?"

Both kittens were inky from their ears to the tip of their tails. "What does that have to do with it?"

Luke stared. How did she not know this? "Black cats are harder to adopt out and more likely to suffer abuse. They are three times as likely to be the victims of violent death at the hand of a sick human."

Her jaw was open. "Why?"

His was almost open, too. He spoke slowly. "Because of their known associations with witches. You're really embracing the stereotype here, Yasmin."

As he watched, she realized what she'd done, and he couldn't help throwing his head back and laughing. Then he couldn't help the sneezing fit that overtook him.

By the time he got himself together, she was laughing, too. And feeling bad for him. He'd taken some medication the second he walked in the door, but it wasn't helping yet. It didn't make things better that he was holding and petting the little fuzzy kittens then rubbing his face every time he sneezed, it was a self-perpetuating cycle. Until Yasmin grabbed both the kittens and put them in her room with the little bed she'd bought. The cat bed held both of them with room to spare.

She found him in the bathroom washing his hands and face and his hands again. As he dried himself off and she apologized yet again for not asking if he was allergic, he thought again that if she was his girlfriend, he'd kiss her now. He would tell her he'd always be allergic to cats, but he'd acclimate to these two and that it would be all right. So when actually she told him he had to take his shirt off his thoughts were somewhere else.

For a second or two he really thought she was starting something. Though his brain told him it was a bad idea, he wasn't able to say no. He started with the top button, working slowly while he tried to figure out what was going on when he hit yet another hiccup with her next words.

"Pants, too. In fact, you should just get out of everything."

He turned away because her words were turning him on. But the next time she spoke it was like cold water.

"I'll grab you something else to put on, and you can just hand all this out to me. I'll de-lint it and get it to the dry-cleaners for you."

Ah, cat hair. She was taking care of him.

That was all.

He reminded himself again that last night had been only a dream, regardless of how clear the memory was. The doorstop had been exactly at the same pencil mark where he'd wedged it again—a block of wood as his protection against witchcraft. Silly though it was, it offered peace of mind.

Yasmin showed up in the doorway once more, this time having changed into tiny sweatpants shorts and a loose top. "I'm trying not to get any cat hair in your room, so I changed before I went in." She laid out his pair of drawstring pajama pants across the sink then closed the door, telling him to just leave his clothing where it fell.

It was an elaborate dance that didn't leave him with any rights he didn't have before. It did leave him shirtless walking past her down the hallway, but her smile was kind, not hot, and the kittens were wailing behind her bedroom door.

In the past, the women he slept with liked his physique, but he was never overly self-confident. Some women liked really buff, ripped guys and he was never going to have the time to achieve that. He was in good shape, but not arrogant—who knew what Yasmin thought was most attractive in a man? He was never going to be that guy that bragged how he was God's gift all the time.

Besides, he was here in a professional capacity. He reminded himself that again. And again. Ignoring what he wanted to do, he put a shirt on. It was harder to ignore the kittens.

She was behind him in the bathroom doorway, carefully rolling one of those tape-thingies over his clothing and picking up enough black kitten fur to make him want to sneeze just looking at it. She caught him staring at her bedroom door, listening to the plaintive wails coming from behind it. "They have to calm down and rest. The lady at the shelter told me they'd likely cry and they could do it early or they could do it while I was trying to get to sleep."

He only nodded. It wasn't the only reason he was looking at her bedroom door.

"Pick something on TV and I'll be out in a minute."

It sounded so domestic that while he waited he imagined it

was more than it was. Then he played into it. "I've got that dinner at my Mom's this Sunday night. You should come. You've been forced out of your house enough while I'm out. And my mom's a great cook."

"She won't mind a random person just showing up?"

"You're not random, you're my guest, and trust me, *no one* will notice an extra mouth. There are so many of us."

Her face scrunched up for a minute and the thought she was going to refuse, instead she asked, "You're all Catholic, right? How big are they on that whole 'thou shalt not suffer a witch to live' thing?"

He laughed. "It has never come up before. But my mother hasn't got a mean bone in her body. It's up to you what you tell her, but worst case scenario, she'll fear for your eternal soul and light a candle for you every day. Then she'll ask me if I've converted. All this will be very dramatic. But that's about it."

"I generally don't bring it up if people don't ask, but if they do, I answer honestly." She looked at him, clearly wondering if this would fly in his big Italian family.

"I got your back. If it gets to be too much, we'll leave."

He spent the rest of the evening beside her on the sofa, eating leftovers from the dinner he'd cooked two nights before. At one point she stood up and bounced on her feet until he got her to confess that she hadn't gone running in over a week.

"Yasmin, we'll go tomorrow morning. You want to run, we run." It wouldn't hurt him any either.

"You don't have to."

Back and forth they went, until they worked it out and wore themselves out. And sometime in the middle of his dreams he turned the knob and let himself into her bedroom again.

This time he slowly stripped her naked before doing the same for himself. He made a leisurely stroll of her body with his hands before using his mouth and when he entered her she moaned his name and he breathed hers. Clinging to him and begging, Yasmin demanded more from him as a lover and he was only too happy to oblige.

This morning he'd woken the same way he had the day before. His alarm went off and he swore he was in her bed, next to her naked body. The sun was on his right as he opened his eyes. But as he blinked, he was in the room she'd assigned him. To his right was not a naked Yasmin reposed in the sunlight that filtered around the blinds, but a computer desk, a note pad and a wall. The sunlight on him came from his left, from the window his bed was nearly under in order to allow any kind of foot traffic in here.

Lifting the covers, he checked to see that he was still wearing his pajama bottoms. Yes, he was.

Brushing aside the dream, he pulled on a t-shirt and running shorts. As the coffee brewed, he went back for his running shoes and met Yasmin in the hallway.

Dressed much the same way he was, she smiled. That sleek hair was pulled up in a ponytail that reached a good ways down her back, but the ends were starting to curl up. Luke cataloged the pink top—tiny and clingy though it was—peeping from under her loose tank. She had on leggings in bright blue that hit her just below the knees and cross-trainers in orange.

He grinned at her, his own colors in white and navy blue, even his shoes were a sedate silver. "What do you think you are? Me?"

It took a moment for the colors to register. "Now is when I want to be seen." She puttered for a few minutes more, setting out food for the kittens, putting them in the litterbox in the laundry room again. She showed them the scratching posts she brought home for them, then told them to be good. Then she thought better of that waved her hand at them and snapped. Both kittens plopped their butts on the ground and watched silently as the two of them went out the door.

Figuring she must have cast some kind of obedience spell, he looked once more at the now docile kittens and followed Yasmin; he was her security detail after all. She had headphones in, which was generally a no-no for a woman running alone in L.A. but she wasn't alone today was she?

No, she had Luke Salzone, officer of the law, running just a handful of steps behind her to keep her safe. Problem was, he kept looking at her ass. The tank top would move and reveal more, since the leggings and the little top were more like a second skin than clothing.

He was supposed to be scanning the area, watching out for the worst guys around. Her home may be hidden, but they were out of the house and she was in her brightest clothes. But a little further down the road and his training would faltered off. He slowly edged into the zone, running, keeping up with the solid pace she set, and the next thing he knew, he was admiring her ass again.

About the third time it happened, he tried to set up a rhythm. Look at her ass, look to the left, look at her shoulder, check the right. He was doing great until her top shifted as they turned a corner and his feet stumbled.

Down he went, barely managing to angle himself across the sidewalk and onto the yard beside him. She'd been deftly hopping up a curb and he should have followed but just then her top had shifted and revealed the small mole on her shoulder blade.

The one he'd kissed the night before in his sleep.

His foot had missed. He'd planted himself in the grass. And Yasmin kept running, earbuds in place. He called to her, but whatever she was listening to, it wasn't him.

Someone in a passing car took pity and waved at Yasmin as they went by. Luke was already on his feet, wiping the grass off and sprinting after her by this point. He couldn't let her get too far ahead. He couldn't fail at the one thing he had to do—the whole point of his being here was to keep her safe.

Ultimately, the day was gorgeous and he had to admit that nothing had happened.

She was looking at him, realizing he'd fallen behind even if she didn't understand that he'd literally fallen, and she plucked out her earbuds. "You should run beside me. Then we can keep better track of each other."

He nodded. Then he wouldn't have to look at that mole. Wouldn't have to think about what it meant.

Trying to lose himself in the music filtering through his one earbud, Luke talked himself out of his original idea—the one that had sent him sprawling. Clearly, he'd seen the mole sometime and his conscious brain hadn't registered it. But his subconscious did and his subconscious dragged those little details back out so that when he remembered his dreams they were alive in full color clarity. Little moles and all.

Last night, he'd sworn there were kittens sleeping on his legs. But that was a detail he'd known even in the daylight, that the kittens were in there.

She was grinning at him as they turned the last corner and he recognized her street even though he still couldn't see her house. Unable to reconcile if that was because of the trees or the spell, he simply followed her lead, walking the last section. Still looking to spot her house, he was unprepared for her to pluck his remaining earbud from where he'd tucked it in his sleeve and start listening.

Her laugh was infectious. "Eighties power ballads?"

"It motivates me."

"To run away from it?" She started singing along to the Scorpions song that was currently coming through his little sound system.

He wanted to make fun of her but she was rocking out—albeit mockingly—and she looked adorable. Luke remembered to look around this time, but the street remained clear. While she opened her mouth wide and sang to what he considered to be a classic, he decided. Monday. If Monday came and nothing had come down the pipeline from the Del Surs, he'd cut her free. And pray that he was right.

Not really wanting to see her celebrate at the thought of her freedom, Luke didn't make a grand announcement. "What are you listening to?"

"Audiobook?"

"Romance novel?" he mocked.

"Nope. Suspense! I'm running from bad guys." She grinned and gave him back his earbud.

Yanking the second one, he bit his tongue and didn't tell her that he was afraid it was more than just her audiobook. But he was standing in front of her house, so he simply ushered her inside where they found that the kittens hadn't chewed any furniture but appeared to be attempting to use each other as playtoys. He could almost see the fur in the air.

Yasmin must have thought the same thing, "Let me shower first. I'll be lightning fast, then we can get out of here with as little cat hair on you as possible."

He checked the whole house, then ate oatmeal while he listened to the water run. The only thing that kept him from playing with the kittens was the thought of having to do his run-downs today with a red nose and bloodshot eyes. No one would assume allergies; not on a cop. Everyone always guessed pot and cocaine. It was not the image the LAPD wanted to project.

As fast as she promised, she was out, her large towel wrapped around her. It shouldn't have turned him on the way it did, but the wet curls springing around her head were as good as gold to him and he couldn't help the smile that formed on his mouth as she told him the shower was all his and turned, flashing him that mole again. He'd made up the one on her hip.

If he saw that, then he'd become concerned. But the doorstop was aligned with the mark and he'd surely seen the mole on her shoulder before. So he grabbed the hanger with today's clothes on it and tugged it into the bathroom with him, giving the set one last steam to get out any wrinkles he'd inadvertently put in it since picking it up at the dry cleaners and he climbed into the shower.

The hot water invigorated his confused muscles. It had been a week since he had run, even though he'd hit the gym during work more than once since then. But the dream sex was leaving him with some satisfied strain in muscles unused in quite a while. The heat stung his shoulders and when he dried off, the towel scraped at his back enough to make him wince and look in the mirror. Fingernail scratches raked each shoulder and Luke's jaw dropped wide open at his image.

Turning one way then another, he tried to inspect his own back, failing miserably at every angle. He tried using the tiny mirror from his overnight kit. While it allowed him to see all the scratches at once, it didn't improve what he could see.

He considered having Yasmin inspect them, but how would he tell her that the must have gotten them during a hot and heavy dream featuring her? Naked. Panting. Begging.

Luke shelved that idea right away.

He'd probably scratched himself . . . somehow. His proof—the doorstop—remained in place each night. Dreams sometimes involved the dreamer altering actual happenings—sounds, feelings, light—to fit the scape of the dream at the time. He must have scratched himself and dreamed it was her.

Doing what he did best, Luke solved his own crime. He'd seen the mole before. The scratches were his own hands. He even reached around his shoulders to prove to himself that he could reach there and that it was possible. The evidence in favor of him staying in his own bed and not breaking every single law of protocol that he'd sworn to uphold was insurmountable. He woke up in his own bed both mornings. His pants were still on this morning. He had no history of sleepwalking. And that doorstop was in the exact right place.

Done.

He dried off, avoiding the scratches, and put himself together. Weird yes, but weird things happened. He dealt with them.

And the next two mornings when he didn't find any more evidence and the door stopper remained in place despite his nightly wanderings, Luke didn't give it much more thought.

He saw only one odd car driving down the street and he even ran the license. It turned out to be registered to a home about four streets over and Luke had to figure that he was just looking for a reason to stay past Monday. But it didn't seem there was any real reason to.

CHAPTER 12

Nothing had happened. Yasmin had a live in police guard who was doing his best to crack the case, keep her safe and not sneeze at the two kittens she brought home with her when she should have asked first or just waited.

They'd gone running twice. She'd worked late the night before as she did every other Friday, closing the shop. It also allowed Luke some time at his own place away from tiny kittens who seemed to enjoy rubbing up on him and he didn't seem to be able to refuse them. Though he was still sneezing a bit, he no longer looked like he'd been doing high quantities of illicit drugs.

She tried to fight the random pop-up memories from her dreams. They'd hit her at odd times, bursting into her consciousness with sharp clarity. Getting dressed in the morning, she would see the iron scrollwork on her bed and suddenly flush hot with the vivid sensation of Luke's hands over hers, guiding her to hold on to the headboard while he knelt behind her and peeled the knit nightie she'd worn to bed wondering if she'd dream about him again.

Yasmin had not been disappointed.

She'd agreed to attend his mother's Sunday dinner the following night as he wouldn't go unless he knew she was with someone. And Saturday morning she'd just had to get out of the house, which meant having her friend Jenn come pick her up so Yasmin could take them to lunch.

Feeling like a teenager getting picked up for an outing, Yasmin stood by as Jenn came to the door and Luke introduced himself. Nothing had happened. No suspicious people had come by her home, her work, anything in between. She was so ready to go somewhere on her own that she was almost prepared to go grocery shopping by herself.

The pinned-down feeling burst out in her voice. "Her name is Jennifer Viviane Lesley, she lives on Poinsettia south of Melrose. Her husband's name is Walker Booth. Did you get all that?"

A war between humor and pity, his pained grin matched his words. "Yes, I did."

"You have maybe three hours. I'll call you on the way home."

"Thank you." He closed her front door behind her and Yasmin fought both the odd feeling of leaving someone at her home and wanting to yell out to him to lock all the deadbolts! Instead, she grabbed Jenn's hand and dragged her to the car.

Jenn wasn't even pulling away from the curb before she bust out, "You're living with that hottie?"

"Technically." While Yasmin was explaining both the man at her door and the satisfied demeanor she was apparently sporting, the whole story came out. In the end, Jenn knew everything, including the dreams and how Yasmin was having both an actual professional relationship with an officer trained to protect her and a pretend, dream relationship with her subconscious's version of the same man.

"I think he likes you." Jenn grinned while putting away about the biggest burger Yasmin had seen her friend ever eat.

"I think you're wrong. I think pregnancy hormones are making your vision cloudy." Yasmin had tapped out of her own meal a handful of bites ago, but she was more than happy to have as much time as possible out of the house and away from her memories. "There is nothing untoward going on between us."

"Except in your dreams."

"Isn't that the way of things? In my dreams!" Yasmin sighed then tried to fight the blush she felt flaming across her cheeks as she was rushed by a sudden memory from her dream the night before.

"You like him." Jenn taunted around bites. "This is much better than the thing you had for Tristan."

Yasmin toyed with a sweet potato fry she had no intention of eating. "Was I the last one to see that? I think even Officer Multicolor figured it out before I did."

"Stop!" Jenn held up her hand and blinked. "Oh God, do you call him that to his face? I love it."

"No. Not on purpose." Chagrinned, Yasmin was forced to admit, "Well, I haven't yet. I have to quit thinking it or I'll slip."

"Okay. Number two: figuring out this Tristan thing was that recent?"

"Yeah. Just a handful of days. A week?" She shook her head at her own foolishness and looked off into the distance. "I was in love with who I wanted him to be."

"Listen, we have *all* done that one. It's kind of a rite of passage. And it's sad to say, I think a lot of women never figure out that they should fall for a real guy—they are so much better than the made up ones."

"You're lucky." Her smile turned soft. Jenn had gotten one of the last of the red-hot guys. Walker was an artist and he practically worshiped the ground Jenn walked on. Which normally would have bothered Yasmin, but it was clearly mutual. Jenn never shut up about Walker.

She nodded, agreeing how lucky she was and making Yasmin even more jealous. "You will be. You'll get lucky, too."

Which just made her face flame more.

"Wow. Those must be some good dreams!" Jenn lifted her hand to fan Yasmin's face, which Yasmin tried vainly to bat away..

"Sure they are. But it's just another made-up guy. He's not any more real than my version of Tristan was." It was impressive how quickly she'd left even the idea of Tristan in the dust once she'd realized the man she wanted didn't want her because he didn't even exist. But it was equally disturbing how her subconscious had immediately turned around and picked another guy to do the exact same thing with. At least she was aware this time.

Eventually, Jenn had to get back to Walker as they had plans and Yasmin had to call Luke and tell him she was on her way home. She almost closed the call with "Yes, Dad." But just thinking about saying it gave her a squirmy feeling of wrongness.

They passed the remainder of the weekend in quiet acquiescence. Luke petted the kittens too much; Yasmin agreed to whatever schedule he set for when she could be out of the house or in it and with whom.

She was close to tearing her hair out by Sunday night. So close that going to Luke's family dinner actually sounded like it would be a welcome relief.

The kittens were crying at being left alone again, so Yasmin cast another calming spell on them and wondered what kind of mother she would make. Then she resigned herself to not getting to find out any time soon, because who could she possibly date while she had a police detail?

As they pulled up to the house in Calabasas, Yasmin thought two things. First, they would have to have a talk about setting her free. Nothing had happened. Second, how did he know he was at the right house? It looked like every other home in the neighborhood, right up to the spindly tree smack in the middle of the front patch of grass. It was still wearing its grow-sleeve.

"I'm guessing you didn't grow up here?"

He laughed. "No one did. Not in my family. My folks bought it after I moved out. I grew up closer to town. Went to Granada Hills High School."

She nodded, everyone knew the area. It was one of the better schools in L.A.

She realized there were a handful of cars of varying ages and styles parked around this one house, and the lights were on. So she trailed him up the front steps wondering just what she'd gotten herself into.

When he pulled the front door open, Yasmin realized no one would have heard a knock anyway. She also discovered several things simultaneously. There were a billion of them. They were all different ages and sizes. They wore all different clothes, but none of them was quiet.

While the house was constrained on the outside by homeowner association rules, the inside desperately wanted to break free in bursts of color and sound and some of the best food smells she'd ever inhaled.

As much as it seemed none of them had paid attention to the new arrivals, it took less than two seconds before her thoughts were interrupted by voices turning their direction.

"Luciano! I was afraid you wouldn't make it this week." The woman must have been his mother, given the worry and the deep hug he was willing to give her. He towered over her as she turned amazing amber colored eyes onto Yasmin.

Though the woman's hair was long, that was the only thing that Yasmin could put her finger on. It suddenly occurred to her that everything she knew about Italian families, she had learned from the movies. She braced herself to have her cheeks pinched or at least to be engulfed in a huge hug that was too personal for a person she'd just met. She was prepared for a barrage of questions about when she was going to marry their son and would she give them lots of grandbabies?

But none of it happened.

The woman had her long hair in a ponytail, and she wore old jeans and a t-shirt that read "Bite me." As she scanned the room she saw that this was where Luke got his love of color. None of them was drab . . . at all. Even the house was in vivid relief, something Yasmin could relate to, though the combinations and shades weren't ones she would have chosen, they were beautiful and welcoming.

"You must be Yasmin." The woman held out her hand. "I'm Luz. Luke's mother."

Yasmin nodded and shook the woman's hand, but wasn't able to say anything before the woman said, "Welcome to our home. We're really glad you could make it."

And it sounded like she meant it. As though this woman was excited to meet her son's latest police assignment. As though she was genuinely happy to feed a total stranger.

Yasmin had no meter to gauge any of this by. Her family was sedate. They rarely invited people outside the immediate family to join them for meals and even when the family ate, Yasmin's own mother often fed Leyla and Maryam early so the adults could have a meal not interrupted by the children.

Here, the children seemed entwined with all the adults. Two little girls hung by grubby hands on a man in a very expensive pinstripe suit while they yelled up at him. "Walk us around, Uncle Donny!"

A toddler broke rank and ran under the table, as a man with pale brown hair, wearing jeans and sneakers ducked right behind the child and grabbed him to the tune of "Gotcha!" and several happy squeals.

A warm hand came around her shoulder, startling her. But Luke's voice in her ear was calming. "Stick with me. No one will fault you if you don't learn all the names in one night, but I'm going to introduce you anyway. Ready?"

She didn't look at him. She couldn't; she was still overwhelmed by the scene in front of her. But she was game to try to learn all the names and people.

"Here we go. This is my oldest sister, Arabella."

Yasmin shook the woman's hand, there was no gray in her hair, but she looked nearly a generation older than Luke. "Her husband, Rafael is . . . Over there." Luke pointed then waved. "They have two sons in college, so they aren't here."

He steered her another direction. "This is my closest sister in age, just a few years older. Savina." Yasmin shook another hand as Luke introduced her then she stepped back as Savina declared how happy she was to have Luciano back for the meal. Apparently he'd missed a few. Then the sister engulfed Luke in another big hug before letting him get back to leading Yasmin around.

She was asking "Luciano?" but he ignored the question and leaned close over the noise to steer her another direction. "Those are her girls, the twins, Casey and Riley, hanging off my only brother."

The brother looked up, dark eyes, thick dark hair and a wicked grin. He easily held one grubby hand in each of his and didn't seem concerned that small, dirty sneakers were killing the high shine on wingtips that had to cost more than her house payment.

The ease with which the man inhabited his own skin, the casual interaction with two small girls who obviously thought the sun rose and set on him, the eye contact that looked into her rather than at her . . . None of that could be faked. She would bet good money that Luke's brother was a hit with women everywhere.

"This is my brother, Adonis."

Seriously? Did he just introduce this Adonis as . . .Adonis? Luke said it with a little bit of an accent. But he had to be kidding, right?

"Don, please." The man grinned again. "I'd offer a hand but I'm a bit tied up."

The girls were ignoring the exchange over their heads and talking to each other. It sounded as though they were planning an "Uncle-Donny-kidnapping."

Adonis looked at her, not Luke, "So *Luciano,* can I ask this one out?"

"No." The answer was firm, but easily followed up by, "She's part of an active case. Can't have witnesses dating my family members."

"Maybe after." Another grin.

Luke steered her away, muttering "Maybe never" and Yasmin stifled a laugh. She met all six of the nine Salzone kids in attendance as well as three spouses who'd made it to family dinner. One daughter was divorced, two daughters and Adonis never married, but one of the daughters had a teenage son. One of the daughters was there with her husband and their two grandkids, one of whom was just a chubby baby. Luke had easily picked him up, kissed him, made him giggle and then the good uncle was roped into diaper duty.

Holding the kid at arm's length, he looked at Yasmin over his shoulder and offered her the chance to come with or hang with the family. It took a moment, but she followed. She wanted to see Officer Multicolor change a diaper.

She herself had never done it until Shori had come over with a baby Leyla, but it didn't seem a person could escape any gathering of this family without getting involved with the children. Here she was, not even a family member, and she was now involved.

The baby was as dark-haired and dark-eyed as the rest of

them. A few of the husbands, Luke's brothers-in-law, were not cut from that rich Italian mold, but something was starting to peck at the back of her brain.

It was the family portrait in the hallway that stopped her dead. There they were, his mother and father with nine kids around them. The oldest was maybe twenty and Luke looked to be about five. He also looked to be an alien from another planet. Every one of them had eyes in varying shades of dark brown, they had olive skin and thick, shiny dark hair. And there was little Luke, clearly the youngest, blond hair and vivid blue eyes, staring up at the camera with a gap-toothed grin from the middle of the crowd.

His voice broke through her thoughts. "I'll explain, but come in here so I don't have to shout."

"Oh!" she threw her hands up as though that would shield the smell and she was on the verge of automatically whipping up a fragrance to cover it when she remembered that she didn't cast in other people's houses. Not unless they'd asked her to.

"Sorry, toddlers are the worst though."

She was making a face she couldn't fight. "This isn't the worst?"

He shook his head and seemed relatively at ease with the chemical warfare coming from the grinning baby. So at ease that he just started talking while she wondered if she was losing brain cells or catching a dread disease. She didn't remember Leyla or Maryam being this foul, but then again, when they were little, she'd never been in a situation to have them to herself. Only an hour here or there while Shori went out. Only if Shori had changed them first before she left.

His words finally punctured through the realization that—though her family considered themselves close—they had nothing on the Salzones. "I'm clearly adopted."

"So you're not genetically Italian? Just raised that way?"

Those were stupid words, and she considered again casting a spell, one to make him forget she'd said something so idiotic.

He didn't take offense, or even blink. "I'm genetically Italian, too."

Her raised eyebrows and disbelieving stare only earned her a chuckle. Done powdering and diapering the baby, he started cleaning up and explaining. "My birth mother is Northern Italian. Blond haired and blue eyed. Only the Southern Italians look like them." He motioned with his head toward the crowd downstairs. "She was a teenager, and she died just a few months after I was born. But she gave me to Mom and Pop. She knew them, knew they were right for me. And she was right about that."

"So . . . was it an Italian thing, here in L.A.?" She was still trying to wrap her head around it.

"No, in Italy. I was born there. We came here when I was two. All immigrants." Luke was leading her out the door, from the little room set up for grandkids, down the stairs and back to the crowd where dinner was being laid out on the table.

Luz was motioning to seats for them and taking the baby out of Luke's hands. There was no high chair that Yasmin could see when she was in her own seat, between Luke and Adonis, and it soon became clear that Luz was going to hold the baby for the meal.

Conversation flowed easily, occasionally in Italian, but never in a rude way. Yasmin was both brought into the fold and easily allowed to tap out when she chose. Sometimes she just watched. The whole family—there were easily more than twenty-five of them at this table—worked over and around each other with the ease of years of practice.

After dinner, she was talking to one of the sisters when she realized Luke wasn't around. Suddenly feeling anchorless, she tried to hide it, but one of the guys came up to her as the conversation with whichever sister wound down. "Luke's in the kitchen with his mother."

"That obvious?" She tilted her head, hoping she hadn't looked flat-out panicked at being left alone here.

"I like to think not. Because I know it's how I looked the first, probably, five or six times I came here." He took a sip from the Chianti he held. It had been passed more times than she could count during dinner. At least that matched her movie-based perception of Italian families. He re-introduced himself. "Randall, engaged to Giada. It's a lot to take in. But don't worry, a handful of Sundays and you'll fit right in. They're wonderful people. Nothing like my family."

Holding back, Yasmin didn't correct his 'handful of Sundays' comment. She didn't think she'd even be back the following Sunday. But she did ask about his family. "Your family is smaller than this?"

His grin was sharp and sincere. "I'm an only child!"

"I'm the younger sister. And this makes my family look positively . . . Emotionless. I mean, they aren't. But we are much more restrained. We're definitely quieter."

"My family is Massachusetts blue blood. We don't have emotions. We don't raise our voices." He lowered his head as though he was sharing a secret. "Having emotions is positively *crass*." He placed splayed fingers over his heart and affected a bored expression. Then he broke and grinned again. "Giada taught me to fight like I mean it and invest in the people around me. I'm less than an inch from being disowned by my own family, but I've never been happier. I hope you'll come to our wedding."

She didn't know what to say. But she tried. "I'd love to. But I don't think I'll be Luke's assignment much longer."

Randall's smile never faltered. "You're invited. Luke or no Luke."

But then, as though he heard they were talking about him, Luke showed up. "Hey, Randall. How many more weeks is it?"

"Less than a month." And the smile widened just a bit. Yasmin couldn't pick Giada out of this crowd, but the woman was lucky.

As Randall headed off to talk to someone else, Luke looked at her and asked, "Are you ready to go home?"

CHAPTER 13

It was nine p.m. when Luke looked over into the passenger seat of his car. Yasmin had her head tipped against the window and was nearly asleep.

He knew his family could be a bit much for anyone. For someone coming from Yasmin's background? Well, he wasn't surprised it had worn her out. Had it been only him that evening, he would have stayed much later; he often even slept over if he drank any of the wine or even if it just got late.

The drive took a while; traffic could pop up anywhere in L.A. at any time. He'd once been stuck in a bad traffic jam on the 405 at 3 a.m. on a Tuesday, so he wasn't shocked by the bumper-to-bumper freeway tonight. Initially, before she'd started to pass out, Yasmin asked about his being adopted again.

He'd heard it all before: didn't he feel the need to find out more about his birth parents? Did he feel like he didn't fit in?

Luke figured he was about fifteen when he learned his then-girlfriend dreamed of finding out she was adopted. Apparently, feeling like you didn't fit in was universal. Adoption was just a handy reason for the emotion. But while he felt different from the rest of his family, so did they all. Donny was a money whore, and no one else understood his need for fancy cars, homes, and women. But he was Donny. Giada loved to cook . . . French Cuisine which his mother always shook her head at. Mom and Pop had taught them all how to feed themselves well and Giada nearly hated Italian food. But they all loved her.

They all accepted Luke's work in law enforcement even if they didn't understand it. He wasn't the only one unmarried; he wasn't the only one who skipped mass far more often than he attended. He was just the only blond.

Right then, there on the freeway, stopping and starting, he realized he wanted more from his life. He wanted a wife and kids. He wanted a smaller version of his own family to add to the bigger one he already had. For years he'd dated off and on, telling himself he wasn't ready for the responsibility of kids, the commitment of staying with one woman forever. Suddenly, he realized he *was* ready. Somewhere along the line, things had changed though he was only just now realizing it.

He couldn't stop his gaze from straying to the woman beside him, now out cold. But he stopped his thoughts. Yasmin Ali was not for him. Yasmin Ali was an assignment. She was literally his dream-girl, but in broad daylight she was friendly and nothing more.

Luke at last understood what Jessica had once said about Friends-with-benefits not being enough. At the time, he told her she was nuts, that it was the best of all worlds. But Valverde was right: FWB lacked security. It lacked future. It lacked the public affection and the declaration to the world that you were in it.

But Luke wasn't in it. It was something he had to accept.

He woke Yasmin up as he pulled into her driveway. He could see the house now as he got closer to the right spot and he hadn't missed in several days. He was learning.

Inside, he sat her down and started "the talk."

She was fully awake by the time he said, "If nothing

happens tomorrow, I think . . . I think you're okay. I haven't known the Del Surs to take time for revenge. Everything I've seen has been quick and merciless. I've only run one quasi-suspicious license plate and it was just a car from two blocks over."

While she took care of the kittens, he drilled her on the people at work. Anyone suspicious? Anyone just look or feel out of place? Did she feel like someone was watching her? Even just good general paranoia was often a hint of something real.

But she didn't have any of it.

"Then, tomorrow, I'll come check the house out when you get home, and if there's nothing, I'll go."

Her nod was rapid enough that her curls bounced in agreement, too. Then she yawned and he shooed her off to her room. Two hours of TV later and he discovered he was well past ready to drop off himself.

Barely doing the minimum to get ready for bed, Luke fell almost face first onto his temporary bed. As the void of sleep pulled him under he offered up a prayer of thanks that it was his last night on the air mattress. Then he wondered if falling asleep in just his jeans would have any effect on his dreams.

Somehow, having Luke declare Monday as her last day of imposed imprisonment—i.e. police guard—let Yasmin drop a load of tension she didn't even realize she was carrying.

She was worn out after being 'on' all night for his family. Though they were very easy people to get along with, she wasn't able to fully relax during dinner. Did she get their names right? Were they always this loud? Would the whole meal turn sour if someone asked her about her religion?

The relief of going home had been enough to set her dozing on the ride back. When she felt the pressure of constantly being on guard lifted, Yasmin felt physically lighter, at first. Then she felt bone weary and told Luke she was headed to bed.

Managing only to brush her teeth and splash some water on her face, she fell onto her comforter, the sounds of the kittens not even really getting through. She kicked off her shoes, letting them fall where they had and pulled the corner of the comforter over what it would reach before she gave up. Her t-shirt was plenty comfortable but a moment later she shimmied out of her jeans, barely opening her eyes and paying no attention to where they landed.

It wasn't long after that she felt the bed shift beside her. Warm hands skimmed up her back and under her shirt while she sighed herself into consciousness.

She knew what was going on.

Luke was here.

In the morning, she'd wake up, muscles well used, tension eased, her attitude sedate. But right now, he would touch her and make her scream his name and beg him for more.

And she would do it. She would be so easy for him. Because there were no real consequences here. Sighing with this first touch, she breathed in the smell and heat of him. She rolled closer and reached her own hands out to touch him.

Yasmin knew she was asleep.

Her knowledge didn't change how real his hot skin felt beneath her fingertips. She heard his breath suck in as she trailed her hand down his bare chest and encountered his jeans, button undone, zipper still mostly up.

She had both hands and her mouth on him as he moved to shove the comforter from where it had bunched between them. As soon as it was gone, he spread his hands across the width of her back, somehow making her feel small but never less, protected but never untrusted. Heat radiated everywhere his skin contacted hers and her body caught fire under his touch as he moved against her, pulling her flush to his length.

Beneath his jeans, his body was ready; it was more than clear that he wanted her. Using his superior size, he moved her one way then another, granting himself access to first her neck, then her mouth.

She didn't protest. Why would she? When had a man last wanted her like this? When had she last been handled with such a combination of need and skill? It was a heady mix and they spoke no words—they didn't need them.

Her arms raised naturally as he peeled her shirt, managing to touch her everywhere as he did. As he tossed it aside, she experienced a pang of need. For the half second he wasn't touching her, her skin was begging for his return. When he granted it, she nearly moaned.

His shoulders were firm where her hands curled there to hold him in place but she happily tilted her head back allowing him room to kiss and lick her. First he played his lips and tongue under her jaw, then traced a path down her neck, all the while holding her hips to him and moving against her as though there were no clothes between them. When his mouth covered her nipple, she couldn't help the noise she emitted and he apparently couldn't help grinning up at her.

Then he did it again.

Unable to wait, needing him now, Yasmin fumbled with his jeans. He helped, or tried to. It seemed difficult for him to complete even simple actions while her hands roamed his ever more exposed flesh and taunted him with soft touches until she pulled an answering groan from him.

When he was naked before her, Luke looked her in the eyes for just a second. In that moment, she agreed to whatever he wanted. Her bra and underwear disappeared then he was touching her everywhere again. Making her beg for more, beg for him.

He pushed inside her, her breath coming in short gasps. His

own breath was hot against her skin carrying sound and meaning, casting some sort of spell whether he knew it or not.

It seemed forever they moved against each other, striving for something together, then finally reaching the tipping point and clinging desperately while they quickly came apart then slowly came back together.

She didn't know how much time had passed when he seemed to realize she was getting cold. Half asleep, she felt him rearrange the covers from where they had been bunched beneath them before she fell into the void of her sleep and his hold.

Only much later did she feel him get up. Somewhere in the distance she heard an alarm, probably his. His fingers laced through her curls as he leaned down to give her a last lingering kiss. His touch filled the volumes his silence could have left.

As he pulled away, she realized he already had his jeans pulled back on and in the dark he stumbled out of her room. The only word he spoke the whole time was a curse as he kicked one of her abandoned shoes against the wall and fumbled for the door.

Yasmin awoke under her covers and naked.

Frowning, she looked around for her clothing. She distinctly remembered going to sleep in her shirt, bra and undies. She also distinctly remembered Luke peeling each piece from her and tossing it away.

Sure enough, she found the three pieces in different places around the far corners of the room. They certainly looked as though they had been tossed against the wall and slid down to where they each now rested.

It made perfect sense that she had shed and tossed each item in her sleep. A hot and heavy dream like that could certainly be matched by her own restless actions. But it was the shoe—now against the wall near her door and far from its companion—that gave her real pause.

She would have had to at least slide mostly off the bed and kick it herself to get it over there. Or maybe she'd just sent it flying when she first took it off and it was simply coincidental that her dream Luke kicked it there. Thinking again, she realized that it was even more probable that her subconscious—knowing the shoe hadn't originally fallen where she thought it had—had corrected the idea while she was asleep by having dream Luke kick it into the spot where it had actually first gone.

All were possibilities. All easily allowed for her strange dream and allowed Yasmin to get on with her day. She played with the kittens, fed them, walked them over to the litter box. They probably didn't need that, but she didn't want to take chances.

She first encountered Luke at the breakfast table eating some toasted bread with cheese baked on it and drinking his five alarm coffee. He motioned that he'd made her some, but kept tapping away on his phone.

The blush she'd so easily felt the first few mornings she'd faced him after so vivid a dream didn't come today. She was over it. It was a dream—her dream—and she didn't have to be embarrassed when that would just give it away. For a minute she wondered if she would continue to have the dreams about him after he moved out tonight. Then she bit into the bread and realized she'd miss having someone cook for her and she told him so.

Grinning, he looked up at her. "Tell you what, since you don't have to go into work until later, why don't we run an experiment? I'll go first and you stay here. You no longer have to stay away from your own home when I'm not here."

That was easy. She'd been wondering how she would fill the morning, if she could take the kittens somewhere and if she'd have to then take them on to work with her because she wasn't allowed in her own home by herself.

He took another bite, then swallowed and said, "I assume nothing will go wrong, and I'll come back and check everything tonight and if all is well, I'll cut you loose."

She took a breath. "What do I owe you?" She figured that initial dollar wouldn't cover everything he'd spent. He'd fed her sometimes, ferried her around, all sorts of things.

"Nothing."

"How can that be?" But she was grateful. Her job didn't pay a ton. It was fine, but she wasn't in the position to just hire herself police security.

He shrugged before he added. "I'm trying to get these guys. The gangs are really hard to take down, and from what happened, they're not only not decreasing violence, they're moving into new territory."

"Are you wishing they had come after me?"

"Oh god, no." He set down his toast and looked at her then. It was a little unnerving. "I'm glad they didn't come back. A lot of times things play out this way. I'll get them through some other thing."

He was a dog and the Del Surs were his bone. Even though he wasn't in the Guns and Gangs unit any more, he still wanted to take them down, she could tell.

Then it was time for him to leave and she struggled at the awkwardness of not having anything to do, the oddity of seeing him off to work while she stayed behind. She was almost tempted to say "Have a great day at work, Honey!" and smile like a chipper housewife and set him off with a peck on the cheek. But she refrained.

Closing the front door behind him, she slid all the bolts into place and heard his voice through the heavy wood, "Good girl." Her curtains were open and through the window next to the door he caught her wry expression and grinned. Then he was gone.

The silence in the house was peaceful—not because Luke had left, but because she was finally alone. A pitiful series of mews reminded her that was no longer actually the case. And a set of claws piercing her jeans and making her grimace at the sharp needles in her calf had her plucking the kitten from the material. "Do you need attention?"

The other kitten sat and wailed at her plaintively from her feet. "Yup. You too!" Scooping them both up, Yasmin headed into the living room and grabbed the fairy wand with streamers. It looked like a leftover from a bratty five-year-olds princess birthday party, but the packaging had been right: the kittens went nuts chasing the glittering ribbons.

She spent the morning listening to her music, not worried about what Luke might think of it. She played with her new little housemates and tried to think up names for them.

She eventually decided on Hex and Voodoo, since they were already 'embracing the stereotype' as Luke had said. Though she was only a few days into being a pet owner, she felt she was doing pretty well. Pets had never been allowed in her home when she was growing up for a variety of reasons, but as with many other things, Yasmin found she didn't believe the same things her parents did in regards to this either. She was beginning to understand what pet owners always said about the rewards outweighing any costs.

Given her good mood, she scooped up her little critters and took them to the pet store where she had engraved tags made now that they had names. She dropped them at home again, thinking she might take them in to work the next time she had a short day and that her house seemed untouched despite the fact that the hiding spell was slowly wearing off.

While Yasmin was certain she wasn't up for another round of that, especially if it wasn't necessary, she was sure she should use her energy for fixing what she'd screwed up in the first place. So she rolled out her pentagram mat and set about setting the universe back in place as much as she could. A balancing spell was as good as she could come up with for something to reset things without possibly further screwing them up. When she finished, she rolled up the mat so Luke didn't have to deal with it when he came to get his things.

The day went perfectly, awesomely normal. Until she called Luke. The frustration was clear in his voice, but luckily none of it was related to her or the Del Sur case. It seemed someone thought they could spray paint graffiti on the police squad cars parked in the lot and get away with it. Luke said he was glad that the security cameras had caught the whole thing and they got the kid even before he finished doing it. The tone in his voice clearly considered this person a complete moron. The problem was, Luke's own car had been parked in the section that got hit.

His pretty car was now evidence and he was involved as a victim in a second case when he was just moments from shedding the last case he'd inadvertently become a part of. He could take one of the squad cars but only after it came back from day shift.

Pity took over. "I'll come get you. We'll get dinner and I'll bring you back to pick up your shiny cop-mobile."

He was upset enough that he just said yes. Yasmine took the on a route up Highland, heading toward her favorite Vietnamese place and realized quickly what a mistake that had been. Rubbing his head as though his day could not get worse, Luke simply muttered, "Hollywood Bowl. Just keep going."

Sadly, he was right. When the Hollywood Bowl had an event, traffic up and over the hill ground to a near halt. Getting in and out of her restaurant then getting turned around to get Luke back . . . That would be a nightmare. So she headed for a place closer to home, her stomach growling while she her car crawled through the crush.

In the end, they gave up and called in a to-go order, taking the food back to her place. Luke didn't seem to mind that she felt the need to check on the kittens and she volunteered to get him back to the precinct later when they finished. She would not take the same route.

They were eating, chatting about how nothing had happened with the Del Surs. How Hex and Voodoo seemed to have already figured out to beg for table scraps. How Luke had to remember the bottle of shampoo and his favorite razor that he'd left in the shower. He was looking at her oddly—as though he was considering saying something—when suddenly his expression changed.

Angry now, his face contorted, he lunged at her.

Before she even had time to be afraid of him, Yasmin was on her back, her head cracking against the hardwood floor, Luke crushing her into the ground. She caught sight of two tiny black streaks as Hex and Voodoo dashed under the couch, suddenly afraid.

He must have smacked at the floor—she heard the wood crack again. Her brain thought it was loud, but she was more concerned with pushing him off her. Luke didn't allow it.

Pinning her, he rolled sideways and twisted one way then another. Her heart was beating rapidly and she found she wasn't scared of him but she was suddenly very afraid. Odd noises came from the entry way as she realized Luke was looking into the living room, still pinning her down but twisted to look over his own shoulder.

Her windows shattered suddenly, the kittens now howling from their spot under the couch. And Yasmin realized Luke had a gun that he'd pulled from somewhere on his body and he was aiming it out the empty window casing.

CHAPTER 14

He was so angry he was shaking with it.

There was nothing Luke could do from his position on the floor but stay on top of Yasmin and keep her from getting hit. He couldn't return fire for a number of reasons, the biggest of which was that he couldn't see jack shit.

His only consolation was the high pitched squeal of tires on road. They were either all leaving or they were leaving someone behind. If the Del Surs did that, Luke would have him.

The sun had set before he and Yasmin made it to the house and he'd been stupid—thinking everything was okay—letting her leave the curtains open after dark. The living room was lit up like a stage, the houses here close enough together and set near enough to the sidewalk that anyone walking by could see exactly what was going on in her living room.

Churning with no direction, but needing something to do, his brain started putting pieces together. She'd walked into the living area several times, though the table was not directly in sight of a window, where she was sitting was—his seat wasn't. He hadn't even paid attention.

Unsure if he was the target or she was, Luke chewed on that

thought even as he scanned the area. He didn't hear anything outside, but he wasn't quite ready to get up and check either. It would mean leaving Yasmin here—in sight of a now-missing window—or moving her.

His brain jumped to a different track even as his eyes stayed vigilant. His car wasn't here either. As if the spray paint incident hadn't been bad enough crap for one day. His brain clicked that fact into place too.

They had been watching the whole time.

Waiting for him to leave.

They saw her inside, no cop car in the driveway, for the first time, and they took shots in this quiet little North Hollywood neighborhood full of first time homebuyers and young families.

Luke was livid.

He pushed off Yasmin, only then realizing he'd completely pinned her to the ground. "Are you okay?"

He started feeling her limbs, checking her head, hoping he hadn't damaged her in the process of trying to keep her from being damaged.

Her hands reached out and slapped at his as she started to roll away. "I'm fine, quit grabbing me."

But he did just that, tucking her under him again. "I'm not certain yet that they're gone."

"What!?" She froze where she was, no longer shoving him away. Now she clutched at his shirt with a death-grip he was pretty sure he wouldn't physically be able to pry open.

"Stay here." He didn't move either. "The neighbors will call it in. Someone will be here any moment . . ." He didn't know this district all that well. He knew the guys in Hollywood, but not here as North Hollywood was a completely separate unit.

He would have called 9-1-1 himself and rattled off his badge number, but he was propped on one elbow, his hand still gripping Yasmin's shirt where he'd grabbed her to drag her to the ground. His other hand was holding his glock, aimed out the front window. Unless someone came through the door, it was the only visual anyone would get on them. He intended to shoot anyone before they could shoot into the house.

Unsure how long he stayed in that position, Luke only knew that his muscles hurt by the time he heard the sirens approaching.

It was just a few moments after that Luke was shouting out to the approaching officers. He gave all the usual info: his name, badge number, that he had a weapon on him and it was unholstered. No he hadn't fired any shots. No he hadn't seen the perpetrators.

As he recognized the blue uniforms of the men and women breaking through the doorway, he fell onto his back in sheer relief.

When Yasmin saw the people coming literally through her front door, she'd initially been grateful. But long past midnight she was long past her point of no return.

While they were at the station, she and Luke each separately gave their statements. But she was pretty sure hers didn't amount to much. Luke rushed her, threw her on the floor—probably saving her life—and she heard some noises. It was pretty much over before she even realized Luke wasn't attacking her but doing his job.

She'd talked to three different officers, called her homeowners insurance and tried to walk her cats. Kittens, it would seem, were not keen on leashes. Had it not been the middle of the night after being shot at in her own home, Hex and Voodoo would have made her laugh.

Hex planted his butt and Voodoo tried to escape the leash by backing up then laying down as though it were pressing on him. While she could drag them along the smooth linoleum flooring, she could not get them to walk. They would pee in the box if she didn't get them somewhere fast.

Eventually Luke took pity on her and her kitties. Talking the force into letting him take Yasmin back into the house to get what they needed, Luke finally got them out but it still took time. They were accompanied by another officer and Yasmin wasn't allowed to touch much of anything.

Her home had become a crime scene.

The windows were getting boarded up by someone the insurance company had sent. It looked hideous and felt worse. There was yellow tape around the fencing marking off the whole yard. Some of the neighbors were still driving by at slow speeds, gawking. Her next door neighbor, an elderly woman, even stepped out and said she was so glad Yasmin was okay. It was followed with "You're such a sweet girl, I can't believe this would happen to you!"

Yasmin was just grateful they weren't drumming her out of the neighborhood because she'd brought the gangs in.

Hex and Voodoo were much relieved to get back to their litter box and Yasmin was forced to confront the issue that they needed more things from the house than she did.

Already in the process of thinking who to call—Delilah and Brandon had a toddler and probably wouldn't want kittens around, Jenn and Walker might be okay hosting her for a few days—but she didn't want the Del Surs to follow her to any of her friends' houses. She would likely need a motel—not cheap in Los Angeles. Luke's voice broke her thoughts.

"We're going to my place."

Turning her head, she realized he wasn't even speaking to her. He was talking to the officer who'd driven them over and would take them to their next stop. Her car was now part of the crime scene, too. Complete with bullet holes.

"Luke, we can't go to your place. You'll get cat hair on everything."

"I'll take allergy medicine." His expression was stone. As though that solved everything.

She sighed. "I can't do that to you."

"You aren't." There was no inflection, no change in volume, but she sensed he was getting angry about it. "I'm volunteering. I'm your guard, you just got shot at, we're going somewhere safer."

"How about I get us a hotel?"

He shut that down immediately and Yasmin found herself bringing her kittens and all their paraphernalia to Luke's apartment.

When he bolted the apartment door behind them, the air leaving his lungs was audible. His shoulders changed level, dropping at least some of the tension he'd been carrying. Too exhausted to be tense, Yasmin instead felt guilty. There was no way to win here.

She offered to set up a spare bed in his office, but he said the futon was ready to go. Both of them bone weary, she trailed along to the back of the unit, kitten box weighing her down physically, the mewing weighing her mentally.

Luke stopped in the hallway and took the box from her. "Let them out." Then he proceeded to do just that. She was ready to tell him to wash his hands before he touched his face, but then realized she'd sound like a pesky mother and shut her mouth at the last moment. He was a grown-up. If he wanted to suffer from touching the kittens, that was his choice.

Apparently that was exactly the choice he'd made. He stroked each of their little heads and talked softly to them, telling them he knew they were freaked out, but they'd like his place. Then he set them down and turned them into free-range allergens.

He then tried to install Yasmin—and the kittens—in his bedroom, insisting that he remake the bed. Though she fought tooth and nail for it—and considered just casting a spell on him to make him agree—Yasmin won the right to the futon.

"Luke, I'm not going to sleep well wherever I am. You should at least be in your own bed. Plus, you don't want kittens all over your bedroom. It's bad enough they're in your home."

She didn't change her clothes, the second night in a row of just falling into bed.

In ten minutes, she was out cold.

Ten minutes after that, she was screaming herself awake.

As tired as he was, he still didn't sleep deeply. His body and brain both seemed to know when he was 'on' and with Yasmin there he wasn't off yet.

He thought he'd have a hard time falling asleep. Luke was pissed at himself for not thinking about his car. The Del Surs—even though he hadn't seen a single one of them—must have been watching. Because the first evening she was in the house without his car there, they opened fire on her.

While it answered his question of whether she was the real target or he was, it wasn't the answer he wanted.

Despite his cell deep irritation with his own miss and his fundamental anger at the Del Surs for shooting at Yasmin yet again, he fell asleep pretty quickly. So when he heard the screams, he bolted.

His brain ran scenarios rapidly, but his hand reached automatically for the gun he was now sleeping beside. Luke had it in hand and was across the hall even as his brain tried to decide how they'd gotten in. The motion sensor in his living room had been set when he and Yasmin came back this way, so no one had come through the front door. Plus, he'd long ago installed two unexpected bolts and the windows were all fitted with security tags. That meant no one had scaled the walls and come in through her window . . . Unless they'd also disabled the security system which . . .

He had her door open and was scanning the room before his thoughts could play out.

"There's no one here." Even as he made the statement, he realized how stupid he sounded. Of course there was no one there. She was obviously having a nightmare and—given the situation—it was also obvious why.

Sitting up now, shaking herself awake, she clutched the comforter to her chest and tried to get herself together. It wasn't really working. He could see she hadn't even made an attempt to get undressed, only taken her shoes off. Luke had barely managed to strip down to his t-shirt and throw on some flannel pants, but still he was way ahead of her. "Are you going to be able to get back to sleep?"

"Sure." She forced a smile that might have passed muster with anyone else, but he could see it for the bald-faced lie it was.

So he just nodded and ignored her answer. "Want to watch TV?"

This time when she nodded to him it was at least honest if slow and uncertain. He could see she was in that state where the dream lingered. Her brain had figured out that it wasn't real but the feelings clung like spider webs and slowed her movements as she stood and started toward the door.

Her movement triggered a wail from under the bed. The kittens must have hidden there when she screamed. That at least brought Yasmin into the world of the fully alert, but Luke beat her to them.

On his hands and knees he peered under the futon frame, quickly spotting two pairs of green eyes cowering behind a box he'd shoved back there a long time ago. He was never going to be able to reach them, but they scrambled to him easily enough when he reached out to check.

There was something stupidly satisfying about that kind of

faith. These tiny creatures were vulnerable to everything around them. A good-sized bird could easily eat them as a snack, they were small enough to get stepped on by most things, they ran under furniture at the slightest sign of discord. But they trusted him enough to climb right into his hand.

"Don't. You're allergic." Her voice was soft, lacking any real conviction. It was nice she was looking out for him.

Luke said "I'm fine. Don't worry." Or he would have, had he not sneezed—epically—right in the middle of it. Still he carried the kittens out to the couch, not complaining when they dug in their claws and climbed his t-shirt to perch on his shoulder.

The four of them settled in on the couch but didn't ever turn the TV on.

"Thank you." Her words were soft, but heavy. "For everything."

"Don't worry about it." It was what he did, still he couldn't quite bring himself to tell her it was just a job. To say he wasn't actually being nice or helpful to her, per se, it was more that he wanted to bring down the Del Surs. He couldn't say it because none of it was true.

There was something personal at play here. Not just between him and the gang he'd tried before to lock up. When they'd shot at her in the parking lot of the grocery store, Luke had felt personally attacked. He still couldn't completely sort out if that was because he'd already developed this deep crush on her or if it was because they were shooting up his neighborhood, or if something had happened in that very moment and everything that happened to her happened to him, too.

He felt that way. He couldn't explain it—partly because he didn't have the words. And partly because he wasn't allowed to.

If he told her what he felt, he would cross that blue line, the one that kept cops professionally but not personally involved in cases.

Also, if he gave voice to those inappropriate thoughts, he would jeopardize the case. If the Del Surs walked free, they would be out there, waiting to finish the job, to take out Yasmin as soon as they had the opportunity. That thought completed the personal/professional loop he was riding: if they got to her, he personally would never be able to live with the loss. Even though she was lost to him the moment he drew his gun and his badge in the parking lot of the grocery store. If she were truly lost, he'd be finished.

Luke simply didn't want to examine that, so when she started asking questions, he just answered them.

"Have you been shot at before?"

He nodded. "But not like this. I've been close to gun fights twice, but in both cases, no one was shooting at me." That was when he was working guns and gangs. "I've been shot at, once, by a suspect, but he was running away from us—me and my partner—and I was too mad to be afraid he'd actually hit me."

"Wow."

Luke shrugged. "People are notoriously bad shots. Even officers and range marksmen. Once you're in it, you go all sorts of stupid. Bullets don't go where they're intended . . . And that's what's really dangerous."

He heard her breathe in, "I'm not sure if that makes me feel better or not. Does it get easier? You sound relatively calm about it."

"Some of them were almost four years ago. I was terrified after the fact, realizing what could have happened. But it fades." Holding on to what professionalism he could while they sat on his couch at three a.m. in their pajamas, he refrained from mentioning that he was still terrified about the two times she'd been shot at. He'd only just ceased to shake when thinking about that gun aimed at her at the grocery store. It was worse that they'd shot up her house.

Yasmin seemed to think the same thing. Her expression

turned from curious to sad. "I'm going to have to file all kinds of things with my homeowners insurance. I love that house. I wonder how fast the windows will get fixed and I can get back in." She wasn't looking at him, her fingers fiddling with the fringe of the throw his mother had placed on his couch as a 'housewarming' gift several years ago.

It was good she wasn't looking at him. "The windows aren't the issue. Your house is a crime scene. You can't go back."

She looked at him now, the disappointment breaking his heart. He understood. Her world was bad enough, she'd been shot at, she needed the comfort of her own home, and he'd just told her she couldn't have it.

"You can't go back until it's safe anyway, regardless of when the techs are done with it."

"Where do I go?" She looked lost. She was lost.

"Here."

Yasmin started to protest, but he just waved a hand at her. She seemed to understand what he meant. The world had gone to hell, what did it matter if she stayed here? She'd be safe—and that was what was most important.

He tried changing the subject. "Tell me about your house? How did you find it?"

She frowned at him until he said, "I'd been thinking about buying a house, getting my own four walls. But it was my first time buying."

"Oh." And that was all it took. Clearly she loved talking about it.

"My friend Delilah helped me. She's bought and sold a couple times out here. And I got a good real estate agent and . . ."

"What?" Smiling now that she was distracted, he leaned in. "What's the secret?"

"I . . .um, cast a spell for the right house to go on the market for the right price."

"You can do that?"

Grinning, she nodded.

"Can I ask? Is that how you can afford the house? Is that okay to ask?"

She laughed at him outright. "You're asking? That means you and Detective Valverde haven't pulled all my bank accounts and checked every deposit to see if I'm not some real target for the gang or something?"

Luke had to concede that one. "Valverde probably has. And while I have a professional courtesy inside track on your case, I'm not really privy to all the intel. I'll be on the stand as a witness and a player in this one, not as the arresting officer."

Thinking for a moment, Yasmin went back to absentmindedly running her fingers through the fringe on the blanket. "So I cast the spell and the agent found me the house. I'd already met with a loan agent and gotten my shit together. Paid off what old debt I could and gathered up a down payment."

He nodded. "Cops don't make much money. I'm doing better since I made detective, but honestly, there were years I couldn't save anything after just paying rent and bills. I have some money banked now, and while it would be plenty to put down on a house somewhere else, I'm not sure about here. Even the postage stamps in the poor neighborhoods are into six figures easy."

Yasmin nodded. "Mine is." Then she looked at him a little oddly, leaned in like she was examining him. Then, seeming to make a decision, she sat back. "I won some money in the lotto. That's how I made the down payment."

"That's lucky! Can I ask how much?"

She rattled off a high five digit figure. "It was the only way I could afford a payment. I work in a shop on Highland avenue. It may be witchcraft but it's still retail." She paused and again looked at him oddly. "Maybe I could pay you back that way."

Only able to frown and shake his head, he couldn't untangle what she meant.

"I can win some lotto money. Instead of just paying you a single dollar. Which, by the way, is not enough." She shrugged this time, as though she were unsure. "I mean, if you'd be willing to take it."

"I can't."

Even as she looked away, her eyes rolled at the statement. "It's not stealing, I'd make sure it was okay with the universe first. It's not blood money or anything."

"No, it's not that." He touched her arm, getting her attention back. "I can't take money from you. It would jeopardize the case."

"Later then, after this is done."

"It could lead to an appeal, if there were large quantities of money changing hands." He had to admit, having the amount she talked about infused into his bank account had a strong appeal. He understood why people stole . . . It didn't make it right, but he understood the urge. The thought of being able to afford a house, even a small one like she had, was another thought that he was ready to move to the next part of his life.

She nodded, then turned back to him. "You can win the lotto. That way I'm not giving you the money." Then she held up her hands to ward off whatever he was going to say next, even though he hadn't come up with the words yet. "I've only done it a few times. The down payment was the largest sum I've won. And it takes a handful of tries . . . But I always come out ahead."

Luke just blinked. "Seriously? You can just go in and play the lotto a handful of times and win enough cash to do that?"

She nodded.

"Why do you work? Why don't you win the whole thing? I—" Lord, if he could always come out ahead on the lotto . . . He'd once read that the lotto was a tax on people who were bad at math. And he'd always believed it.

"I can't. I'm not allowed. I mean . . . You wouldn't understand. When you get into real Wicca, you always work under the tenant 'harm none.' Sometimes there's this . . . Universal push back when you try to do something. I usually get a deep, bad feeling if I try it on the big lotto. Like I'm messing with the real winners' mojo. So I play scratchers. And I like my job. I —" She shrugged.

So she couldn't win the big thing, but she could win five figures? It didn't make a lot of sense. And he asked what he wanted to all along. "If you can win the lotto almost at will, and you can create a world of your own making, why couldn't you keep from becoming a random target in a gang war?"

CHAPTER 15

It was all pretty embarrassing. Yasmin was used to the standard "If you're a witch and you're so powerful why aren't you rich? Why aren't you living in a mansion in the hills and visiting the spa all day?"

She always answered, "I could, but the price is too high."

The energetic work alone to maintain that would be astronomical. She'd literally pass out from exhaustion at trying to move that mountain. Also, it was horridly hard to work against the universe, and there was always a kickback. Which is exactly what she told Luke. "The problem was, I deserved the kickback."

"So you brought it on yourself? It's just as hard to believe that you could make yourself the target of a gang you have no prior association with."

It took a big sigh before she could bring herself to say it. When she did, she blurted out the words, "I cast a love spell."

It was almost worse that he nodded. "I take it that's a no-no."

"Yeah." Feeling like a kid confessing to some family crime, she had a hard time looking at Luke. The fact that it was the middle of the night and he was being nice staying up with her only made it worse. "You're not supposed to try to change other people's lives."

"And you did that?" He was tilting his head sideways, as though he were trying to get her to make eye contact. "On your boss?"

That worked.

Her head snapped up, her open mouth and wide eyes cleanly giving away that she'd thought that was a secret. She didn't have to speak. Luke did.

"That's what I thought." This time he looked away for a moment. "Did it work?"

"Yes and no." She picked at the fringe on his throw blanket for something to do. Yasmin was hoping he wouldn't ask anything more, but of course he did.

"You have to tell me what that means . . ."

"Well . . ." It took her a moment to get going, but once she started, the words just seemed to fall out of her. Cleansing in the telling, they tumbled of their own accord. "I couldn't just cast one on him—both because it's not good Wicca, but also because Tristan is a much stronger witch than I am. He totally would have seen any spell I cast directly on him and traced it right back to me. It would have been more subtle and more effective to walk in wearing a T-shirt that just said so."

Luke nodded as though that all made sense. "So you can just 'see' spells and who cast them?"

"Oh, no, not me. But Tristan is really good at it. Delilah, too." Without being prompted she chattered away at the rest of her cathartic confession. "So I cast this grand universal 'Bring My True Love To Me' spell rather than just casting on Tristan."

"And it didn't work?" His head tipped as though he were thinking a bit.

She had to laugh. "It backfired. It sure brought something

though, didn't it? Bullets weren't what I had in mind. But it was no less than I deserved, trying a love spell like that. They are always bad news. Like money spells."

Again, Luke nodded as though she made perfect sense. Yasmin had to agree—she did make sense, just a lot of people didn't agree. They were too closed-minded to really listen. Luke wasn't like that. He seemed genuinely interested.

Then again, Yasmin had heard doctors say they were nice to the crazy patients to get them to talk about what they were hallucinating. She didn't put it past Luke to be using those same skills. In fact, she'd bet they came in really handy as a detective trying to get people to open up to him.

Still, when he asked her "So, playing lotto scratchers isn't a money spell?"

She fell right for it, it sounded so genuine, and she just spoke. "No. That's more of a question-and-answer kind of thing. I ask the universe to give me money and it answers either yes or no. Sometimes the answers is 'no' and I struggle to pay my bills just like everyone. But sometimes the answer is yes, and I get a down payment for my house."

Yasmin was very grateful they'd gotten off the topic of her ill-advised crush on Tristan. Somehow talking about the limits of her Wiccan powers and the repercussions of her bad decision seemed safer.

She blabbered on, answering questions, feeling wide awake until the light bothered her. Only then did she realize that she'd fallen asleep, her head draped over the arm of the soft—if ugly—couch. Her feet were tucked up under her and the throw was tucked around her. Luke.

She looked up to find him looking at her.

His eyes looked as sleepy as she felt and—given that his position on the couch mirrored hers—he was only just now awake himself.

Her voice sounded thick to her own ears, but she pushed through the words. "What time is it?"

Eyes darting as his head lolled to one side, rather than lifted, Luke spoke in a voice that sounded sinfully rich. "Almost ten a.m."

It wasn't fair that he sounded and looked so good when he woke up. Her curls had probably gone full Orphan-Annie on her while she dozed. Reaching her hand up, Yasmin patted at the soft springs. She wondered why she did it. She had no particular skill at determining how good her hair did or didn't look just from touching it. She sighed.

Then sprang directly up from the couch. "I have to get back to the house. I have to get to work."

Luke just shook his head. Stayed calm and didn't react to her outburst. "Nope. Please call in and take a personal day."

"No, I—"

He didn't let her finish. And though he interrupted her, he was really polite about it. He just held his hand up to stop her, using the motion alone to make her interrupt herself. "Please. Last night was awful. You shouldn't be at work anyway. We don't know if they found you there."

"They wouldn't come after me at work!" That didn't make any sense.

But his nod was soft and sad. Clearly he thought the Del Surs just might. And if his silent belief didn't sway her, his next words sure did. "Are you willing to bet your life—and the lives of your co-workers—on that? Your friend Libby? *Tristan?*"

Plopping back onto the couch she actually felt her curls bounce. "Tristan doesn't matter." Immediately she woke up, realizing what she'd said. "I mean—he *does* matter, but not like that! Not anymore." Another deep sigh. "I'm over it."

Luke only raised his eyebrows and managed to refrain from commenting. He still hadn't moved from where he'd clearly spent the night draped along the opposite end of the big couch. "You should call the store and leave them a message that you're not coming in. You can tell them what happened. It may already be all over the news."

That sent her into another tizzy to race back to the office and search the futon covers for her cell phone. She'd gone to sleep with it, thinking that someone might hear about what happened and text her or call. Then, when she'd gotten up and followed Luke out to the living room, she forgot all about it.

Her blurry eyes were clearing as she looked at the screen. There were and handful of texts and two missed calls. All from Delilah and Libby. Not Tristan.

Both Delilah and Libby admitted to not knowing what was going on. Messages from Delilah at least stated that Tristan had called her with concerns just as she had been struck with sudden worry about her friend. Over the course of the texts the tone changed from 'call me back to let me know you are okay' to 'I know you're okay' to 'I see you're sleeping with a hunky police officer but it's not quite that . . . What's going on?'

Libby apparently hadn't gotten the final message from the universe that—though things were bad—Yasmin was actually fine. Physically.

So Libby was her first call. It took about ten minutes to explain what had happened and that she was safe. Luke peeked in and made a motion at his throat indicating that she shouldn't say where exactly she was. Thus Libby only learned that she was safe and she was about to call Tristan and tell him she wouldn't be in today.

Almost able to hear the gears in Libby's brain, Yasmin wasn't surprised at the final question. "Fine. But if you're really okay, you'll give me the code word."

"Of course. Marshmallow." At last her friend and co-worker was satisfied and let her off the phone.

Blessed Be was next. Tristan was already in the office and picked up before the first ring even finished. "Yasmin, what happened?"

She explained getting shot at, being detained at the police station, and finally being at a 'safe house'—she figured that was as good a name for Luke's apartment. And it was as good as she was willing to say with Luke himself standing in the hallway, listening in to the conversations as though he were just loitering in his own hallway for no reason.

Forced to consider his reasoning, she wondered if he truly thought any of her friends or co-workers could be involved in some way. She sighed, just wrong place, wrong time. Something that wasn't supposed to happen to her.

As she hung up, Yasmin closed the door to get dressed, not that she had anything to get ready for.

What had she been thinking? Falling for Tristan. For a moment, she forgave herself. After all, he was hot, talented in the field she wished to go into, ran a successful business, and was just generally a good guy. But . . . well, it was a big 'but.' He never had feelings for her. He didn't flirt with her at all, and he was a wicked flirt. The man clearly had a type and it wasn't her. Shiny blond hair, long legs, sweet smile and just a little slutty. Tristan liked his girls media-hot and media-stupid.

Somehow, Yasmin had managed to believe—for far too long—that she would be the one to break the mold. The one who would make him realize that being a man slut wasn't what he really wanted. Instead, she'd learned that he really enjoyed being a man slut. He like his women hanging on his every word and on his arm. And Yasmin was not going to be that girl—she couldn't and she wouldn't.

Getting dressed in jeans and a t-shirt, she fumbled her way through finding her things, taking care of the kittens and finally calling her friend Jenn just to keep her up to date. Jenn had absolutely zero Wiccan skills, so she hadn't gotten any 'concerning feeling' updates as bullets had ripped through Yasmin's front window.

At last, she stopped and sat on the couch, dressed and stroking Hex, who had finally eaten and calmed down, curling into a tiny ball of black puff in her lap. Her brain wandered to her windows, the trim she'd painted herself, the home she'd worked hard for. Sure, she'd played the lotto for the down payment, but she'd scrimped and saved to have it repainted and she—like everyone—had months where making the payment was hard. She'd eaten her share of Ramen noodles and cereal.

Now it had bullet holes.

Now she wasn't allowed in her own home.

Now she was sitting on Luke's couch having called in to work and with nothing to do today but stew about how horribly awry her life had gone and how it was completely her own fault. She knew better and she did it anyway.

Luke wandered into the living room having gotten dressed himself. Today he was in a fuchsia shirt that managed to cling like a girlfriend with low self-esteem. His jeans didn't respect themselves much more than the shirt, their deep blue hugging his ass and leading down to a pair of shoes that burned her eyes in bright orange and yellow.

She wanted to look away, but he was mesmerizing. She wanted to ask "how can you wear that?" but he did and somehow he wore it well. Instead she said "Clearly you aren't going to work today either."

"Nope. I'm off too while they investigate yet another shooting I was present for."

Her breath choked in her throat at the sudden thought this could hurt him. "You won't lose your job or anything over this, will you? You were *supposed* to be there. You saved me!"

As she said it, she realized it was true. He'd figured out what was happening just moments before her. He hadn't been angry when he dove at her, he'd been scared, reacting. "I didn't say it last night, but thank you. There's no way to ever repay you."

He tipped his head. "I didn't save you. Not that time." He sighed. "Their aim was so bad. They shot through the window but I don't think any of the bullets made it to the dining room. You would have been fine without me."

Yasmin didn't think so. He'd pulled out his gun the first time and talked them down, while her spell seemed to have worked, she didn't know how long it would have held. And this time? She hadn't seen, heard, or sensed it coming.

She was getting ready to say so when he suddenly pitched to the side as though he were going to fall and simultaneously opened his mouth and squeezed his eyes shut.

Her own mouth opened to ask what was wrong. She was starting to jump up off the couch to help him, too, but the tiny kitten on her lap made a heavier weight than one would think. By the time she had it figured out, so did Luke.

He was sucking in a breath and starting to smile. He tipped his head awkwardly to the side as a small black form made his way onto Luke's broad shoulder. "You know, bud, all you had to do was ask."

As she stood to get her pesky new child away from the allergic man, Luke reached up and plucked the kitten away before pulling it in toward his chest like one would a baby. "Hey Voodoo, I think you may have drawn blood."

Jeez. The man helped her dodge bullets and was nice to her dander producing kittens when they climbed him like a tree. She took the kitten back and tried to stay quiet and not cause trouble until she heard him swear a few times from the bathroom.

He was clearly trying to clean up any blood Voodoo may have drawn. And she felt obligated to knock on the door and see if she could be of help.

Just as she suspected, the poor man was bleeding from a few short scratches in inopportune places on his back. She had not prepared herself for Luke with his shirt off and her tongue almost got away from her and asked if maybe the kitten had scratched him through his jeans too and could she help with that?

It wasn't fair. Men weren't supposed to look as good with their clothes off as you dreamed they did.

The other thing she wasn't prepared for was the band-aids. Three lay crumpled on the counter from his clearly misguided attempts to put one on his lower right shoulder blade. She almost laughed out loud, "Hello Kitty?"

He tried to glare at her. "My nieces visited a while ago. It's what I have. I don't want to ruin that shirt. I like it."

Of course he did. It was bright enough to make up for a cloudy day and for now-obvious reasons his manhood never seemed threatened by pastels or pinks.

In a moment, she had several smiling white kitty faces covering the deep claw mark on his back and she had managed to not run her hand down his flesh. She'd done well in her dreams . . . Gotten the form right, the slight freckling on his shoulders, the abs that weren't gym-dog ridiculous but on the right side of awesome.

He had the shirt back on in a moment and she managed to keep the drool in her mouth and her heart firmly in her chest.

The man kept Hello Kitty Band-Aids for his nieces. Just another nice—no, great—trait to add to the list. He cuddled her kittens and treated the females around him by the same code he did everyone else. He saved her from bullets.

But a list of nice traits wasn't enough. Hadn't she learned that from Tristan? So she told herself that she had indeed learned it and learned it well. And she followed Luke down the hallway and out to his car.

~

Luke tossed and turned in his bed. He'd spent the entire day with Yasmin and it had been the best kind of hell.

She was friendly and easy with him. She bought him a late breakfast before they headed into the station to see what Jessica had on the new shooting.

It turned out, two of the neighbors reported that they thought their cars had been stolen and returned. When Valverde sent people out to canvas the neighborhood several others turned up. They hadn't called in because clearly who would steal a mid-level sedan and then return it? But one was the car that Luke had called in.

His timeframe for running the license plate as the car drove through Yasmin's neighborhood was directly in the window of time that the owners thought something odd had happened. The seat wasn't set right, the front door hadn't been bolted, the keys were hung wrong. And he couldn't tell Jessica really *why* he'd run the plate. Maybe partly because he hadn't really seen anything he could put a finger on, he'd simply been suspicious.

But the Del Surs had been there.

They had been watching.

His blood ran cold at the thought. They had waited for him to leave, which meant they knew he was a cop—her protection. They wanted her alone, and he wouldn't let that happen.

As he tangled his covers by way of sheer restlessness, Luke considered a really stupid question Giada had asked him years ago. She'd been reading some romance novel and said the cop had to pose as the witness's boyfriend and would that ever happen?

Luke had laughed out loud at his sister. Commented that surely both characters were too hot to be believed, and when the danger had passed they looked into each others' eyes and decided to get married. Giada had slunk away, huffing and spitting out "Fine!"

But he was starting to see the appeal of the story.

They problem was his prediction wasn't coming true.

He'd developed this sudden and crazy crush on her while following her through the grocery store before he even knew her name. But when things got tangled he reminded himself of his past: something would turn up about her that was unappealing. Maybe he'd learn she was mean to old people. One girl he dated was sweeter than honey to him then manipulated her friends and bitched about them behind their back to him. She'd suddenly gone from crazy hot to just ugly.

He kept waiting to learn that one awful thing about Yasmin that would set him free.

But it didn't come.

She rescued kittens on a whim and gave them silly names. She was willing to dole out some snarky comments and didn't pull her punches, but she was kind. She read fantasy novels with dragons and clashing armies as well as sci-fi. She defended her own religion fiercely but never pushed him to abandon his. She accepted people as they were and—while the whole spell casting thing was wildly out there—she seemed to be relatively unselfish with it.

Sometimes he watched her get a parking space. But she always prefaced her short spell with "an it harm none" as though her parking space was never more important than the greater good. He knew people who would literally kill for the power to always have a good parking spot open up for them.

At dinner that night he bought, heading for a mid-level Mexican place. The server referred to Yasmin as his 'girlfriend' when she'd stepped away from the table. He'd gotten a thumbs-up behind her back from another misguided man. What would he say? "Nope, she's not my girlfriend. Want to date her? I don't think she's seeing anyone."

So he'd smiled politely and not said anything.

It was as close as he'd come to crossing the line with her.

By the time they made it home, his body was exhausted; he really was tired and he wanted to climb into bed. The adrenaline from twenty-four hours ago hadn't been completely made up for. Luke finally felt the pull of sleep.

He reminded himself that his job was to keep her safe. That meant getting the Del Surs responsible locked up. That meant perfect protocol.

But he could dream about her.

He imagined what he wanted while he finally drifted off. Then, fully asleep, he wandered across the hall, quietly opening the door to his office to find her sprawled on his futon.

He stood there, looking at her for a moment. She should have taken his bed. He could be in here on this thin mattress. But she'd refused on the grounds of kitten hair and his allergy. Luke was grateful in his own way—he didn't know if it would amazing or torturous that his bed would smell like her.

Hex looked up at him and meowed. It was even harder to tell the two of them apart in the dark. The sound made Yasmin stir, pulling the tiny kitten to her a little closer.

She'd kicked the covers back and as she rolled over he saw that the nightshirt was actually a button down in some creamy shade of blue. It had rucked up her legs, leaving them bare and begging for him. And he quit fighting it.

It didn't count when he was asleep, and it was the only way to have what he wanted. So he brushed her hair back out of her face and leaned down close enough to kiss along her jaw line.

At first she responded with little sounds much like the kittens, but by the time he reached her ear she was whispering his name.

Her sigh hit his ears and something in his chest at the same time as he stood up and held his hand out to her. Accepting, she followed him into the living room where he proceeded to kiss her as though he could lay claim to her that way.

Then he did what he'd been wanting to do since he saw her sitting on his couch during her first visit. The vision had come back with a vengeance when he'd woken up to find her curled up opposite him that morning. And he proceeded to unbutton the cotton shirt and peel her open like a present.

CHAPTER 16

The noise broke her dream and Yasmin bounced onto the bed. It felt that way when she was suddenly yanked back into herself. Not that it had happened a lot to her.

Try as she might, she hadn't been one to master astral projection of any kind. And she'd tried. Even managed to accomplish a few short flights. But the fact was, they'd all been random, nothing was ever able to repeat.

So it was a shock to her system to get pulled back like that. She'd been in the middle of another *very* steamy dream, featuring none other than her own version of the man asleep across the hall.

Or he had been asleep. She heard him slamming through the door to his room, the wailing noise piercing her brain and yanking her from her thoughts as surely as it had pulled her from her dream.

Was it really a dream? If she was yanked back—

She didn't complete the thought. As she sat upright her nightshirt gapped, all the buttons undone—just as they had been in her dream. She was grabbing it and pulling it together as her bedroom door slammed open and Luke filled the doorway, his cotton pants riding low and concerning her with their familiarity.

She had not seen them before, not in reality, but she knew they were soft. Her frown formed as she ignored the mechanical beep that signaled something bad. A fire? She looked around, didn't smell smoke.

He still frowned at her, ignoring the noise, barking out his words. "Are you all right?"

Nodding, she held the shirt together with just her grip, the open buttons useless, but he didn't seem to notice. He took her at her word and turned, military sharp, and stalked into the living room.

She was still doing up the last buttons as the noise stopped. Right at the same time she stepped into the living room and saw what had happened.

Her heart stopped cold as all the pieces clicked into place.

Luke had no such revelation, he was simply frowning at everything.

He stood by the door, where he had clearly punched in the code to turn off the alarm. For the first time she saw that he was holding his gun along his leg. On the surface he appeared almost calm, but she could sense he was more like a leashed storm.

His voice held the same controlled tone. "The motion sensor went off." Then he pointed at the couch, his eyes looking where his finger indicated, at the furniture scooted back from its original position.

He still seemed as though he hadn't put it all together, but Yasmin had. Her breathing went shallow as she realized how everything fit. Luke's voice rumbled through her and the sound shot along her nerves much the way his touch had just a few minutes earlier.

"How did the couch move?"

But he didn't wait for her answer, just clutched the gun and walked the border of main room again. He ducked just out of sight as he checked the dark corners of the kitchen.

She almost fell to her knees, her hands clutching the front of her shirt again even though it was now buttoned.

Coming back into the room he spotted her there, sinking down the wall, her breathing now shallow. His arm—the hand not holding the gun—went around her shoulders but she shook him off.

It was that touch that had caused all this.

His alarm was real—he still didn't understand.

Shitshitshit.

"Yasmin?" He looked in her eyes and she didn't want him to. "I think it's safe. I don't know how the alarm went off . . ."

He looked around the room, but ignored her squirming. Instead he held her tighter. "Maybe the cats did it?"

No way had her tiny kittens moved his couch. No, she knew exactly what had and her mouth ran before she could think better of it. "We did it. We moved the couch."

That got his attention right back.

In for a penny . . .

"You're a dreamwalker, Luke."

Sensing the topic was bigger than he might have liked, he slid to the floor beside her asking his tentative question. "What do you mean?"

"You can do actual things in your dreams, including finding other people and bringing them along." She paused only for a heartbeat. "We moved the couch."

"We? I was asleep."

"Yes . . . And no." She couldn't look at him. The things she'd done. The things she'd allowed him to do to her. She'd wanted them. "You have the ability to pull other people into your dreams."

She was starting to say more, to attempt an explanation, when he pulled back and just stared. "Did you do this to me?"

Shaking her head, almost violently, Yasmin denied it. "No! I don't mess with people that way. I don't even make the clerks give me extra change or anything. And if you had *asked* me to conjure it for you I still wouldn't have done it. What advantage would it give me anyway?"

She realized what she'd said only as the words left her mouth.

His brows rose at her. Then he snorted at some other thought he had. Finally, some odd third expression changed across his face and he relaxed. "It's not right. It was just a dream. I wasn't even sleepwalking. I put a doorstopper under the door and *marked* it. It never moved. I checked. It was only a dream."

"It wasn't. I was there." She had *really* enjoyed those dreams, but she wished now she hadn't been in them.

He shook his head. "They weren't real."

Though she would love to let him go on thinking that, she couldn't. They were probably in enough trouble as it was, and he should learn to control it rather than go around thinking there were no consequences.

"Luke, it wasn't a dream."

Again with the eyebrows and the expression that simply did not believe.

"What color is my underwear?"

He almost laughed. "Red with little white and pink hearts."

She lifted the edge of her shirt but didn't say anything else.

Luke shook his head, still in denial "Lucky guess."

Yes, surely when asked for a 'color' a lucky guess was the right main color along with the details in the right color and shape. But she didn't say that. "Where's my birthmark?"

"Back of your shoulder, but I saw that when you were in a towel . . . A week ago."

"It's not that memorable of a birthmark. You remembered it because you'd already seen it in a dream and you were shocked that your dream got it right." She'd been guessing that, but the look on his face told her she was spot on. Then she went for the kill. "And the other?"

"Left hip." His shoulders slumped.

He knew because he liked to bite her lightly there. Yasmin could feel her face turn red and she scrambled for something else. Before she could talk, he suddenly scooted back as though she might burn him.

"You did this. You pulled me into your dreams." His eyes were wide.

She got it. She really did. People were afraid of what they didn't understand. She already demonstrated some power to him in the past. Of course he thought it was her. Of course he was afraid of it, of her. But that didn't make it hurt any less. "It's not me . . . Believe me, I've tried and I have no talent for it. It's *you*. You have to have done it before, maybe when you were a kid?"

Luke's eyes glazed as his thoughts turned elsewhere. "My best friend and I would dream the same thing sometimes."

Prodding a little, she asked another question. "Did you ever see evidence from those dreams?"

It took a moment of Luke gazing into the middle distance before he answered. "My dad was building a shed once and he had put these stakes out in the yard where the corners would be. Jason—my childhood best friend—and I dreamed we were digging up treasure in the yard and that the stakes were markers. In the morning the stakes were all out. . . But the yard wasn't dug up." He was frowning at her again as though she had done this to him.

"I wasn't there when you were a kid. I didn't even know you then." She could ward off his accusations if not his fear. Maybe she could help fill in some of the gaps he had. "I can't do it, I've tried. What I understand is that when you're in that state, especially if the two dreamers are really in sync—" her face flared red, she could feel it, "—then you can move things. But you can't break them."

For example, the first night he'd ripped open her shirt, sending buttons flying, and when she woke up the shirt had been open, but the buttons intact. Not that she was going to say that out loud and remind him just how steamy it was between them.

He was still keeping his distance, and from his perspective she really couldn't blame him. "So we moved the couch and that set off the motion sensor?"

Yasmin shrugged. Just when she'd thought her life couldn't get much worse. She answered him first, "Yes, I think we moved the couch. Check if there's any other way it could have happened."

While he checked, she looked upward, as though the universe and all its powers were over her head. Silently she pleaded.

Look, I'm sorry. So sorry. I knew casting that love spell was so wrong. But even so, I didn't alter anyone's feelings. I just wanted my love to notice me. I won't do it again. Believe me I got the message the first time I was shot at. The second time was just mean. And this? Finding out my steamy dreams weren't even dreams? Just stop! I've learned my lesson. I've learned it very well, thank you.

She had no idea if it would work. It wasn't even much of a prayer, by the end it had turned into a bit of a rant with a touch of sarcasm. Maybe the universe wasn't done with her yet. Maybe the punishment for bad casting was far worse than she'd thought. Right now, Yasmin wished Delilah had been a little more clear about the gravity of casting on others.

Luke stood in front of her, having swept the whole apartment while she sat there. "I don't see anything else."

Then he almost crumpled in front of her. She was leaping forward to catch him but he fell into a cross-legged sit, the gun almost smacking the ground beside him and making her wince. The look on his face was so defeated she almost cried.

She wouldn't have done it if she'd realized he was dreamwalking. Especially since he had no idea what he was doing. But she didn't think it deserved this look . . . As though he had cheated on someone with her and it had destroyed his life. Her breath sucked in and came back out on a barely audible whisper.

"Are you seeing anyone?" She thought he'd said he wasn't, but the look on his face said otherwise.

He shook his head no, but ran his hands over his face and refused to look at her. When his words came out they were as defeated sounding as she felt.

"The case is fucked."

That was not at all what she was expecting. "What?"

"I've apparently been sleeping with the victim-slash-witness. I'm going to get fired for it. And the Del Surs will walk. Which means not only do I have no job and can probably never go back to police work of any kind, you have no protection from one of the nastiest gangs around."

Her blood ran cold at his words. Then she took a moment and unscrambled her thoughts. "No. No none of that is true. We didn't actually sleep together. . ." Even though it had felt like they did.

This time Luke did look her in the eyes. The too-blue color seeing straight into her. "What if you're pregnant?"

He was right that they hadn't used any birth control in those wild moments. But he was wrong, too. "I can't be. You can move things but you can't alter them. Can't break them, glue them together, or *impregnate* them by dreamwalking." She sucked in another breath. No matter how good it had been, no matter that they had shared the experience, the experience hadn't really happened. "You shouldn't lose your job. The case is fine. You've been the model of professionalism."

His disbelieving snort interrupted her but she went on, ignoring it.

"But whatever we may remember, none of it was real. We weren't really together."

Yasmin was surprised at how much that thought hurt. It shouldn't have hurt at all. She'd thought of those dreams as stress-relief, as steamy free-for-alls with zero ramifications.

Once again, she'd been wrong. So wrong.

~

Luke had no idea how he kept himself together the next day.

Eventually, he and Yasmin had talked themselves out and fallen asleep. In separate rooms. His with the door locked and a chair underneath it, even though she'd told him that wouldn't help. Instead, all he needed to do was make a different decision. Instead of coming to get her, do something fun.

He came awake in his dreams again and stood at the foot of the bed. This time he didn't wander into her room and peel her clothes. He didn't get the brilliant idea to dream-christen the couch. Or he did, but he didn't act it out. Apparently, realizing you were asleep was the key to being mentally awake inside your dreams. The irony was not lost on him.

It was much more difficult being around her now. In the past, he'd woken up remembering how she tasted. How she would bury her face against his neck and kiss him there, how he could smell her hair and feel it tickling his chest.

He survived it then by talking himself down from every memory. Told himself it was only the way he imagined she'd feel. That her actions were all conjured from his own subconscious.

Before, he'd wanted her.

Now, he needed her.

Now Luke knew how she felt in his arms. He knew the

weight of her breasts in his hands. And though in the cold light of day she offered him nothing but apologies, he knew what she was like when she wanted a man.

He had to get rid of her.

Still not allowed back at work, he handed off some of his cases. With each call to explain what parts he finished already and what still needed work, he asked if the officer was able to take on a personal protection client.

No one even said maybe.

That would have been barely the first step. Most of them had heard about the squished bullet. Most knew that she considered herself a witch. Then there was the added problem that she'd actually been shot at twice, which was twice more than most officers and they wouldn't touch the assignment with a ten foot pole.

His third call was to one of the other detectives in his unit. Harry Jasper—terrible name, Luke thought—had laughed and asked, "What? Did you bang her and she got too clingy?"

Luke had been rubbing his hand down his face for probably the thousandth time that day when Valverde's voice had popped up in the background. "Salzone? Salzone wouldn't sleep with a hooker if that was her method of payment for protection." And she'd laughed. Deep and hearty, like Jessica always did.

Jasper had chuckled too. "That's a good point. Sorry bud, can't take that bullet for you."

No one could.

Luke would almost rather take an actual bullet than deal with smelling her faint perfume as she walked by. Seeing her ass in those jeans and knowing what it looked like out of those jeans. Dealing with the bland expressions she let float his way, letting him know that whatever they had done together in the dark of the night didn't affect her the way it affected him.

Nope, she was still trying to get boss-boy to look at her. Luke was just for fun. Just in the middle of the night. Just something that she hadn't thought was real either until they'd moved the couch.

She sure hadn't come to get him. He'd stood at the foot of his bed, wandered his room. Eventually he'd walked around the living room, thinking how the carpet felt under his feet, the sound of the neighborhood at night. He stood in front of the motion sensor and waved his arms around while the alarm stayed silent.

Then he'd searched out a dusty spot behind the TV and swiped his finger. Just as Yasmin had said, it was there the next morning. Had he been sleepwalking, the alarm would have gone off.

Once again, Yasmin was right.

It wasn't real, the two of them being together, but it was real enough.

And once again, he was wanting what he couldn't have.

CHAPTER 17

Yasmin didn't know what to do. It was a week before her house was fixed. A week that she spent at Luke's apartment.

They ate breakfast together like they always had. Occasionally had dinner. On the surface, nothing had changed, but underneath everything had.

They were like a string stretched too tight.

It made perfect sense that they would feel that way—after all they'd been shot at, more than once. It was enough to make anyone tense. But they had been at ease with each other. At least while they'd been screwing like bunnies and each thinking it was all in their own little fantasy world.

Luke hadn't handed the case off to anyone. Not that he hadn't tried—even though she'd been in the guest room at the time, she heard him on the phone trying to pawn her off on everyone he talked to. No one had bitten. She'd even considered casting a spell to have someone come forward, but she didn't want to begin to contemplate how much worse her life could become if she tried something like that again.

So she kept her spells to herself, thank you very much.

And she just dealt with the tight smiles he gave her, the stilted conversation, and the knight-in-shining-armor complex.

She'd be alive at the end of it. Luke would see to that.

But more and more she was starting to realize that all the things she'd thought she made up about him were real.

With Tristan, she'd filled in the parts she didn't know about him with whatever she wanted. She fell in love with a man who didn't exist.

With Luke, she told herself that her crush was a literal dream lover. She was quite convinced that he was just as made up as her Tristan had been, only this time wearing a different man's face. Despite her beliefs, Luke had proven time and again that he wasn't just the made up version she wanted.

He avoided squirrels in the road and stopped to help people stuck on the side of the freeway. Even when he wasn't on duty. They'd stopped twice while she was with him and he hadn't even once said he was a cop. He'd just helped.

He was nice to his family, good to his mother and father and all his brothers and sisters. He accepted them even when he didn't understand them. He was gentle and kind to her kittens despite the fact that they made him sneeze and he only bonked them on the head when they tried to shred his couch.

He got mad, furious even, at the world around him, but it never translated into violence. Yasmin never worried. She was safe with him.

The control alone wouldn't have done it. It was the banked fire that slayed her. She knew he'd pull the trigger if he had to. Didn't doubt he'd fight to the death with his bare hands—and win—if that's what it took. But he'd never start that fight. No, what he started was just as volatile though. The way he'd handled her . . . she got warmer just thinking about it. The way he'd *wanted* her—no one had ever wanted her like that before.

It wasn't about her looks, that she fit some mold or idea he had. He certainly seemed to like her looks, but it was about *her*. All of her.

Or it wasn't. Because in the daylight he was only embarrassed that he'd gotten his rocks off with her. Here she was, falling crazy in love with him and he was just a professional doing his job. Just a guy with some girl he had to keep by his side 24-7, so he was getting his jollies the only way he could. While he was asleep.

So she smiled back at him the same tight smiles he gave her. And she only went to work when he could go with her. He stayed through her class, halfway listening, but mostly browsing the store and playing with the kittens and occasionally sneezing. He even let Tristan kill the allergy for him.

Not her, though she had offered.

But one offer from Tristan and Luke said "Sure, if you think you can do it."

Yasmin found herself wondering how she'd ever fallen for Tristan. Sure he was hot. Sure he had skills she wanted and worshiped. But he'd never put himself out for her. He hadn't noticed her in any way—other than treating her as a valued coworker. He clearly didn't have any feelings for her. Her feelings for him seemed weak in the light of his only mild concern that she'd been shot at. And when he offered to help Luke it sounded kind of arrogant. Like Luke was some disbelieving muggle and Tristan would make it all okay for poor sneezing Luke.

Yasmin was now wondering how she'd fallen for Luke. While he was a much better candidate than Tristan, certainly more worthy of her feelings, the fact that he didn't return them should have warded her off.

It didn't.

With Tristan she hadn't been able to see that he simply didn't —and wouldn't ever—think of her that way. With Luke she saw it. And she still couldn't shake the feelings.

Maybe the problem was that she had memories of Luke wanting her, needing her far more than the made-up fantasies of Tristan. Those fantasies—she could see now—consisted of things Tristan would never do. Actions that were so far out of his realm of behavior that even if he loved her it wouldn't be like that. Luke was . . . Luke.

And it was killing her.

So she kept her mouth shut about it. Didn't bring up the dreamwalking.

Well, except one time. Luke had turned positively to stone. She'd never seen anything like it. Clearly it was not a topic he wanted to discuss. So she dropped it like a hot rock and stuck to safer ground.

Yasmin had trailed him to his parents' house for Sunday dinner again. It was both easier the second time—she knew them now, recognized faces, understood the traditions of the evening a bit—but it was also harder. This time his mother not only got on his case for bringing a woman to dinner but for bringing the same one back.

Both Yasmin and Luke protested heavily. She was just a case to him. But his mother figured he'd never brought a client home with him before. And such a pretty one, too, she'd said, so smart and clearly good people. Yasmin had beamed a bit at the praise. In her own home, the praise was not for what you were yourself, but how you represented the family line, the name, followed the path your parents had laid out for you.

The clear and heartfelt praise from Mrs. Salzone was a balm to Yasmin's undernourished soul. But then she remembered what she knew of Italian families—loud, boisterous, everyone was beautiful and good. Until they weren't. Then they were spoken of in hushed whispers.

Maybe she'd simply seen The Godfather one too many times. Or maybe she'd misread it. Either way it dampened the feelings. Even when Mrs. Salzone told her she'd make a fantastic daughter-in-law.

"Mom!" Luke had yelled, nearly dropping the bottle of beer he was politely drinking. His brother had brewed it. The family didn't seem to have the heart to tell him that it was clearly a first attempt.

His mother had responded to her own outlandish statement that she'd seen a psychic the week before who said the next woman Luke brought home, he'd marry.

Yasmin had felt her own eyebrows go up, but tried not offend the woman who was an otherwise wonderful hostess. Luke had no such compunctions and Yasmin watched as he obviously brushed aside his mother's statement. "One—I can't believe you gave that woman your money again. And two—I didn't 'bring Yasmin home with me.'" He even made air quotes while managing to hold onto the beer. "She's an assignment, Mom."

"I just know what the psychic said." His mother hmphhed at him, patted Yasmin's cheek, winked at her as though the two women knew a secret and then served dinner.

Luke had looked at her like "Do you believe that?" and Yasmin had only shrugged. Sure, she believed that psychics existed. And some used the skill to earn money. But she didn't think that just because some unvetted woman took Mrs. Salzone's money and told her what she wanted to hear that it was accurate.

On the way back to his apartment, Luke had apologized for his mother's outlandish statements. Yasmin really hadn't minded. It was harder to deal with Luke and his cold attitude than Mrs. Salzone and her honest pushiness.

Each night, Yasmin curled up with the kittens, grateful she had something to snuggle with if not someone. And her dreams remained unaltered.

~

Twelve days after her house had been shot at, Yasmin got good news.

Jessica Valverde had been working tirelessly to put the pieces together and she'd finally gotten enough. Homeo and Doddo—the initiate and the leader of the Del Surs—were being brought in on charges.

Fingerprints had been found on the 'borrowed' cars and traced back to the two. Enough trace evidence had been gathered from the original shooting scene to put the two there. And bullets at Yasmin's house had been matched to a gun in another subsequent crime the Del Surs had been hauled in on.

Valverde had woven enough tiny threads together to make the tapestry she needed. On the thirteenth day, Yasmin, Luke, and the eyewitness from the grocery store were called in to the station to identify the two men in the original shooting. The three positive IDs all lined up and Homeo and Doddo were awaiting bail hearings.

There would be more. Luke had briefed her about the trial. How time consuming it would be. What her role would entail. But Yasmin was ready.

She was getting her life back.

It happened slower than she wanted it to.

Her house was repaired. Though it smelled musty from disuse and the energy of her life there had faded to only the traces that clung in the bones of the house, she was happy to reclaim it.

Luke insisted on staying with her the first few days. He made her drive; they entered by the back door, kept the curtains closed and stayed away from the front window. He ran every license plate of every car that drove down the street until he recognized the makes and models that belonged to a few of her neighbors. And he made sure he recognized the neighbors driving them.

Yasmin got back to her full time schedule at work, no longer bound by Luke's schedule. He didn't have to be there—guarding her—every waking moment of every day.

To her surprise, she found she was breathing easier when he wasn't there. Especially after the first night when nothing had happened. Why should it, when the two men who'd shot at her were finally in jail?

Luke had expressed concern that gang members would come to even the score, but then again, they might just consider her as Homeo's failed initiation attempt and leave her alone.

Piece by piece he disengaged himself from her. Always making sure she had what she needed, always making sure she was safe, but getting further and further from her life.

His first step away was to leave in the morning before she did, and arrive later at night. Luke eventually let her sleep in her own home, by herself. He called to speak to her at both midnight and seven a.m., but she was—very nearly—her own person again.

She would become completely her own if she would just shake the lingering need to hear his voice, to want to talk with him over dinner even if it was stilted and cold.

Yasmin considered casting a spell on herself.

Lord knew she'd cast close to a hundred those first hours she'd been finally left alone.

Though she cast in front of Luke before, he obviously wasn't comfortable with it. She'd done small things in the comfort of her bedroom. After the shooting—after she'd moved into his apartment—she shut it down even more, limiting herself to the basic protections for herself, him if he wanted, and for the furniture and carpets from her kittens.

Pulling out her mat, lighting her candles with a deep breath and raised hands had set her free. She protected her house, herself, her car. She didn't need to do Blessed Be, Tristan might get offended that she didn't think his spell was strong enough. Of course it was, so she expended her energy on other things.

Gearing up to cast a cast-off on herself, Yasmin gathered all the supplies from the shop. She didn't have the lavender, crushed quartz, and coral for that at home . . . Both were for altering memories. Things that Blessed Be sold but only carefully and in small quantities. Tristan kept a list of names of people who bought them. And he only sold small quantities, like a pharmacy hoarding cold medicine.

The combination she was buying was particularly damning, so she fessed up and told him it was for her.

From the look on his face, it was highly possible he thought she was trying to get over him. She almost laughed. But it would be easier if he believed that, so she simply offered a bland smile —she'd had plenty of practice in these last weeks—and waltzed out with everything she needed to stop dreaming about one Luke Salzone.

Not that he'd come to her. Not once since the motion sensor alarm went off. Not once since she explained what was happening.

Had she known what the alarm signaled—the end of a relationship she hadn't known was real, and one she hadn't realized was as deep as it was—she might have paid it more attention. But gone was gone. Or it would be in a spell.

She set out small cauldron—really more of a Dutch oven, but cool looking, perfect for a burn in the middle of her re-claimed guest room. It seemed the ideal place to cleanse her thoughts of him, since she almost believed she could still smell him here.

The ritual of it seemed more important and less rote than the other spells she'd been casting. Those had been almost thrown to the wind, this one would be carefully sown.

She would strip not her memories but the way she clung to them. She would take his calls and texts, stay up to speed on his news of the trial, but rid herself of the need to hear his voice. That in turn should relieve her of the daydreams, the curiosity that Mrs. Salzone's psychic was anything other than a crackpot. Hopefully it would also lessen Delilah's concern for her.

A strong witch like Delilah could smell it on a person. Apparently Yasmin's yearning for a man she couldn't have was almost like a haze that followed her around, a flag for anyone with the power to see it. Delilah had the grace not to say anything, but Yasmin long suspected Delilah was up to speed on all things related to Yasmin's ill-fated crush on the eldest Goodman. Maybe she just wasn't up on the fact that it was gone. So Delilah only twisted her mouth as she noticed these things and held her tongue.

Setting out the candles carefully, Yasmin then laid out her athame, the small cracked glass bowls for salt and water, the lavender, quartz dust and two pieces of orange coral.

With a whoosh of her breath the circle came to life around her. All but the four pillar candles at the four corners lighting bright, tall and near blue. Those she turned to one at a time and called the four corners, the rush of feeling coursing through her and lending strength to the spell to come.

For a moment she stood there, truly herself again for the first time in far too long. Yasmin breathed deep the scents of candle wax and herbs. She was back in her own home and she had some work to do.

While Luke had never asked her to be anything other than what she was, she'd hidden it from him like she had everyone else. And though she'd always known she didn't fit the mold others wanted her to slide neatly into, she hadn't celebrated who and what she was either.

She wasn't Delilah and Tristan, born to the craft and brought up in it. She was new, and yet she was good, powerful, strong. And before she forgot the feelings she owed Luke Salzone something. After all, the whole mess was likely her own doing.

Though she had no proof, the only time her life had been this kind of a mess was after she played in magicks she knew she wasn't supposed to.

Pouring the water into the pot, she snapped her fingers bringing it to a sharp simmer. She added the whole of the salt and watched as it fizzed and frothed and nearly boiled over, the thin layer of water becoming such volume from the magick. With a smoothing wave of her hand the froth regressed and the water became glassy clear.

Yasmin unhooked the charm she wore on her mother's chain and began scrying. In reality, what she was seeking was material and silly seeming, in the truth of things, she sought to pay what she owed.

The weight of the charm worked as a pendulum, swinging back and forth over the surface of the water. The images changed, scenes of Los Angeles, then further out, Orange County, the Inland Empire. She wasn't surprised by the distance, these things weren't everywhere.

When she had a location she sought her clues and two numbers. Seven, it was. And three.

Sitting back on her knees, the information stayed in her head. Tomorrow evening after work, she'd head out and get what she'd looked for.

She slid the necklace back into place, its job done for now. Together, she snapped both hands, bringing the water to a rushing boil. Palms toward it, she pushed and the water receded, disappearing into steam and then into nothing.

Now, for the release spell.

Yasmin fortified the circle again, bringing the flames higher. Not that she needed it. Spells cast on oneself were often easier, then again, they were often harder, too, as the base of all magick was intent. If hers wasn't truly aligned, it might be harder to push through. So she turned a full three-sixty, checking all the flames and finding the circle intact and tall.

She sprinkled the crushed quartz into the now empty cast iron and held the coral to her chest. Into the coral she fed all her memories of Luke that grabbed at her and held her tight. His genuine kind streak and all the examples she'd seen of that over the weeks. The way he had leapt at her—no decision, just reflex—the moment he'd heard the first shot. The way he'd pulled his gun that first day and, with her, stared down a man attempting to become a killer. The breakfasts he made her, served up with a care.

Lastly, she let all the memories of their shared nights wash over her. The way he'd stared into her eyes as though she was the only woman in the whole world. The sound of his voice murmuring her name. The touch of his hands on her bare skin.

She didn't know how long she sat there, reliving it, getting nearly overheated at just the thought of it. But she poured it all into the coral. Then she set it into the pot.

Or she tried to.

It took three tries to let go of the damn thing.

She went to add the lavender and couldn't pick it up. By the fourth attempt she couldn't even touch it.

And when she tried to start over, she discovered she could pick up the coral but not set it back into the pot to burn. Finding she could set it in her lap, she did just that and raised her hands to bring the power of the circle higher.

As she did, it all went black.

CHAPTER 18

Luke had done everything he could—for the case, for Yasmin, for himself.

So he sat back into his deep comfortable couch and popped the top on a beer and put the game on TV. In a few moments, he got up, headed to the kitchen and grabbed some tortilla chips. A few moments later than that, he realized he just couldn't eat them without dip.

His mother would be sorely disappointed if he had store bought dip. So, with the TV paused, he pulled out salsa and cream cheese. He added a scoop of salsa to half a block of cream cheese and hit it with the stick blender. Then he folded it back into the salsa, letting the white and red swirl together.

He put the game back on, pushing aside thoughts that he hadn't ever made Yasmin his favorite dip. It was a 'girlfriend test' of sorts. It often came out vivid pink if he folded it too much. Most looked at him like he was nuts. One had gotten mad at him for ruining all the salsa. Few survived.

Though, if he was being honest, it wasn't the salsa test that killed it. Most didn't understand what he did and they didn't want to. Cops were fun to nail apparently, but living with one?

No thank you. Even dating one for an extended period of time was clearly a hardship. One woman had asked him on the fifth date when he was going to get a better job. He'd looked her right in the eyes and said, "There is no better job."

There was a better job, for him at least, even if it was much the same job. He wanted to get into the DEA—detective work, more group cases, some homicides, but a much bigger jurisdiction. It sounded right up his alley.

He'd taken and passed several of the written exams, a medical physical as well as the agent physical assessment test. Now he just had to wait for his application to go through. Last year, he'd been rejected. Well, he'd been offered a position lower than the field agent position he wanted. But he was another year more experienced now and he'd keep applying until he got in. He was still young to be accepted for the path he'd chosen. He wasn't sweating it. . . . Well, he was, but it wouldn't break his heart.

He hadn't told date number five any of these things.

He'd told Yasmin all of them. Then again, maybe it was easy for her to encourage him, obviously it had nothing to do with her. Girlfriends were looking to be with someone, thus what he did and where he wanted to go was an important assessment for them. It made perfectly logical sense. Yasmin, on the other hand, couldn't wait to be rid of him. She'd almost pushed him out the door.

She'd thanked him profusely. Repeatedly. Told him she'd be there for every minute of the trial that she didn't have to be at work and of course she'd testify. But then she shut the door before he'd even walked away and Luke had heard the three bolts slide firmly into place.

He'd ignored the way his heart had sunk. Told himself it hadn't.

Then he told himself that he wasn't following the game

because he was too hungry. Chips and doctored salsa weren't going to cut it.

Pausing the TV again, he went back to the kitchen. Noshed on more chips while he pan fried a fish fillet in breadcrumbs and parmesan and reheated a leftover rice/grain mix with peas.

He was sitting back down and looking at his plate later when he thought to himself that he was a catch. Sure he made no money as a cop, but it would get better once he was DEA. It would never be great, but he didn't have any issues about a woman out-earning him either.

But he could and did cook. He had no compunctions about changing diapers and—unless future wife was working at a daycare—he'd have way more experience with it. He was relatively neat. In Luke's mind, he was the right mix of old world chivalry and new world equality. He was smart, generally kind, never abusive. Why wasn't he married with a kid?

Maybe because it was only recently that the thought had come to him that he was ready for that. Maybe because no woman had roped him in yet. Maybe that was because he had a job where he might not come home one night. But he wished people would be honest, this was LA. Everyone here had a story of being robbed at gunpoint or being right there when someone else was. This was not small town America, so his chances of getting shot on the job were only slightly higher than that of the average Angeleno going about his daily business.

None of the women he dated seemed to agree with him on that point, though.

He finished his dinner, happy with the tasty results and managed to stay relatively involved in the game. But his thoughts still wandered.

This morning they'd set bail for Homeo and Doddo. Both Luke and Jessica had been there. Yasmin had shown up, too—he figured since it was an 8am hearing she'd made it before work.

She must have come in after him, because even though he looked for her, he didn't see her until he was leaving. He didn't get to say anything, he only saw her walking away, but it hit him in the gut that—even at a distance—he'd know that walk anywhere.

Bail was high enough that Homeo and Doddo were returned immediately to their holding cells. Homeo's court date was set for one week away. Horribly fast given the system. Luke got the impression that the judge wanted him to plea out quickly and get into prison right away or just get it done with. Another trial had cancelled and Homeo was scheduled right in.

It wasn't a problem at all; the evidence was solid. Luke had his hands in it as much as he could without compromising anything. He wasn't the investigating officer after all. Still, Valverde and the prosecutor had built a tight case.

They were ready. Both Homeo and Doddo would be going away. Homeo for attempted murder. Doddo for the lesser crimes of being an accomplice, shooting Yasmin's house, and grand theft auto.

Still forcibly pushing thoughts of work and Yasmin from his mind, he polished off his dinner and watched the end of the game. He was just contemplating that the win should have felt a lot better than it did when his phone rang.

He didn't do ringtones, just left it on the assigned tone that came with the phone, so his heart jumped a little and his brain tamped down the excitement that it might be Yasmin. He had to look at the phone to see. But it wasn't. It was Valverde.

Frowning, Luke answered, "Jessica?"

Why was she calling him this late at night? He was breathing in, thinking nothing good could come at this hour, when she told him he thought right.

"Doddo just made bail."

"What?"

"Yeah," There was a deep sigh in her voice as though she were put out. But it was more than that. The fact that she was calling him and not waiting until the morning to tell him spoke volumes. Jessica understood the possible severity of the situation. "My friend at the jail was on tonight and he called me to let me know."

"When?"

"They just processed him. Richards handed over his belongings, closed the window and called me." The sigh had left her voice. She was now a detective relaying facts. "He's possibly still walking the sidewalk waiting for his ride."

He barely eeked out a 'thank you' before he hung up on her.

Yasmin's number was in his speed dial, and the memory was in his muscles. His finger just hit the button and he was waiting for the ringing to get picked up.

"YasminYasminYasmin . . ." He muttered it over and over, as though he could incant her to answer the phone. He paced the floor, his feet rapid and harsh with his impatience. Six rings in he got a sweet answer from her recording.

Or he heard the start of it and knew it was sweet. He'd listened to it before. Luke hung up immediately and tried her home line. She was a smart girl—it certainly cost extra—but having a land line was important to personal safety, especially for a woman in her own house in Los Angeles.

But she didn't pick up there either.

He went back to the cell phone, but before he hit the button he pushed his feet into his sneakers and checked very briefly to be sure he was dressed. Sweatpants and bright long-sleeved shirt would have to do. He grasped his heavy keychain, the motion of pulling it off the hook in the kitchen systematic. He had the door open before he remembered his wallet. And then his badge.

It wouldn't do to get pulled over for speeding—which he most likely would do, the way his heart was racing—and not have his driver's license on him. LA was not a small town, not all the police officers knew each other and he sure didn't know the whole force in Yasmin's district yet.

His sneakers rang on the cement steps down to the garage. His cell signal in the back corner—his spot—pretty much sucked. He could get one, but no one could decipher anything. So he didn't even try yet. Luke pounded his fist on the steering wheel, narrowly missing the horn in his frustration and he tried to push back thoughts of what the Del Surs might do. It was unlikely any of it had happened yet. Yasmin was probably fine.

The garage door was a solid fence of metal that tilted upward—Luke gunned the engine and spun the tires as soon as it cleared the height of his car.

Out on the street in the dim light and white noise of the city at night, he reached for his cell phone again. Hitting Yasmin's number he waited and waited.

Two rings.

Three rings.

He took the turn up Highland and over the canyon, toward her house, his heart pounding harder than it needed to.

Four rings.

Five—

"Luke?"

"Where are you!" He barked it. It wasn't a question at all but a demand. And realizing what he'd done, he switched tacks. No more politely, he barked another non-question at her. "Are you okay!"

"Yes." She was clearly confused. "What's going on?"

"Where are you?" He was clearer now. Surely it was easier to understand his words, even if he couldn't speak calmly. He again asked a second question before she could answer the first. "Are you at home?"

"No. I was out . . . shopping."

"At this hour?" Now he was confused. Maybe she was at the

grocery? Although he didn't see her doing that shopping late at night, not anymore. "Where?"

"In Alhambra." Another pause. "I'm on my way home. What's going on?"

She seemed to at least understand that whatever was wrong it had him worked up. His breath was slowly leaking out of him. He was talking to her. She was alive. Safe. In her car. "Doddo made bail. He just got out."

This pause was lengthy. He almost asked if she was still there, but then she spoke again. "And you think he'll come after me?"

Actually, he didn't think it was that likely. It was just that the consequences if Doddo did come for her would probably be fatal. So he forcibly calmed himself down and told her just that. "You should come here and stay with me again."

Something seeped through him as he said the words. Luke didn't like admitting that having her here felt good to him. It wasn't right. It was all on his side. But she needed to be somewhere safe.

"You don't think he'll come after you?"

"He might, but that's why I'm in this building. It's a good neighborhood—Doddo and his ilk would likely be noticed hanging around here. All the units are on upper floors. Motion sensor, all my locks. It would be hard for him to get in without us having enough time to be ready."

"Okay . . . I was coming by your place anyway."

Her voice sounded stilted. It didn't matter. His heart stuttered. Why would she becoming by?

There was no time to dwell on that question, he'd have to find out later, she interrupted his thoughts.

"I'll swing by my place and grab some stuff and the kittens."

"No!" another bark. He had to stop that. Jessica wouldn't bark at her. Jessica would be calm. "I'll swing by and get them. I'll get you some stuff. You shouldn't go there." He brooked no argument by posing another question before she could tell him no. "Is anyone following you? Is there anyone suspicious around?"

"No and no." He heard the noise of her engine starting, the ding of her GPS giving her instructions. Wherever she was, she was unfamiliar enough with it to need the inhuman voice telling her which turns to take.

After asking her arrival time at his place, he gave her a nearby location, a well lit parking lot with reasonable traffic at this time of night, told her to meet him there. Then he hung up.

He couldn't let her disagree.

And he hoped he didn't run into Doddo or any of the other Del Surs at her house.

Staying on the route he'd chosen to her house, Luke thought through the particulars of the case. It had seemed that Doddo and Homeo were the ones to shoot up Yasmin's house. They had been the ones to steal—and then surreptitiously return—the neighbors cars.

Killing Yasmin was Homeo's initiation fee into the Del Surs. There was sometimes a gangland version of 'sponsorship' that went with it. Because the gangs were into illegal activities, they were often tight about who got in and who didn't. In most cases, you were either recruited young or someone had to vouch for you. If the new recruit turned on the gang or turned out to be an undercover cop, well then, the 'sponsor' went down with him.

So if Doddo was Homeo's sponsor—which made sense as Jessica had uncovered a family tie between the two—then it was logical that they were hunting down Yasmin.

Doddo shouldn't kill her. If he did, that would remove Homeo's ticket into the Del Surs. He might get another one, but it wasn't smart for Doddo to remove that option in the first place. But Doddo could hurt her. Take her somewhere and hold her for when Homeo got out.

Luke's blood ran cold at the thought.

Gang activity was brutal. The men—if they could be called that, though they certainly didn't fit Luke's definition—were indoctrinated in that brutality from an early age. It was what they saw on the streets where they grew up and often in their own homes. There was no telling what the Del Surs could or would do to Yasmin, and they would do it without a second thought, without any remorse.

It took a great effort to push those thoughts away. She was in her car. No one was following her. Doddo likely wouldn't do anything. Jessica and the DA would lock Homeo up good and tight, maybe even Doddo, too, and Yasmin could go on with her life.

Luke repeated the thought like a mantra.

He would keep thinking it—believing it—until he saw her in the flesh. Saw for himself she was alive and safe.

Her house loomed in front of him before he even realized he arrived. If there was cloaking on it he was immune to it now. So he grabbed his personal gun from the glove compartment, scanned the area for anything out of the ordinary and when it checked out, pulled the spare set of keys she'd given him weeks ago.

Luke let himself in through the back door and found himself greeted instantly by two little black puff balls who meowed and curled around his legs and generally acted starved and neglected. He almost chuckled.

First he shoved the kittens into their box, before they suspected anything nefarious from him. Then he gathered their things into a cloth grocery bag, quickly mentally running through a 'day in the life of Hex and Voodoo' and grabbing supplies as he thought of them.

Secondly he had to think through a 'day in the life of Yasmin Ali' and tried to gauge what she would need. It was intimate, packing her toothbrush, hairbrush and a variety of items from her bathroom counter. Luke thought back in an attempt to recall the things he'd seen at his house, tried to duplicate what she packed for herself the first time she came to stay.

It was harder still to plunge his hands into her underwear drawer, to pull out a bra, a shirt . . . And he found he couldn't do it. It was a violation, just his being here. In the broad light of day, he could bring her back here, or he could get a big box and just dump all her things in it and let her sort through what to wear.

His watch told him it was time to head out. He didn't want her waiting for him in some parking lot, just in case she had been followed and didn't know it.

Loaded with bags and kittens, he considered taking a second trip to the car. But he came out behind the house, which would protect him a bit, and he was now concerned with speed.

Hex and Voodoo mewed their way over the hill, letting him know what they thought of his shoving them right into their carrier. Luke sneezed at them several times in response even as he tried to use his most soothing voice to tell them—and himself—that they'd all see Yasmin in a few minutes and everything would be just fine.

Luckily they made it to the parking lot before she did, but not by much. That didn't matter. It only mattered that she didn't sit and wait for him.

Pulling her car up to where their windows aligned she waited until his went down, then she smiled. "See? I'm safe. I'm fine. Do I need to get out of the car?"

His heart rate crashed back to a normal level and he matched her smile while trying not to look crazy. Even knowing the instructions sounded curt to his own ears, he couldn't help himself.

The situation was getting out of hand. Well, it was, but only in his own mind. In reality, everything was professional. Everything was on the up-and-up. He was her hired personal protection—cleared through two precincts. Just an officer picking up extra cash (that whole dollar) and working on a case he was involved in because he was a victim as well. No other reason.

In sharp words he gave her instructions to his place and told her park first in the garage, he'd follow.

Not much later, he set the kittens free in his living room, explained what he thought the likelihood was that Doddo would cause problems. She frowned at the restrictions he thought should be set back in place on her life. He offered her something to eat, which she refused. Then he offered her something to sleep in, which she didn't.

So they stood there in the hallway, her clutching the large t-shirt he'd handed her. He noted it was from some charity event he'd attended several years ago while he explained that he didn't get her any clothes. He tried to be professional about telling her that he couldn't bring himself to go through her drawers and that he'd take her back to her place in the morning, gun in hand —just in case—and help her pack some things up.

Yasmin only nodded.

She didn't look at him like she knew he wanted nothing more than to bury his hands in the weight of her hair and lean her against the wall. That if she made the slightest move toward him, he'd probably throw all the professionalism right out the window and kiss her until they were both senseless with it.

They'd done that before. Kissed like that. And more. He knew how she felt pressed to the length of him. Knew what it was like to hold her in place for his mouth.

But he didn't do it.

He couldn't. The case would be compromised and that would put her in danger. It wasn't worth a kiss. Wasn't worth her slapping him with a whopper of a sexual harassment suit. So he offered her yet another tight smile and she turned and closed the bedroom door behind her.

CHAPTER 19

Luke was counting down the days.

He had tried to get someone else to take over Yasmin's protection once before. And he tried now a second time to get her to an official safe house provided by the precinct. She'd be better protected there, have a constant guard, stay at an address that wasn't associated with either her name or his. . . and she'd be out of his hair.

It didn't happen.

Luke had learned a long time ago that the law was the law. It wasn't always right, it was just the rule. As a policeman he was an officer of the law, not a keeper of justice as he would have wished. The two overlapped just barely enough to keep him happy.

In this case, not enough.

The other problem, even when the law was on the side of justice, the budget usually was not. Even though Yasmin had been shot at in her own home, because she provided her own security detail and maintained it, there was no clear reason to begin to provide one for her.

Luke tried again to get departmental coverage. It was

hopefully more necessary now with Doddo out on bail. But Doddo was only ever the accomplice—at least as far as the law was concerned. Because he had not previously pulled the trigger at Ms. Ali, it was not budgeted to protect her on the possibility that would change. Luke couldn't seem to make a strong enough case that it was a likely outcome. Luke was left guarding her.

And his heart.

He was back on the job and so was she. They were arranging their schedules around each other—mostly her around his—so that he could drop her off, pick her up, and sometimes ferry her to her house. While they were there, he would stand guard with his gun drawn and the safety off in case Doddo or any other Del Surs came by.

Unable to block traffic at both ends of her block when they were there, he simply had to deal with cars going by. He watched each of them, no free hand to run license plates as fast as he would want, and try to keep his heart from racing.

His home was no longer a bastion of silence and peace. He had a constant guest. She cleaned his place for him, which was nice, but he pretty much didn't let her cook anything. They ate breakfast and dinner together, and Luke figured it was much like a marriage that had gone sour but no one would leave.

They spoke of mundane things. They spent a lot of their time planning—who would be where when, and how Yasmin would never be alone.

That was eating at her. The woman needed some solitude and the best she was getting was going into his office/guest room and closing the door. He couldn't offer her anything more.

Luke spent a good portion of his time fighting the urge to just say something to her—to tell her how he felt. But he was betting everything on this case. He had to lock up at least Homeo or he had no idea how she was ever going to be safe.

If the new gang member was free, then the best-case

scenario that Luke could come up with was that Homeo would kill someone else (probably in front of a large group of children to make up for missing Yasmin in the first place) and then—fully initiated—he and the rest of the Del Surs would simply forget the miss in the grocery store parking lot. They would forget the ring of blue fire around her, the gun handle that burned hot enough to melt nylon and burn Homeo's hand. He was still getting medical treatment for that while he was in jail.

No, they likely wouldn't forget.

The only other option Luke could figure was that Yasmin could maybe conjure something so big as to make the Del Surs afraid of the Hollywood shop girl. That seemed unlikely.

Maybe she could simply make them forget her.

But from the way she spoke of the spells, it seemed as though that would be quite a bit of work to put up and maintain.

If it didn't work, she should probably leave the city.

Luke didn't see her agreeing easily to that. So he left her shut behind the door in his office. Hated that she was sleeping on that awful futon. And prayed that Homeo got locked up good and tight and then that Doddo did, too.

He was sitting at the table, looking over the notes for his testimony in Homeo's trial, now only one day away—but who knew how long it would last—when Yasmin came up to him.

She was wearing pajama pants and . . . his shirt.

For a moment he wondered if that meant anything.

Then Luke was forced to conclude that it most likely meant that the shirt was old, soft, and available. Nothing else.

Yasmin held out an envelope to him. "I got this in Reseda the night you called. It's why I was headed here then anyway."

Taking it, he looked and saw that his name had been written on the front, probably prepped before she went out, before she realized she'd be stuck here again. He frowned a bit.

A thank you note? He didn't have any idea what was in it, but he opened the flap and all made sense as a handful of lotto tickets fell out.

"Yasmin, you didn't have to do this." He looked up at her, surprised to find her expression completely neutral. Besides, what were they likely worth anyway?

She didn't really answer him—maybe a habit she'd picked up from him. "Sign the backs. Now. That way they're yours and only yours."

Yasmin stood, straight and silent, in his t-shirt, waiting. So he picked up the pen sitting nearby and dutifully signed the back of each scratcher. He would have expected those digital yellow lotto printouts, but instead he held two strands of perforated tickets, one much longer than the other, both folded accordion style and stuffed into the envelope. Dutifully, Luke signed the back of each of the ten tickets then looked at her as though asking what he should do next. He never bought lotto tickets.

She smiled at him. "Get a nickel or a quarter and scratch the silver off according to the rules."

Then she turned and walked away before he could ask if there was a reason not to use a dime or a penny. If maybe the cards were enchanted and the other coins wouldn't work. Then he wondered if maybe she'd suggested that simply because the penny and dime were just too small for the work.

He checked his pockets and easily came up with a quarter. It was a distraction for sure; a welcome one . . . he wasn't certain. The three smaller ones were some kind of "Bag of Coins" limited game. And there was no strategy or psychic ability to it. He was simply to scratch all three bag logos off to see what he had. If all three matched, then he won what was showing.

Starting at the top card in the short string, he scratched the foil covering, releasing a combination rubber and metal smell that was entirely unfamiliar to him and creating a mountain of what looked a lot like eraser dust. He checked partway through the first card and saw his coin was still intact.

The first gold bag told him he'd won a million dollars, the second agreed, and the third said $100. Not a winner. The second was much the same with the first bag revealing a very large prize that the later scratches revealed to be nothing but a tease. Not ever playing the lotto seemed once again like a wise decision. But he kept going.

On the third card, the first removed section revealed $5000. He was no longer scratching off the entire gold foil bag and only starting in the middle and removing enough to show that he had, as expected, lost. The second bag revealed another $5000, but Luke wasn't about to be fooled, despite the fact that Yasmin said she sometimes won five digits of money. She also said she often went and struck out. That option seemed far more likely to Luke.

But the third bag revealed an identical $5000.

Frowning now, he scratched all the foil from the bottom card in the chain and read both the front and the back again. According to what he read, he could exchange the card for five thousand dollars, check to be issued by the California State Lottery Commission in Sacramento.

His heart beating a little faster, Luke started on the second chain.

This one was more complex. There were nine squares on the card and the bearer had to scratch three squares off and match two to claim a prize. So he could hold a winning card and still screw it up. He had no psychic abilities at all. Though he was beginning to think Yasmin did.

Sitting back, Luke thought long and hard before he took the coin to the first card. He deeply contemplated getting Yasmin to come and tell him which squares to remove. She should have far better luck than he. But he thought she had gone to sleep and he didn't want to wake her up. Besides, she handed him the cards and left. Obviously, she didn't expect to be here when he used them . . . so she must expect him to do with them as he would. If there was money here, he should be able to find it, psychic skills or not.

He was definitely a 'not.'

So he made a pattern. On the first card—at the top of the chain—he took out the top line of the nine-grid. And quickly lost. For posterity's sake, he scratched all nine silver squares and saw that there was nothing to win on this card even if he had been completely psychic. Well, if he had been, he wouldn't have bothered with this card in the first place, would he?

The second card he scratched every other square. And promptly added a second loss to his tally. The third, he took out every third square, making a downward line, the fourth made a diagonal. He scratched all the squares off and saw that all the cards had been losers anyway. On the fifth card he had to stop and flex his hand. Not only the scratching but the tension of thinking there was money here to win if he could just do it right was making him grasp the tiny quarter with a strength well beyond what was necessary.

He lost on the fifth card, too. But it was his fault. That card had a one hundred dollar prize had he removed the right combination of squares. Despite the loss of the C-note (which the card told him he could claim at any lotto dealer) he stuck to his pattern for cards six and seven.

Six was also a loser, and as he scratched off his second $8000 marker he wondered if she had bought the string knowing the last one was the winner. Sure enough his third block revealed the last $8000 square.

His jaw hung open.

Eight grand? Along with the other ticket he had thirteen thousand dollars in his hands.

For a handful of moments he just stared. Desperately he wanted to scratch all the squares on the last card and see what they said, but it would invalidate his win. He immediately placed each winning card in a zipper baggie. The first card was set, but the second had to be protected.

He was walking down the hall to tell Yasmin when he thought for the first time about taxes. He'd probably only get to keep about half of it. Still, it was a nest egg the likes of which he would have to work months to save.

Knocking softly on her door, he whispered "Yasmin?" as though he wasn't really waking her up by being quiet.

Luke was shaking his head, thinking he should have left it until morning, when he heard her voice, awake and alert. "Luke? What did you win?"

"Thirteen thousand dollars." He couldn't believe the words coming out of his mouth. He was still half convinced that he'd read the cards wrong. Maybe he miscounted his zeroes or had suddenly forgotten how to do math.

From the look on her face, Yasmin wasn't shocked at all. She smiled at him in the now open doorway. "I thought it was over ten. Good for you."

She smiled blandly waiting while he couldn't think of anything to say. Then finally he blurted out. "It's your money. You bought the cards."

That felt better. He sighed again. It was her money. Then he didn't have to think about it.

Yasmin only laughed at him. "Nope. It's yours. You signed them, and I'll testify in court that I gave them to you as a gift. So you can cash them or not as you wish. But they aren't mine." She paused a moment and her laughter died. "I owe you my life. I know that. More than one occasion. You haven't complained as I invaded your home—"

He attempted to interrupt, but she held up her hand to stop him and simply didn't let him get a word in. "And my protection has taken over your whole life. If you have a girlfriend you haven't seen her in several weeks, at least that I'm aware of.

You've barely seen your family. And for most of this time if you were off duty at the precinct you were on duty with me. Even when you were asleep. This is how I can pay you. It's yours."

Her benign smile was the last thing he saw before she shut him out and left him standing there in the hallway staring at the closed door to his own office.

~

Yasmin was off work for the trial. She put on some of her better clothes, but not the one suit she owned. A lovely powder blue that set off her hair, it looked fantastic and was to be saved for the first time she was on the witness stand.

She'd been all set to wear it on day one, but Luke had set her straight.

No one would be televising this trial—it was L.A. and there were gang initiation shootings all the time. Not usually in Hollywood, but not unusually either. They were trying to keep the whole witchcraft thing quiet, as that might blow up in their faces, but so far, Luke said it was successfully staying low.

While Yasmin thought it was ridiculous, she didn't balk. Not out loud. She also considered that she was 'of middle eastern descent' not a 'natural born citizen' and that her entire family aside from her Wiccan self was Muslim. Nope. America would not feel kindly toward her.

She muttered under her breath as she walked into the courtroom, "Melting pot, my ass."

So for the entire first day, she'd sat. The trial had begun. She was in the third row of seats. The DA was prosecuting, by herself. Detective Valverde was in the first row. Luke beside her, having the odd distinction of being both an officer and a witness and a victim. Yasmin, as the actual person the bullets were aimed at, seemed to only rate a 'find your own seat, miss' at the trial of the man who shot at her.

Homeo sat at the defendant's table along with his lawyer, a disturbingly well-dressed man. It appeared that either the public defender was independently wealthy with a deep seated need to spend his life and time helping the underdog—the guilty as hell underdog in this case—or the Del Surs had bought Homeo a real slick lawyer.

Both lawyers made their opening statements. Basically they spent several hours telling the jury and everyone who managed to stay awake what they would do over the coming days. No one actually did anything, they just talked about it.

Yasmin rescinded that thought for a moment. Homeo's lawyer did in fact introduce himself and say he'd replaced the public defender only recently and that he would like the trial pushed back by several weeks. Yasmin had almost leapt to her feet and yelled "I object!" herself. There was no way she could stand living with Luke that much longer. Homeo's ass needed to land in prison—preferably in another state—and soon. She had a life to get on with and love spells to not cast.

Luckily the judge agreed with Yasmin, or the defense lawyer —whom Yasmin immediately decided she didn't like—was an idiot. The judge smirked down at him and almost laughed. "Honey, I'm sorry you're slow to the trough here, but you get what's left of the slop."

The laugh, the colloquialism . . . Even calling that grown man "Honey" all floored Yasmin. Even if she completely agreed.

Later the defense moved for a change of venue. The judge again laughed at him and he grinned an oily grin and said, "I had to try."

Yasmin felt her skin crawl. She'd have to ask Luke later if that gave Homeo a better chance to get off on a technicality or not?

By the end of day one—which was only really a half day of sitting there—she was exhausted. No one had paid a lick of attention to her. Not that she wanted it, but wasn't this all about her being shot at? Apparently she was mistaken because if Luke hadn't been there and rounded her up to take her to his apartment, no one would have noticed whether she was there or not.

While they checked out through security, Luke reclaiming his gun and pepper spray, Yasmin asked if they should invite Jessica along for dinner.

"Oh no." His voice was tired, definite. "I'm going to cook. I don't even want to be out. Trials like this kill me. And we really shouldn't be seen hanging out personally with Valverde."

"What?" That made little sense. They weren't to be decent people and be nice to the other detective that he worked with every day?

He was already closing her into the passenger side of his car when she asked just that. While he jogged around the front of the car, she wondered if opening car doors was chivalrous or just part of her paid protection. She couldn't tell.

Luke picked up the conversation as he closed his own door. "If it looks like we're friends, then Homeo's lawyer can claim that we are acting as friends and not as officers of the law. It's stupid really, but since you can't prove intentions . . ." He shrugged.

At first she nodded. It made an odd kind of sense, given what she was seeing of the legal system. Luke had even told her early on not to expect what was 'right' only what was 'legal.' Apparently a lot of people confused those. Yasmin thought she was one of those 'a lot' given that she always believed American law was designed to uphold and defend justice. Luke had almost laughed at her. Then she thought about something else.

"Wait, we can't eat dinner with Jessica, but I can basically live at your apartment?"

"Different thing. You and I have a professional relationship. I protect you; you pay me." He navigated the last turn, pulling into the slim driveway and clicking the remote on his visor.

She watched the gate go up, thinking how stupid the whole thing was. They didn't have a 'professional relationship' they had a basically 'naked relationship' that only didn't continue because it was 'unprofessional.'

Luke ignored it because he wanted to. She agreed because where else was she going to find someone who would jump in front of bullets for her for the low, low price of one dollar?

So she smiled her way through a dinner that Luke cooked. Yasmin cleaned up afterward and went to bed thinking that she had this whole trial to make it through. Though she wasn't the one being tried, it was definitely going to be a trial for her, too. Tristan had let her off work for as long as she needed, but she wanted to go back. She needed to resume her regular life. And she couldn't.

She was being held back by forces beyond her control and frustrated by a man and a circumstance that she felt she had earned but more than paid for.

Yasmin had had enough, but it seemed the universe wasn't done with her.

Hex and Voodoo followed her dutifully into the room, now quiet. It seemed the little performance artists had used up all their meows during dinner when they tried, albeit somewhat successfully, to beg scraps . . . It was the only thing that kept Yasmin from breaking down and crying and thinking just how far off track things had gone.

CHAPTER 20

Yasmin was practically homicidal herself. The trial was nothing like she expected. It was long, dull, and full of lawyers talking mostly about how they'd like to talk. Or how the other lawyer should talk. Or shouldn't talk.

The defense added a psychologist to the witness list who came in and talked for four hours about Homeo's traumatic childhood. Then he was cross-examined for another two. Yasmin boiled the whole day down to: Poor Homeo, well actually, no, he didn't have to join the gang or shoot anyone.

Why was no one concerned about poor Yasmin? There was no psychologist being asked for hours on end about the trauma of getting shot at in front of your nieces as a random victim in a club initiation. There was no one commenting on how traumatic it was just to have to sit and listen to this drivel all day.

To top it off, she was still lamenting the loss of her nighttime stress-relief sessions with Luke. That's what she was calling them these days. They were firmly filed in the category of 'not real.' Her feelings were labeled 'not returned' and the whole thing was being called 'hot casual sex' that didn't really happen.

Had it been a real booty call, she would have knocked on his door again. Instead she was sleeping in a shirt that smelled like him. It was a poor choice. But she made it again each night.

She played games on her phone during the breaks. Sat on the hard bench for hours on end and worried.

Occasionally, she snapped her fingers, the smallest thing she could do to bring a spell about. Well, she could blow out a gush of air, like she was rapidly taking out her birthday candles, but that would earn her weird looks. Apparently, so did snapping.

She did consider casting a spell on Homeo's mother. Then thought better of it and cast one on herself so the woman wouldn't annoy her so much.

Mrs. Dudley—Homeo was apparently some concoction she thought resembled the name Romeo—planted herself in the front row and cried as often as possible, as loud as possible. She yelled out what a good boy her son was until the judge told her that she'd be permanently removed with one more outburst. The woman then limited herself to sniffles and silent tears.

Each day, Yasmin became more concerned.

Luke and Detective Valverde assured her that this one was in the can. There was no way they could lose. Yes, she should keep the witchcraft on the downlow, but the case was sewn up tight.

So why didn't Homeo and his lawyer plea out? Wasn't that their best option? Or had she been basing all she knew on TV?

In the evening, Luke would assure her everything was on track. Homeo would go away for a long time, then she would no longer be part of an initiation and she could go on with her life. She would sleep relatively well, believing what they told her. But in the daylight, she would worry again. Why was Homeo's lawyer acting as though he could end all of it? Acting like Homeo would walk out of here a free man?

Her butt was going to be shaped like the hard wooden bench before anything even happened. Did it matter that the jury looked as bored as she did?

She worked as many hours as she could on the weekend and still ran her class in the evenings. Yasmin even closed the shop two nights for Tristan and managed to get a three-quarter schedule in despite sitting in court all day.

Being at Blessed Be was freeing . . . both from watching the back of Luke's head and listening to the trial. She was ready to start skipping—it was going to come out how it came out. But when she was good and ready to just stay home, it was suddenly her day.

Luke and Valverde had prepped her. The DA had even gone after her in mock practice, trying to break down her testimony and destroy Yasmin as a credible witness. She knew to breathe, think before answering, and wear her nice suit.

The morning it was her turn, she couldn't eat breakfast. Both because she was afraid of getting something on her shirt and because of her stomach. But Luke grabbed her by her arms and held her still. He told her that the case wouldn't turn on her testimony, even if she screwed it all up.

That helped, a bit. But she'd never been on the stand before.

When she finally made it, it was like being on stage—something she avoided at all costs. She was okay teaching her class, but that was about the limit. The stenographer was probably the worst—someone recording her every word for all time. But the upside was that made her always stop and think about what she said. If she blurted it would go down on the courts permanent record.

She was questioned by the prosecution first. These people were on her side. And the assistant DA who handled Yasmin's testimony was a sweet guy, looked like he was pretty fresh off the law school boat and handled her with kid gloves.

There was a lunch break, during which she ate very little, despite both Valverde and Luke trying to get her to finish at least her sandwich. Then she was sworn back in—as though lunch made perjury possible—and this time the defense lawyer had at her.

He asked her to identify the man who shot at her. She pointed to Homeo. Then he went round-about for a while that she'd never met him before, hadn't seen him in the store, etc. That maybe she'd been shot at by someone else and was just overlaying poor Homeo's face on the memory.

Yasmin leaned forward a bit, already having learned that too far made the mic feedback and that made everyone jump. "I did not see him inside the store while I was shopping . . . with my very young nieces. I did see him outside the store when he got my attention then aimed a loaded gun at me."

"But how did you know the gun was loaded? Are you a weapons expert?" The man was even more smarmy than she'd originally thought.

"No sir—"

"Thank you."

But she kept talking. "However, the crack of a gun being fired—at you—is a fine indicator that it is, in fact, loaded."

She sat back and stared at the lawyer.

He stared back, obviously a little perturbed.

Once when she didn't respond fast enough, he asked if she needed time to compose her lies.

Yasmin thought so as not to say 'yes' or 'no,' but replied, "I'm not lying. However, I'm not at home in this courtroom like you and your client. I don't do things that land me in court. So I'm taking my time to be sure that I don't get caught in your double edged questions."

She thought she saw Luke's jaw tic.

Then she thought she shouldn't be looking to Luke. Yasmin shifted her gaze to the DA who was silently drumming her fingers on the desk, code for 'you're doing well.' A single finger tapping meant 'no' or 'not like that.'

Yasmin fought a smile.

Even though she felt she had done a good job, she could barely walk as she exited the stand. It was important that she stand tall, confident, and not leave the jury with any ideas about the importance or conviction of her testimony. But her knees buckled as she sat in her spot on the bench.

Luckily, court was dismissed for the day with no time left for another witness. Luke checked on her first, then professionally led her out the door and to his car. Only when the door was closed did he look at her and ask, "Are you okay?"

"I'm exhausted." And she was, more than she ever would have thought.

"You look like you're about to cry."

"Thank you." But he was right.

They hit a drive through for sodas and fries. Sugar and fat and starch, he said, to keep her going until he could get a reasonable meal in her.

"I can't. I'm on at the shop tonight." In fact, she was due there in two hours. With traffic she had barely enough time to get to his apartment, get changed, then get a slice of pizza from next door before she started.

"No. You are not working tonight. Call in." His voice brooked no argument from her. But she did it anyway.

"There was no way to predict which day I would be called up, so I had to pick a schedule. I'm on today."

"Then switch with someone for tomorrow, or just call in sick. I'll call for you if you want."

"No, no." She batted his hand away as he reached out offering to take her phone and call in like a mom with a sick kid.

Sooner was better and she got Tristan on the line. Luckily he was sympathetic and offered to cover for her himself. The stress of staying upright almost folded her, and she leaned her head back against the seat and almost fell asleep to the music of tires on manhole covers, starting and stopping, and the occasional horn.

Luke's voice nearly woke her, though it couldn't have been more than a few seconds since she set her head back. "Is it okay?"

"Yeah." Her head lolled back again. "Tristan will cover the shift himself."

"That was very nice of him."

There was something in his tone, something almost sarcastic, but Yasmin wasn't looking at him and she just didn't have the energy to figure it out.

She barely remembered climbing the steps to Luke's apartment, or changing into her pajamas. She did have a clear vision of lying down on the couch and offering to help with dinner. She didn't.

Luke woke her when it was ready and fed her a hearty, well balanced meal with chicken and green beans and a rice dish. She was blinking at the food for a moment trying to make sense of it all.

"Is something wrong?"

Finally she looked at him, really at him, for probably the first time that day. "Yes. Did you conjure this? I don't remember you having this food in the fridge, and I just laid down." She was motioning to the couch when he bust out in laughter.

"It's been an hour. You were out cold. And the chicken was in the freezer until this morning." Then he dug in, the smells of the food teasing her until she couldn't hold back. After all, she'd hardly eaten today.

He nodded at something. "The way yesterday went, I figured out pretty early that today would be all you. I should have told you to call in to work last night. I just didn't think of it."

The DA had talked to Yasmin before, hoping that her testimony would get broken up over two days. But yesterday had dragged on—like every other day, Yasmin thought—leaving her examined and cross-examined all in one day.

She nearly inhaled the food, having eaten almost nothing all day and worried away what little energy she might have stored. Yasmin didn't even wait for Luke to suggest she go to bed, but she did try to clean up after dinner.

Pushing her hands away, he shooed her out of the kitchen. "I've got it."

"You sat there all day like I did."

"Yeah, but it's different when you're on the stand."

She nodded, having learned that lesson in spades today. "But you're on tomorrow." And his testimony would likely be just as long as hers, if not longer. He was not only a witness, but a professional one.

He sighed. "Let me rephrase: It's different the first time you're on. I do this a lot."

"At big trials like this? That go on for days?" She was still trying to help clean up and he was still trying to block her. Yasmin managed to get a few dishes into the sink.

"Not that often, but enough that I have practice." He rinsed and slid plates, bowls and glasses into the dishwasher. "I keep hoping he'll wise up and plea out, but his lawyer wants to try a run for it." Luke shook his head, "I think it'll go badly for Homeo in the end."

"What do you mean?"

"Well, in a plea bargain, we agree to a lesser sentence in exchange for admitted guilt." He absently wiped down counters and rinsed out the sink, clearly a man comfortable in his domain. "It's an imperfect system, but it saves a lot of time and money. If Homeo doesn't bargain soon, we'll have him dead to rights and there won't be any time or money left to save. The jury will declare him guilty as hell. Juries generally aren't kind at all to gang members, and the judge will lock him up and throw away the key."

"So why run at it, then?" Yasmin didn't understand.

Luke sighed, leaning against the counter. For the first time she saw that he too had changed into plaid flannel pants and a t-shirt. Clearly both of them were exhausted.

"I guess it's like the difference of you on the stand and me on the stand. It's easier on me. I've seen this go down a ton of times and I don't see a lot of options for how it turns out. But you're nervous." He shrugged. "The lawyer wants to make a name. If he loses, it's just a black mark, and not that bad, it's a pretty unwinnable case. But it's Homeo's life he's playing with. It's worse for you because it's not my case, really. For Valverde, for me, it's one of many, for you it's hopefully the only one you'll ever have."

And didn't that just sum it all up?

She was attached to him and he saw her as just another case. Never mind what they'd done to each other. This was professional. Even that silly dollar, it was because he felt responsible since it had happened at his grocery store, right in front of him.

So she cast a spell on herself before going to bed. She protected herself, her poor kittens left alone these long days, her home that she hadn't seen in nearly a week. Then she crawled into bed and passed out cold.

It was two a.m. when she woke up screaming—she didn't even know what from.

The door slammed open. Luke simultaneously blocking the wide beam of light even as he let it in. She could see the outline of the gun he held and Yasmin looked around for the source of his need of it for a moment before she realized it was all her.

"Was it a dream?"

He didn't move from that spot in the door. He could have been almost anyone, she couldn't see his face, though she would recognize his outline anywhere.

Yasmin nodded and, being the polite gentleman that he was,

he asked if she was going to be okay, if she could get back to sleep all right, then he closed the door.

Still shaking from the remnants of a dream she could feel but not remember, Yasmin took the lumps she doled out to herself. He didn't even come into the room as she screamed.

Luke's day was as frustrating as one had ever been.

He'd hardly slept. First because Yasmin had screamed and he had to play the professional. Police officers didn't hold crying women. Not ones that looked like that. Besides, that's what he'd done the first time she'd needed him—pillowed her head on a grocery bag, stared into her eyes and played knight in shining badge.

Then he hadn't been able to sleep because he felt like a tool. She'd needed someone to hold her. He wanted to. But as he sat on the stand—his day looking to be longer even than Yasmin's—he was almost glad he hadn't.

The lawyer was a sleaze of the worst kind. This was the kind of person Luke was always tempted to leave at an accident or say 'not much we can do' if his place got vandalized. Luke wouldn't *do* that, but he wanted to.

As the morning wore on, it became more and more clear that the lawyer had played softball with Yasmin the day before. Either that or he'd simply dismissed her as a source. For some reason he found a thread with Luke and he started picking at it.

Luke was pissed. He explained again the first time he'd seen Yasmin, right before Homeo's failed attempt at murder one. "I saw her in the produce section of the grocery store. She had two little girls with her. I thought they were her daughters; it turned out they were her nieces."

It was the vegetables that got to the lawyer. Luke saw that as the sign of an undeveloped soul. "Why was a bachelor in the produce department . . . Unless you were following the beautiful Ms. Ali?"

Luke blinked and kept his expression as bland as possible. "I was buying vegetables. I'm quite at home in my kitchen." Then he said something he regretted. "Would you like some tips on a proper diet? You look like you don't get enough vegetables."

It was stupid. Juvenile. And completely out of line. He knew it. The judge and DA knew it. But the jury and the audience tittered. And it made the defense lawyer pissy. Which was just as juvenile as Luke saying it in the first place.

He asked about the first shooting. Picked at the circle of blue fire Luke saw. And Luke shot back, almost coming out of his seat a few times. "I don't know what it was I saw. But several people saw it. How am I supposed to know?"

Forcibly he calmed himself. Reminded himself repeatedly that he told Yasmin last night that he was a professional. It was time he acted like it. The thing was, it wasn't just any case. It was Yasmin.

Several times the DA would object, and it got to the point where Luke would look to the prosecution before answering. What a farce.

He was asked about his one dollar fee, even though the DA had already clearly established that both precincts had approved, the fee was known in advance. Luke had to answer that no, Yasmin had not paid him in any other way.

And he hoped that his body language didn't give away anything about the lotto tickets sitting in his desk drawer. Because surely Mr. Sleaze Defense Lawyer here would assume Yasmin had whored herself to pay for protection.

That's exactly where he went.

Was there anything unprofessional at all about their relationship?

No. Thank god he could say that.

Did he have any feelings for Ms. Ali?

Luke looked to the DA with an expression that asked "Is this guy for real?"

The DA objected soundly and Luke felt like he was watching a tennis match as he turned back to the judge, then to the defense lawyer. The judge was in the process of laughing down the question and upholding the objection when Mr. Sleaze interrupted.

Though the judge clearly didn't like it, she listened.

"Mr. Salzone here—"

Luke gritted his teeth. He was in court and that was just rude. It was all he could do not to spit out "Detective Salzone." But he kept his mouth shut and listened.

"—has made a series of decisions and recommendations about the protection of Ms. Yasmin." Sleaze spread his hands out as though his meaning were obvious.

The judge was having none of that. "The woman was shot at. More than once and evidence points to your client. I'm not sure where you're going with this."

"I'm simply saying that he extended protection when the PD did not feel it necessary."

Luke's neck snapped as his gaze volleyed to the other side of the room. The DA was on her feet. "The PD did not find that protection was unnecessary, they simply did not have the funds to cover it."

"Actually," Sleaze shook a finger at her, the conversation having turned away from the judge who seemed to realize it but let him go on. "The PD ranked Ms. Ali's protection as not worthy of the limited funds they did have to protect high level witnesses."

The DA tried to hide her irritation and Luke tried to hide his, too.

"Ms. Ali's protection was clearly a proper decision and warranted by the number of bullets removed from her domicile

. . ." She went on to rattle off statistics and even got through some of it before Sleaze popped back in.

"Still, Mr. Salzone offered protection before any of that occurred and for just one dollar."

The judge popped in this time. "It's not unheard of."

"But it is rare. In part we believe Ms. Ali was in danger because Mr. Salzone convinced her she was. I'm simply trying to establish that his decisions may not have been solely based on her actual danger." Sleaze, attorney at law, stood before the judge, penitent with his palms out, up, as though it were all obvious.

Luke's heart beat faster. This was ridiculous. Yasmin had been shot at, repeatedly. Protection was clearly necessary. And it was his job to determine so at the outset. He'd done exactly that and he'd been right. He was ready to say so.

But the next question floored him.

"Mr. Salzone, are you in love with Ms. Yasmin Ali?"

CHAPTER 21

Frantic, Luke looked to the DA. But she only stared back at him blankly. He looked next to the judge, trying to look calm but clearly failing terribly.

It was his obvious panic that seemed to make the judge frown at him.

The DA had already objected and been overruled.

And she had gone over everything with a fine tooth comb. She'd asked Luke and Yasmin every question in the book prepping them for this trial that wasn't supposed to happen. Homeo should have pled out. Luke shouldn't be asked this. He'd done everything right. Dammit, he hadn't touched her, hadn't held her last night when she screamed out so that he could come in here today and say "No, nothing unprofessional ever occurred."

Instead, he wasn't asked about his actions. He was asked about his feelings. In his head a barrage of swear words careened back and forth. Turning to the judge he asked, "Can he ask that?" and tried to look nonchalant. He wasn't fooling anyone.

The judge told him to answer the question.

So he sat forward, faced the courtroom even though he looked into the middle space at no one in particular, "At the time of the decision to offer protection for one dollar, no, I was not in love with her."

The swear words in his head almost blocked the sound of the defense attorney asking a follow-up question. It was—of course—accompanied by a satisfied smile. "But you had feelings for her? You were . . . interested in her? That's why you noticed her in the grocery store."

Luke adjusted his tie, a nervous tic he couldn't seem to counter. "I thought she was married with two school aged children!"

"You didn't answer the question."

No, he hadn't. Taking a deep breath, Luke tried again. "Yes, I found her attractive. I think Ms. Ali's attractiveness is more a matter of fact than of my personal opinion though."

Sleaze walked back and forth across the open space bracketed by the judge, the witness stand, and the counsels' desks. This time he stopped in front of the jury. He spoke toward them, though his question was clearly for Luke. The fifteen people in the box, twelve jurors and three alternates, leaned forward. The case had just gotten good. Luke tried to ignore the fascinated expressions on their faces.

"Mr. Salzone—"

Luke snapped. "It's Detective Salzone." Though he didn't yell it, the words were sharp enough to make his point. Unfortunately, they also made the defense attorney's point: that Luke was on edge. This topic was a touchy one. That he'd hit a nerve.

The DA was sitting so motionless it was clear that she was trying not to put her head in her hands. She was actively searching for a spot to object, he knew it. But she didn't find it.

Sleaze started over, saccharine dripping from every word,

his tone as disbelieving as it could possibly be. "Detective Salzone, are you or are you not in love with Ms. Yasmin Ali?"

Luke breathed in. Looked up.

There she sat, several rows back like she always was. Watching him like he was a monster, mouth open, fangs inches from her face. Like a rabbit that—if she just sat still enough—might go unnoticed, or at least die quickly. There was nothing left he could do.

But he couldn't look away. "I am."

He could hear her intake of breath from where he sat on the witness stand. In half a second, she had popped up from her seat, drawing the attention of the jury finally away from him and his answer. But Luke wished they'd keep looking at him.

Instead, the whole courtroom watched as Yasmin fled out the door, the carved wood nearly slamming behind her as she made a grand exit.

Inside Luke seethed.

He'd done everything right. Dammit, everything.

And because Sleaze wasn't done with him yet, he was stuck on the witness stand while she fled.

Yasmin couldn't breathe.

What the hell had just happened?

The lawyer had just asked Luke if he'd made decisions about her safety based on the fact that he was in love with her.

When he'd started squirming, she figured he realized she had feelings for him and didn't want to embarrass her in public. Or else he thought the line of questioning was so far out of the line of reality that he just stared at the defense lawyer like he was stupid.

Then he said yes.

She couldn't breathe. But she tried to walk around like she

was a normal person. The L.A. County Courthouse had a paved central area for foot traffic . . . And food and coffee carts. She stepped up to one and ordered an iced fruit tea, just for something to do.

While the man behind the cart poured hot water, steeped her fruit infusion and scooped up ice, she tapped her foot and tried to control her runaway thoughts.

Luke had just destroyed her case.

Well, the sleazy defense lawyer had found a weak point and yanked it wide open. If they thought there was no evidence of her danger and that she and Luke had just been getting it on this whole time then Homeo might walk free.

She wondered how much it would count that her home had been shot up?

Clearly there was a danger to her. But if she couldn't prove it was Homeo and Doddo who had shot her home then they wouldn't get convicted.

It seemed like an eternity before the tea was ready, poured thick over ice pellets. She worried it in her grasp rather than drinking it.

Surely the case would be saved by the other witness? The man at the grocery the first day who would say he'd seen Homeo and Doddo. He had successfully picked Homeo out of a lineup. Doddo, too. She repeated to herself that the case was safe.

In a short time she had wandered the entire perimeter of the foot area. Any further and she'd have to cross a street. As silly as it sounded, she wasn't up for it. She was still under Luke's protection—his legal, paid for with a dollar and some lotto tickets protection. He wouldn't want her crossing the street.

So she sat on one of the cement retaining walls that held back raised areas of grass, trees and the occasional flower and doubled as seating space. And she let herself wonder at what Luke had said.

He was in love with her?

It was crazy.

And had to be a lie. Didn't it?

Maybe it made sense in a way . . . Given the way he'd acted—as though she was nothing more than a project, a task to complete. It made some kind of logical sense that he had acted that way because she was his charge and he had feelings for her that he couldn't show . . . But it still blew her mind.

It boggled the brain that she hadn't sensed any of it.

She'd been pining away for him, telling herself that he wanted nothing to do with her that he was just a nice guy when it was all there.

Finally, she took a sip of the cold tea and shed her sweater. It was one of those L.A. days that made people want to move here. Yasmin acknowledged that there was nothing that would have changed about her life, even if she had known about Luke.

As he'd said, it was all about the case. That if Homeo didn't get convicted she might always be in danger from him. Nothing could happen between them because Homeo had to get convicted.

While she sat and sipped at her tea, she reconciled what she knew. Luke couldn't even tell her how he felt. Doing so would compromise the case. It would bring questions to bear on all his decisions regarding her protection, regarding the threat the Del Surs posed.

However stupid that idea was, in the end it really didn't matter, did it? Luke had done a stellar job of keeping his thoughts and feelings to himself. Well, while awake, he had. He'd been so professional that Yasmin, living with him, had no idea he had any feelings for her at all. But the lawyer had picked up on something. And put Luke on the stand to say so.

She hoped it helped that Luke had acted nothing but professional. She hoped that it really mattered that Luke had been right. The Del Surs had shot up her home with her in it. A shudder involuntarily ran through her at the thought that Luke had saved her that night. Had he not thrown her to the ground, bullets might have taken her right out.

But now the case was the case. They had to finish it.

So Yasmin figured she couldn't say anything now. The more she thought about it, the more she wanted to throw herself into his arms and tell him she loved him, too.

Or maybe she'd ask first if he was serious? He had to be, didn't he? He couldn't lie on the stand.

Her happy heart suffered a bit of a dive. Luke sure hadn't sounded too pleased regarding his feelings for her. If he was in love with her but didn't want to be, or if he found those sentiments to be a burden then it wasn't something she wanted a part of.

She would have to ask him. Have to see what he said when the case was over. When it was just the two of them left standing. See if he meant it. See if he wanted it. If he really wanted her. Then she would decide if she should throw herself into his arms or slink off to cry for a month or two.

A strange noise alerted her that her tea was empty and she looked down at the cup, a bit startled.

With a sigh she looked up at the doors that led into the maze of corridors that housed all kinds of services for the public. She hadn't seen Luke or Jessica come out, but she hadn't been looking. Either of them should have seen her sitting here if they had come through those doors, though she wasn't sure that had been her intention. The DA might not recognize her right off the bat but . . . Yasmin figured they were still in session.

Another deep breath, another attempt to get the last of her tea from around the ice and she gave up. Standing, Yasmin headed to the trash can then figured it was close to lunch time and she was getting hungry. She tossed the cup into a recycling bin and started off.

Her thoughts remained on Luke as she headed across the open space. She wanted him to want her. Not to be put out by his feelings like it had sounded from the witness stand. He had looked pained in the telling of it, but Yasmin was trying not to judge. She couldn't say how she would have reacted had she been the one on the stand.

The sunshine felt wonderful on her shoulders and—maybe just a little—began to make up for the turmoil that was her life. She wouldn't even contemplate what things would be like if Homeo walked free.

Just as she thought that, she thought something else.

She was outside, not paying attention.

So lost in thought, she'd wandered away from any protection the building itself might offer. She was away from her champion, from the man paid to keep an eye on her. No one could have come after her without being held in contempt of court. She'd known it and she'd left anyway.

Stopping cold, there in the middle of the sunny day, in the middle of the concrete park, Yasmin turned and looked over her shoulder. It would not be unheard of for Homeo's gang friends to be here for his trial, would it? She had no idea how that worked.

But no one was there.

She wasn't being followed. And if someone was lurking, they were doing a good job.

Luke and Valverde weren't there either, so she thought for a moment. Standing there like she was, she was interfering with the flow of traffic. As the day passed into afternoon, more and more people were amassing in the front area for lunch breaks. But still, Luke and Jessica didn't appear. She couldn't stand here forever waiting.

So she turned back toward the street and had a clear shot of the car pulling to a stop.

Even before the door opened she was slapped backward by

the menace coming from the passenger. He slammed open his door and ran toward her.

Yasmin barely registered the squeal of tires as the car drove away. Her attention was held by the black gun aimed right at her.

She breathed twice before her brain or her instincts started to work. Yasmin wasn't sure which it was, but she didn't care. She drew the circle on the ground around her with her right finger, chanting her protection spell as she went.

It was Doddo with the gun this time. He was yelling at her though she couldn't really distinguish the words much more than "bitch" and "You won't do this". He seemed to think she was "getting away with something." And in her heightened, fully adrenaline-fueled state, she contemplated that, wondering where the hell he got off thinking that getting out alive was the equivalent of 'getting away with something'?

There was a bit of distance between the street and where she stood. She'd had the whole quad area to cover, but it seemed Doddo had recognized her from the passenger seat as the car had pulled up. And he closed the distance quickly even though she was carefully cataloging every moment.

She tried to make the gun hot, but got no response. Maybe it was plastic? She tried to push the air away from her, but that didn't do anything until something was coming at her. He hadn't fired yet.

Maybe he wouldn't.

Screams sounded around her, though they seemed to be in the distance. The noises of voices, the blur of other people receded in her mind and—she thought—in reality. They were leaving her standing in the middle of the open space facing down the gunman.

Then again, she was the only one Doddo was after. If she ran, she'd just pull his fire toward others. If he shot anyone it should only be her.

He was maybe twenty yards away now, having closed the distance quickly. His hand, the gun, were still toward her and his face came into clear view though she'd seen all along the rage that clouded his expression.

Yasmin held her palms out toward him, telling herself that he hadn't fired yet, when she heard the crack of the bullet.

Her head spun, looking first left then right.

Around her a cacophony of screams responded to the call of the gun and she was forced to look at herself to see if she'd been hit.

She didn't feel anything, but she knew that shock would keep her from being aware. She was just cataloging the lack of blood on her when she heard another crack as Doddo tried again.

The air ripped beside her face, but again she didn't feel anything. For a split second she thought that maybe she had died and simply didn't know it yet. That she hung suspended in that moment between when the bullet yanked the soul and the body crumpled. But she didn't fall and behind her a sharper, deeper scream answered back.

Doddo hadn't hit her.

But he had hit someone.

Furious that she hadn't stopped him, Yasmin screamed herself, only hers was a war-cry, full of power. Aimed at Doddo.

She chanted low and heavy words. "Demon go, return to flame, back to hell from whence you came." Over and over she repeated the spell to cast out a demon.

Doddo kept coming.

But he was having to work for it.

Where he'd come rushing from the car, gun aimed, he was now fighting through the thick air she conjured, having to push for every inch he gained. Yasmin held him back.

Despite that partial success, the gun cracked a third time, sparking more sharp screams and drawing her attention.

For a moment, he sprung forward, and Yasmin redoubled her efforts. She didn't even check to see if he'd hit her this time, she only yelled, her chants having risen in volume until no one within earshot could have any doubts about what she was doing.

"Drop your weapon!"

At first, she startled, thinking the call was to her. But Doddo looked to his side, so she did too.

A guard, an officer probably, had pulled his gun and was stalking up toward Doddo. Slowly he was swinging right, and it only took Yasmin a split second to see that he was lining up to pull the trigger in the place least likely to take out a bystander.

"Drop your weapon! This is the LAPD, we will shoot to kill."

This came from another side. Another officer, gun drawn.

Yasmin barely registered that it was a different uniform before a blur of color came between her and Doddo.

She smelled him before she recognized the size and shape of him.

Luke.

Suddenly between her and the man trying to kill her.

Unlike the other officers he didn't speak to Doddo. He breathed heavily through the words, "Are you okay?"

"Yes."

She, too, was breathing heavily, glad they had Doddo surrounded. Starting to see that it was coming to an end, her adrenaline began to seep out. Her breathing was changing to deep gulps of whatever soap Luke used, a comforting and deeply familiar smell.

Her eyes were drifting closed as she accepted that others were handling things when she heard Doddo's voice one more time.

"Bitch!"

There was a crack of a gun. Followed by a series of sounds signaling a volley of return fire. Somewhere in the distance more screams rent the air, vying for space amid the sharp retorts of the guns.

She watched over Luke's shoulder as Doddo's body jerked and flailed with the barrage of bullets entering his system. He was finally falling to the ground when Yasmin registered the sudden searing pain in her right leg.

CHAPTER 22

Luke woke up alone. The unfamiliar room coalescing around him in the darkness, the strange noises breaking through his consciousness and forming memories. Still the right memories didn't come.

Luke was miserable.

And it wasn't a state he was comfortable with.

Normally he was pretty happy. He was content. He liked food, good company and enjoyed the satisfaction of a job well done. He liked helping people. He had a disturbingly soft spot for well-behaved children and small, fuzzy creatures.

He understood and was used to frustration, anger and even sadness. He worked through each in his own way.

But this? This he didn't deal with well.

Finally he gave up and hit the call button, summoning a nurse in to give him pain medication. It wasn't the pain that bothered him so much. It was the frustration at the fact that he couldn't do anything about it.

The night nurse came in and asked a few questions, but didn't immediately give him the bump he needed. Instead, the man in blue scrubs checked every possible vital sign as though he were a student testing into the profession, rather than a real nurse. Then he said he'd be back and left Luke to stew in his own thoughts while he waited.

Bullet to the right leg.

That bastard Doddo had shot him in the leg. When his leg collapsed, Luke had apparently gone down firing. He'd hit Doddo twice according to the trajectory of bullets pulled from the man's corpse. He'd also apparently hit his head on the concrete.

Luke remembered none of this.

He was told, by several different people, that he'd run from the courthouse as though his ass was on fire as soon as he was released from testimony. Other accounts said he blasted out the front door of the building—he had no eyewitnesses telling how he'd gone through security on the way out, but Luke guessed it wasn't calmly.

He arrived on the scene between Doddo and Yasmin and inserted himself between them, right in front of Yasmin.

Given that he had his gun in hand and that he shot Doddo with it, Luke figured he'd gotten out through security somehow. But he had no actual recollection.

He'd even seen a video someone had uploaded online. He could see himself running. Yelling for Yasmin to get out of the way. She didn't even react.

He had stood right in front of her, just as he was told he did. And Doddo had kept coming. The video didn't capture the circle of blue fire, the pulse of air . . . But he knew they were there because—even given the distance from which the video was shot—he could see her hands moving, see her lips chanting.

He watched the video over and over, hoping to recall some of it. But none of it came back. Being conked on the head would easily remove recent memories. All the doctors told him this. And they all told him that he may or may not ever remember.

At the end of the video was Doddo doing his final dance.

Luke had seen it on film in training—a man jerked and pulled oddly as a body absorbed gunfire—but he'd never seen it in person.

Well, given his memory loss, he still hadn't.

The video hadn't captured his own shooting. He was told his blood would be cleaned off the courthouse square before he would be able to get out to see it.

He was the only person Doddo had hit. Which was why the other officers had held their fire. Adding to gunfire wasn't wise, not until it was deadlier to hold fire. But Luke got the distinction of being the only injury.

While it was a bad injury, it could have been much worse. Apparently the bullet had slowed miraculously as it had entered his leg, stopping at the bone and pressing against his femoral artery. The surgery to remove it had been dicey, the doctors had all come in exclaiming that the bullet should have shattered the bone given the close range. It should have gone right through him.

But in the video, not only did he spot Yasmin's mouth and hands moving, but also he saw that Doddo seemed to be fighting elements that were only against him. It was as though he was going uphill and very heavy. Commenters on the video speculated what disease the shooter had. But Luke knew what was going on. Yasmin had slowed him down. She couldn't stop bullets but she'd possibly saved his leg.

Rehab was still his next stop. But he knew it could have been worse.

The bullet could have hit Yasmin.

It should have gone right through his leg. By everything he could see on the video, that would have then gone right into Yasmin. He was more than happy it wasn't her.

So he would lay in his bed and wait for the night nurse to bring him something to put him back to sleep. And he would be glad it was him and not Yasmin here.

He hadn't seen her.

Five days. Touch and go surgery—the doctors marveled, thinking that the bullet must have nicked the artery. They had readied for a possibly fatal bleeder as they pulled the bullet from him. Instead, it had merely pinched the vessel slightly and come away cleanly. No complications.

Thank God. Everything else in his life had come with complications.

Yasmin visited frequently, but never when he was awake. Luke was beginning to think that was by design.

His mother and father took turns sitting with him as though a grown man needed company to watch TV and read manuals. At least they brought his laptop. He answered emails. And some he didn't answer because he was pretty sure he was somewhat high most of the time.

Several of the detectives from the unit had come by. A couple had praised him or expressed jealousy over his getting to jump into gunfire and save the girl.

Since he hadn't seen the girl in five days, he was about ready to tell them he, too, wished it had been one of them.

Valverde had stopped by several times. And she brought news.

An officer had been upstream of traffic and had witnessed the drop-off when Doddo came out of the car at the courthouse. This officer had followed the car, recognizing it from one of Luke's earlier BOLOs. And the two guys they pulled out of the car had cracked like nuts.

Clearly not hardened gang members, and clearly not ready to do hard time, they had rolled on everyone. Valverde grinned like a schoolgirl. These two nailed Homeo to the wall, collapsing the remainder of his trial under a deluge of evidence. They put Doddo at the shooting as well—not that the information changed anything for the dead man. And they coughed up some evidence associated with another shooting, thus helping to do enough to bring down the Del Surs. They did it in exchange for lessened sentences in a lower security prison out of state. The DA also demanded gang tattoo removal.

Luke thought it was a fair deal.

Luke was mostly happy that Yasmin would get her life back.

Luke was happy when the night nurse came back with that horrible little paper cup with the little white pill in it. He tossed it back and let the crazy come at him from the edges.

He would fall asleep soon, he knew. But in the meantime his thoughts would dodge and fall apart. Though he'd held it off while he had control of his brain, now his heart sank at the memory.

The last thing he knew before waking up in the hospital post surgery was being on the stand and having to answer that he was in love with Yasmin.

Clearly, he could see her face, startled, shocked. He would re-watch her stumble to standing and race out of the courtroom, the door sawing in the void she left.

He saw it play in his brain three times, four, before the blackness came closer than just the edges and overtook him.

She sat by the bed, watching his sleeping form, wondering if he'd think it was odd that she was here.

Yasmin had been here plenty. But she'd always managed to be here when he was asleep. And he was asleep a lot it seemed. The bullet had left a dent in his bone—though it was lucky it wasn't more, it still hurt. Not to mention they'd filleted his leg so they would have access to the artery that the surgeons had firmly believed would burst and gush as soon as they dislodged the bullet.

Luke's artery had done nothing of the sort. Though Yasmin was proud that the bullet was slow enough not to have shattered the bone or given him a life-threatening artery tear, it didn't change the fact that the surgery had been almost as damaging as the bullet.

She could feel it.

When Doddo had shot, Luke had been in front of her.

She'd felt the bullet so clearly that for a good number of minutes she'd been convinced that she, too, had been hit. But Luke had dropped like a stone in front of her and she worked around the shooting pains radiating up from her right leg, in an effort to save him.

All she knew at the time was that Doddo fired and Luke dropped. For several heart stopping seconds she was convinced he was dead. And that it had happened because she hadn't slowed Doddo enough.

Her feelings for Luke hadn't diminished, but there wasn't much she could do. He was in here. Out cold most of the time. She also had heard the reports on his status. It seemed the knock to his head—which she could still recall with a sickening clarity—had taken out some of his short term memory.

It was a pretty common phenomena apparently. A psychologist had come to check on him, and found Luke asleep while she was keeping watch several days ago and informed Yasmin all about it. This woman believed it was self-preservation against the scary moments that led up to whatever got us knocked on the head in the first place. She said it was incredibly common in shootings with head injuries, car accidents and even in faintings if the person hit their head.

What she wouldn't tell Yasmin was how far back Luke remembered.

That was the fifty-thousand dollar question.

Yasmin told herself that she didn't sit here every day and wait for him to wake up so she could ask him that herself. But she didn't think it was all altruism either. Though mostly she just wanted to see his blue eyes smile and know that he was okay.

Maybe the knock to his head had completely erased her from his memories. Unlikely, but she'd contemplated the possibility. Maybe he'd simply changed his mind or his heart. She would deal with that if it had happened. Mostly she wanted to look at him and have him look back at her and know that he was all right. She could live with that.

So she sat, and read, and stepped outside of the room when his mother came to check on him.

She was immediately engulfed in a big hug and—if it were possible—bigger smile. "You're a good girl, checking on my Luke like this."

Then Mrs. Salzone held her at arm's length and smiled knowingly. She nodded once before beginning a normal conversation as though Yasmin was not left thoroughly uncomfortable. "How is he doing today?"

"I don't know. I haven't seen him awake since he got here." She knew he woke up sometimes. He stayed awake, spoke to visitors. Everyone else had managed a conversation or more with him, but not her. Not the one who really needed answers. "I come in the mornings before work when I can, and I tried the afternoon on my day off."

She shrugged. It hadn't worked out. She'd been able to stay several hours each time. At first it seemed like a coincidence. Now she was getting to the point where she was about to pinch him to be sure he wasn't faking.

Yasmin had heard the update from Valverde. After the shooting, she'd immediately been taken into protective custody at the station. Apparently a second point blank murder attempt was enough to finally create enough need to expend the necessary budget for protection. Yasmin wasn't mad about that. Luke had explained it all—the budget problems, the issue that they hadn't been able to explain who might be after her or even if there was a credible threat. Not until her home had been targeted, and by then, she had protection firmly in place. The city couldn't afford to provide it while she had a viable option. Luke explained that she could throw him off and the city would pick up the tab, but her restrictions would be severe and he wouldn't be able to say where they would take her or what might constitute her 'safe house life'. She'd been okay with it.

She was even quite sure she'd made the right decision after Valverde had taken her in. Being kept in an interrogation room for several hours with only her phone for company and Valverde checking in on her when possible. She ate chips and soda from the vending machine when an officer became free to escort her. Luke had been right about all of that and she'd like to tell him so.

Eventually she'd been cut loose, after Valverde told her about the other gang members who'd turned. They were in jail now on their way to a plea bargain and time in another state. Homeo was in jail now, and the trial was essentially over. Sure, Homeo and his lawyer could continue with the proceedings, but the case stood less than a zero chance of Homeo being exonerated. The two members had all kinds of information on activities the Del Surs had been involved in. So continuing the trial would only cost Homeo his chance to plea bargain.

Yasmin was free. Finally.

But she didn't feel like it.

She felt like she was wooden. Getting up in the morning and going to the hospital. Checking on Luke. Some days she sat around and waited for him to wake up. Some days she saw that he was out and didn't have the heart to just wait.

Hex and Voodoo seemed none the worse for wear, though Valverde had to let Yasmin into the place at two a.m. after Luke came out of surgery, after the gang members had turned, after everything was done.

Yasmin had found what little energy she had left and packed

up her kittens, their things, her things, and even cleaned a little so Luke would see she'd left the place better than she'd found it. Then she'd woken Valverde where the woman had fallen asleep on the ugly couch and had her drive Yasmin over the hill into the valley.

The roads were never as clear as at four a.m. though they could clog even then. There was no predicting traffic in L.A. Other places in the country the weather changed and affected daily lives. Out here, it was the freeways. The weather itself rarely offered anything other than a few degrees of temperature difference.

So she slept quietly in her own bed, kittens usually piled on top of her. She woke up to them mewing in the morning as she now left her bedroom door ajar thinking that would save her from their morning cries of hunger.

No, it just changed them from 'let us out, we're hungry' to 'we went out and ate all our food and now we need more'.

She taught her class, happy to have that back on schedule. Though she identified two promising students, she didn't have the joy for it she wanted. It would come back, just like the life would come back into her house.

Bullets hadn't stopped anything, they'd just slowed it down it seemed.

They had sure slowed Luke.

She knew he slept a good number of hours each day. Between the meds and the lack of things for such a go-getter to do, she wasn't surprised. But statistics suggested she should have caught him awake at some point. Instead, here she was, standing outside his door with his mother hugging her and giving her that look that said she knew more.

Yasmin wanted to press her for details, but she didn't. Whatever she heard, she needed to hear it from Luke. So she told his mother that she had to go and left the woman sitting at his bedside just as she had done for the past thirty minutes. Only he would wake up for his mother, Yasmin was certain.

Covering the distance from the hospital deep in Los Angeles to her home over the hills in North Hollywood, Yasmin thought long and hard. She wouldn't go back to the hospital. Luke seemed to not want to wake up for her; she was clearly wasting her time and gas.

She entered the house to two small, fuzzy black creatures winding their way around her ankles by way of greeting. She didn't have to be at work today at all. She could have waited Luke out, sat by his bedside and been stubborn.

She didn't really think that would work. So she pulled out her mat and her materials and she started with simple protection spells.

Yasmin hadn't cast on Luke; in general she didn't cast on anyone who hadn't given her specific permission. So she went with something general, she cast to the universe for her permission since Officer Multicolor wouldn't wake up and give it.

Then she cast protections for Luke. She offered him faster healing powers. Anything she could muster. And the air swirled around her, flickering the candles, making tiny waves on the surface of her dish of water, all while Hex and Voodoo politely watched.

CHAPTER 23

Two weeks since he'd been shot and Luke was sitting on his couch, staring at his laptop, debating hitting the 'send' button.

Left to his own devices, he was limping—badly. He had a crutch he could use, but it was one of those handicapped ones with the single metal shaft and the arm cuff above the grip. It sat —unused—propped in the corner of his living room.

Instead, he'd opted for a cane. The staff had suggested one of the silver, four-footed kinds for stability. Luke had taken it and had his brother drive him first to an eclectic store where he purchased something wooden and left the silver, old-folks-home monstrosity as a gift for someone who needed it. He did not.

Still on medical leave, Luke was about to go positively insane. That bullet had changed everything.

One minute, he was over-crowded, spending every waking moment either at work with his usual too-full load of cases and court appearances and every home minute on duty with Yasmin. At home he was torn between keeping his hands off her and keeping her safe. He managed that. But just for numbers, when he added in driving her around on top of his normal commute, it was a wonder he had any time to sleep. Then, a bullet to the leg and suddenly he's on medical leave. Stuck in a hospital bed, unable to do . . . Anything.

Yasmin was now safe, which was good, but Luke was left at home by himself. Unable to drive, and unable to work, and about three inches from getting declared clinically insane.

His siblings were taking turns taking pity on him. He'd never been so grateful to be from a large family. Giada had offered to come over and cook for him, but he'd begged her to take him back to her place. At her apartment he'd hobbled up two flights of stairs then breathed heavily for about an hour. Not from the exertion but from the waves of pain he refused medication for. He'd spent enough time loopy, thank you.

In case it wasn't bad enough that he'd confessed his love for his client in front of God and all, and on a stack of bibles, he spent nearly a week so doped up who knew what he'd told people. The only good news was that no one would believe him.

Giada had stuffed him with French cuisine before returning him home to sleep it off. He woke up hours later in the dead of night petrified he was going to turn into one of those lumpy men he saw if he kept letting people take him out to eat while he couldn't really exercise. He did about fifty baby pushups from his knees before even that got to his thigh.

The doctor told him he was healing miraculously fast. But to Luke it was still far too long. He got Donny to take him to the health club where he did every sitting exercise he could find and became afraid his ass would form into the shape of a seat.

One day, so bored he could cry, Luke hobbled to the bus stop, the cool cane not nearly enough help, and took the bus down to the precinct. His chief informed him that his job was waiting no matter how long his healing process took. When the chief quoted what he'd found on the average time, Luke felt the blood drain through the soles of his feet. He almost literally swayed.

If he was out of work that long he'd . . . Go numb? Learn to knit penguin sweaters? Mastermind a criminal organization and wind up on the other side? He was suddenly grateful the doctor had told him he was healing quickly.

That day, Valverde had taken pity on him and driven him back home. She managed to do it without acting like she was taking pity on him. Luke was grateful.

In all that time, he hadn't seen Yasmin. Not once.

In full combat with his overall sense of boredom and ennui, was the decision he had to make.

He'd read the email in the hospital and had been smart enough not to respond while he was stoned on pain meds. Hell, Luke hadn't even been sure he was reading it correctly. But he'd read it three times.

The DEA had offered him the spot. They had invited him to Quantico to train as a Special Agent.

It was a dream come true for a man who'd worked hard to get there. To pass all the written tests, to build his resume toward that one goal, to have been rejected in the past—which did sting a bit even if it was the norm.

The kicker had been that the man who applied was not the man who got the letter of acceptance. The man sitting at his desk now was nursing a bullet wound in his leg and couldn't pass a physical for elementary school let alone the DEA.

He'd nearly cried when he'd written the return letter to that first acceptance. Luke had been forced to say that he would love to accept but had taken a bullet to the leg, was recuperating . . . Blah blah blah.

That was it. He was sure they would tell him to re-test on the physical test next year—if he was up to it—and then he could re-apply.

Instead, they had shocked him by asking for his medical

records and expected recovery time. They needed agents with his background. So he'd sent the material in waited. Just this morning he'd gotten a reply. And Holy shit, he was on the way.

So three days ago, he'd stumbled to the bus station and ridden to Sacramento. There he'd had one goal: go to the lottery commission and cash his tickets. Instead, he had a check that would be coming in six-to-eight weeks. Every time he thought about it, he sighed.

Not that it mattered. While on medical leave, he was still drawing full pay, so he was fine where he was, except for the mind-numbing boredom.

Today, he wasn't bored though.

Luke hit 'send' on his acceptance letter. A moment later he had to remind himself to breathe. They believed he'd be well enough to enter the second class coming up. His new recruiting officer even said they had hoped Detective Salzone would be attending the training starting in three weeks, but clearly that wouldn't work given his injury.

So in nine weeks, he would be cleared to sit in class and work toward the physical goals. He would have to make the certification requirements by the end, but it was an eighteen week training program, he would have plenty of time to recover and get up to speed.

Staring at the screen didn't do him any good, and he didn't have much else to do . . . So he got dressed. He used his cool cane to hobble very uncool-ly to the bus stop. It was slow going and he saw the bus pass him about a block before he got there. Since there was no way he was going to run and catch up to it, he simply resigned himself to waiting.

He could have gotten Savina or Arabella to drive him, but they both lived out of town. Savi had young kids, Bella had a job. And Luke had all the time in the world to wait for the bus.

While he waited, he contemplated his life. Knew he was doing the right thing, but knew his mother would cry. Still,

Donny and Giada had gone away for years for school. Savi had moved, following her husband for five years and had only recently come back to the L.A. area. It was his turn.

If he needed leverage, he only needed to tell her what had happened on the stand. His mom would understand that he both needed to get away and to follow his dream.

So he finally arrived a block from the precinct and headed in to wait for a moment with the chief. Luke was gritting his teeth against the dull throb starting in his leg. Radiating outward, the pain made his leg feel as though the bullet were still in it. He'd swallowed his allotted dose of Tylenol before he left his apartment. Though it felt like forever, it wasn't long enough to warrant another dose. So he thought about other things—like the conversation before him—and used that to keep his mind off the ache.

When the chief finally called him in, Luke had planned words. He knew how to say what he needed. But the chief only took one look at him and grinned. "You got in, didn't you?"

"What?" Stunned and at a loss without his prepared words, Luke could only stutter. "Um. Yes. How did you know?"

"It shows." His boss looked him up and down. "Will you stay on medical leave until it's time to head out to training? Or . . ." It seemed the man started to offer some other alternatives, then stopped.

"I have nine weeks. Then I head to Quantico." He shook his head in regret. "I don't think there's any way I could be fit for duty before it's time to go."

"Nine weeks?" Chief grinned. "I'm sad to see you go, but I'm happy for you. The DEA will be lucky to have you. Tell me it means a pay raise!"

Luke threw his head back and laughed so hard he literally almost fell over. Though given his cane and his bad leg he was always near to toppling these days. Tension he didn't know he'd been holding seeped away. He'd been ready to have a heavy talk with the chief about his need to move up, to not deal with the day to day of this paperwork, graffiti artists marking up his car, that kind of thing. He was ready for bigger problems, bigger solutions, bigger wins.

"Well, I'm behind you . . . except for one thing." The chief looked him square in the eyes and Luke felt the weight of the man's stare. "You have to tell Valverde. Now. Before she hears it from anyone else."

That was the right of it. With a salute, Luke thanked the man who had been his boss since he'd emerged green and ready from the academy and went off in search of the woman who'd been friend, partner and long-time sounding board.

Jessica did not bear the chief's dignified happiness. She squealed like a schoolgirl, so happy for him. She was a little younger than Luke, and almost ready for her own move up. Valverde just hadn't decided which direction of up she wanted yet. "You'll have to tell me what it's like! I may follow you in a few years."

"Or go FBI." Luke could see her doing it. She had the right demeanor and the brains. And he tried to give back the hug she threw at him, once again without toppling over.

He left the station happier than he'd entered. Though he had mentioned the DEA, and asked for recommendations, he hadn't realized the others had paid attention as much as they had. They had been ready for this day, maybe more ready than he was.

Still, he had one more job.

Another bus took him over to Highland, and he hobbled the slope as best he could. He was slow and foot traffic went around him. Luckily, foot traffic in L.A. existed only between one store and the next; Angelenos were notorious for driving any distance over two blocks. So he didn't have anyone too seriously held up by his snail-like pace.

When he finally stood in front of the door, he was toasty warm from the walk. Not quite uncomfortable, but ready for the artificial cool of the indoors. Realizing he should have checked first, Luke pushed open the door to Blessed Be, hoping Yasmin was on shift.

There she was, helping a customer choose dried herbs from a variety of bins. "Here's a binding tape. You'll want this . . . It's a little safer for beginners."

She didn't see him, or she didn't acknowledge him, he wasn't sure. So he hung back and watched as she rang up her customer. Just after the girl left, Yasmin looked up and caught his gaze dead-on. She'd known he was there all along. He could feel it. "Hi Luke. What brings you by?"

"I . . . Do you have a minute?"

She nodded, and pointed at his leg. "You're healing fast right?"

"Yeah, how did you—?" Oh, God, he was an idiot. "Thank you. There's no way to thank you for that." She'd done it. Of course she had.

"Oh, I think pushing in front of me and taking a bullet that was meant for me more than covers anything we might owe each other." She motioned to where they could stand near the back of the now empty store, seeming to just know that he'd be happier standing and leaning on the counter. She didn't even offer him a seat. "Actually, I think the balance is still in my favor."

He nodded, wondering what else she might have pushed through for him. But he had a job here, so he sucked up his fear and started. "I came to tell you that I'm sorry."

"About what?" She began toying with a stack of inventory papers on the counter, those amazing curls fighting to cover her face. He didn't know if he should push them out of the way so he could see her or if it would be easier to let her hide.

"About what I said at the trial. I don't remember running outside. Seems the knock to the head took out all that memory. At this point the doctors said it was a crapshoot whether I'd ever get that memory back." He was babbling. He was off track. Luke steered it back. "I do remember what they asked me on the stand, and I do remember what I said."

She nodded. But he still didn't see her face.

"I'm sorry." He sighed. He didn't know what to say, how to make it right. It seemed almost like stalking someone, that by falling in love with her and keeping her close and not saying anything, he'd somehow infringed on her personal space. "I didn't know how to say anything to you, and anything that happened would have compromised the case. So I never said a word . . . And the case got compromised anyway."

She looked at him. Whiskey eyes, smooth skin, no expression. "And you're sorry."

"Yes. I just wanted you to know." But she didn't say anything else, so he filled in the gaps. "I heard you came to visit me several times at the hospital. I'm sorry I wasn't awake."

"Me, too."

But the conversation dropped off to nothing and he said a hasty goodbye even if he couldn't make a hasty retreat.

Yasmin watched him leave. Clearly miraculously fast healing wasn't fast enough for a guy used to being on the move.

While he admitted to what he'd said in court, he also apologized for it. Not really what she wanted to hear. A second apology for not being awake every single time she stopped by didn't help. There hadn't been a single word about wishing he could have visited with her.

Luke didn't ask her out. If their professional relationship had held him back before, there was no telling what was holding him back now. She wasn't his client and hadn't been for two weeks. There was no reason to believe she would have need of protection services in the future as the Del Surs in the area were all but gone and she didn't go around pissing off people with guns on any regular basis.

But Luke couldn't get away fast enough.

Which was a damn shame.

She was hopelessly in love with him.

And she'd never really kissed him. Sure she'd done far more while dreamwalking and it had felt real, had even to a certain extent actually happened. But it only embarrassed him.

Clearly she'd brought him to her with the spell. It was Tristan her net had caught after all. However, catching her true love, bringing him to her just to be able to watch him walk away? That was a cruel universe.

Her leg throbbed.

Right where the bullet had hit him.

It was no shock to her that she felt it. As Doddo shot Luke, Yasmin felt the bullet and even believed she was the one who was shot. Each time she came into any proximity with him, she felt the pain in his leg. She almost believed it was psychological—just a sympathy pain—but she'd felt it before she'd even realized what had happened. And today she knew he was off his pain meds and just gritting his teeth because so was she.

Wishing to tell him to take something, that she would drive him home, Yasmin had instead kept her mouth shut. Luke seemed to want little if anything to do with her. His entire visit seemed only to be about getting his need to apologize off his chest. So she let him do that.

The rest of the day went by with a mild layer of depression over it. Yasmin hadn't realized she held out hope that Luke was just recovering. Maybe he didn't want her to see him with a cane or something. And she'd created an elaborate fantasy where he walked in tall and proud and claimed her. Or asked her out. At least said in some way that he'd meant what he said on the stand.

Instead she got this stilted apology and truncated

conversation. She saw his back as he walked away with no plans to ever see her again. The woman he claimed to be in love with just two weeks ago.

This sucked.

First Tristan, now Luke.

She closed up shop, still happy that she didn't have to worry about more than the usual after-dark in Los Angeles kind of trouble. She and Libby went to their cars, keeping only the usual eye out for each other, making certain that cars started and each other were safe inside before leaving.

Her home was another matter. Yasmin entered to the kittens rushing her. They didn't try to go outside, but that may be because she had enchanted the doorways to look unenticing to kittens. Hex and Voodoo wanted only to wind around her ankles while she poured their food then did only slightly more work to prepare her own meal. Hers was a full step above kibble but nowhere near what Luke cooked for her. Yasmin sighed. She needed cooking lessons. Delilah would do it. Her friend would take pity on her.

Yasmin considered casting on herself in an attempt to remove her feelings for Luke. She'd screwed it up again. Shouldn't she start over from scratch?

But neither Delilah nor Tristan would approve.

As much as that sucked, it was the hallmark for making those decisions. The Goodmans were raised in the craft, steeped in the old ways and trained to make the right decision, to work through what shouldn't be cast against and to understand that there were repercussions for using spells and magicks the wrong way.

Didn't Yasmin already know that? Hadn't she learned that herself?

So she sucked it up and spent her evening pining away for a guy she couldn't have, just like any other girl would. She ate ice cream. She watched bad TV. And she tucked herself into bed at a reasonable hour, reading herself to sleep.

She was shocked when the bed dipped beside her.

Eyes fluttering open, she found Luke smiling down at her. His hand reached out, brushing her hair away from her face as he leaned in to kiss her.

It had been so long since he touched her. She was certain he didn't want to. But here he was.

She kissed him back, wildly, fiercely, until she took a deep breath.

Pushing his shoulders back, she looked into those too-blue eyes and said. "No."

CHAPTER 24

Her heart beat fast enough that she thought it might jump out of her chest. Yasmin hadn't even gotten dressed.

While she'd decided at least fifty times on the way over to turn around and go back home, she hadn't. She came straight here and now stood with her hand up, but hadn't yet knocked on the door.

She said no.

But she wanted yes.

He was awake—maybe walking around—she could feel the pain in her right leg. Nothing too bad, it was definitely getting better. Still, she could feel it radiating up to her hip, down to her knee. It happened whenever she got close; maybe he was as close as the other side of the door.

Thinking maybe he was already looking out the peephole at her standing there, undecided, hand up but not knocking, Yasmin took a breath and rapped on the door.

He hadn't been looking through. She could just make out the uneven gait as he came to see who could possibly be here at three a.m.

Bad idea, she told herself. Bad idea. But it was too late to turn and run, too late to pretend she'd never been here.

In a flash of regret, she ran her hand over her hair. It was taking him a long time to get to the door. Of course it was, she didn't hear the cane. The lag gave her time to think that she should have brushed her hair, smoothed the curls down. She probably looked wild as she'd just pulled on pants and a t-shirt, no bra even. Yasmin stuck her arms through a hoodie and hopped in her car. She was partway here before she realized she was coming to see him.

The door swung open, interrupting her train of thought. Her breath caught. He looked good.

A little haggard maybe. A little less than clean shaven. A little under perfectly groomed, but really good.

His pants hung low on his hips, obviously an old comfortable pair of running pants, which made sense given the leg injury. His t-shirt was old enough to be almost sheer in places. She didn't—couldn't—speak.

Luke stood in the doorway for a moment, just staring at her, before he softly said, "Come in." Stepping back, he let her pass, clearly favoring the healthy leg.

Her heart still pounding, though she tried to look calm on the outside, she stepped inside only far enough for him to close the door behind her.

The nice thing to do would be to sit, to offer him a chance to get off that leg, but she didn't have it. Part of her wanted to be near the door, to be ready to bolt because she still wasn't really sure what she was doing here.

His voice cut through her growing panic. "You said 'no'. I respected that. Why are you here?"

Deep breath. "Because I don't want dreams."

Luke didn't look her in the eye and she didn't look at him either. This time he continued the conversation going nowhere. "I don't even know what that means."

He should. He should know what it meant. And the floodgates opened. She looked at him, through him, into him. "It means that I understood you didn't know what you were doing originally. Neither did I. And you quit once you did understand. But now you know what it is. . . I'm not your dream girl booty call."

Okay, that wasn't what she'd meant to say.

"That's not what I meant."

Yeah, this conversation wasn't going the way she'd thought. She actually harbored some idea that she would show up at his door and he would just kiss her, for real, in person. Clearly, that had not happened. "I got it that you had to keep things separate because of the case. I was crazy surprised by . . . What you said in court."

Luke only nodded so Yasmin continued on the roll she was on. "But you never spoke to me in the hospital. You woke up and talked to everyone else who came to see you. I went every day. Then you were out and you never said anything except that you were sorry. Sorry you said it? Sorry you felt that way? What?"

"Sorry that it disturbed you." He looked away again.

She was still standing in his doorway, still in jeans and an old t-shirt in the dead middle of the night. She nodded. It wasn't going to go well. So Yasmin delivered what she thought was here final volley. "If you want me, you have to want me for real."

Silence.

Just dead silence.

Turning, she put her hand on the knob to leave. She hoped she could hold it together long enough to get to her car before she just lost it.

"Real sucks."

Wow.

So he loved her but he didn't want to do anything about it?

She was shaking her head, and started to turn the knob, but his voice stopped her.

"I know how you respond when it isn't real. But real means I have no idea if you have any feelings for me at all. Real means possible consequences. Real means giving you the chance to get up and walk out and say 'thanks' and just go. Real means I have a crap leg that doesn't move well and I'm not the guy I can be . . . When it's not real."

She didn't look at him. It took enough guts to say it, so she spent all her energy just getting the words out. "If you want a dream girl, go get one. That ability, it's all you. You can have anyone you want. Not me. I'm . . . I'm crazy about you. I'm in love with you. But I want the real thing."

When he didn't say anything, she turned the knob. Only nothing happened.

When she started to pull, the door resisted.

An odd click directed her attention up, to the oddly placed deadbolts he'd installed. The ones that a criminal wouldn't look for because they were too high up.

He'd turned it. Bolting the door. Keeping her in.

Using the door for support, Yasmin turned to look up at him.

He looked upset more than anything else. "I can't carry you to the bedroom. I can't even keep up with you going down the hallway. I doubt I can function anywhere but the bed and you're going to have to do most of the work. My leg won't . . ."

She smiled. "I know. Take some Tylenol, it won't kill you."

"I don't need it." He shook his head. Typical response.

"Yes you do. I can feel it."

A sharp jerk brought his gaze to hers and he really looked at her for probably the first time.

"I can feel it. I felt it when it hit you—I thought I'd been shot. I felt it each time I went to the hospital and when you came to Blessed Be. Take some damn Tylenol." She sauntered into the kitchen to check the cupboards and returned quickly with the pills and a glass of water.

He watched her warily as he swallowed them. Then she shooed him down the hallway. It wasn't like she'd have trouble catching up.

It wasn't romantic, feeding him medication, waiting on his slow, uneven passage, but it was real. Her heart swelled. That unevenness was for her, from him taking a bullet in an attempt to save her life. She messed everything up and he unscrambled it, at a cost to himself.

When she finally walked into his room, she had a moment to look around before he reached the edge of the bed and plopped —unceremoniously—on the mattress. It was as though he was trying to ward her off, trying to convince her she was better with dream-Luke.

Dream Luke was awesome, but he wasn't there when she woke up. Nothing he said mattered in the light of day. And Yasmin wanted everything.

She slid alongside him, tucking one leg up so she could face him. A pose he could no mimic in his current state. For a moment they just stared at each other wondering what was going to happen.

Then he leaned forward and kissed her.

Full on for the first real time.

Quickly it went from tentative and sweet to passionate and driven. Though his leg wasn't overly mobile, there was nothing wrong with the man's hands.

Yasmin heard rather than felt the zipper of her jacket, and then she heard the sound of it hitting the floor. She might have gotten cold where her arms were bare, but his hands were hot and she leaned into his touch.

Luke peeled her shirt, leaving her bare to his gaze, then—without taking his eyes off her—clumsily pulled his own shirt over his head. This time when he kissed her, they were skin to skin. While she'd kissed him this way before, more than once, real was different. There was a depth of sensation that dreamwalking could never duplicate. There was a need in her that was satisfied that he was willing, even wanting her, in reality.

He was right, he couldn't take charge completely, couldn't balance himself the way he would if his leg could have borne the weight. She peeled her jeans herself, then his.

They fumbled their way through their first condom and slept the night together for the first time.

She woke truly in his bed, naked beside him and aware of the dull ache in his leg.

Yasmin smiled at him then made a face—she had been responsible for his overexerting himself. "I'll be right back."

She popped up, naked and happy and he pointed her to the extra bottle of Tylenol on the bathroom counter. She brought the pills back and tried to refuse him when he reached for her again. "I don't want to hurt your leg."

"Then don't." His grin was lethal, reaching up to deepen the bright of his eyes and down into her soul—grabbing her and holding tight.

They made love again, this time more adept at working around his injury. This time she held on fiercely after, knowing that he wouldn't disappear when she closed her eyes.

Falling back asleep was easy. Luke was worn out, still healing. She'd been up a good part of the night, woken by Luke in her dreams. It was noon when she pulled on what odds-n-ends clothing she'd brought with her and suggested she drive them to her place so she could shower and change.

Yasmin was off today. Luke must be on medical leave; there was no way he was going to work, even at a desk, with a bullet injury. They could eat a late lunch . . . She started making plans. Asked him about them and accepted a soul searching kiss before he slowly made his way into the master bath for a shower.

Thinking she was going to be a while, and unsure what to do —she could hop on his internet, but wasn't sure how he felt about her being on his laptop—she decided to watch TV.

Stepping into the living room, Yasmin stopped dead.

She'd missed this last night, too high strung to look around. Cardboard boxes lined the wall. Some closed and taped. They were labeled in Luke's neat writing. Books. Collectibles. Office Supplies. Computer Stuff.

There was a pile of clothing, still on hangers, stacked under an index card taped to the wall. Store at Mom & Dad's.

As she looked around, she'd seen what she missed. He had colored index cards, labeled and taped to furniture, cabinets, etc. Even his labeling was Multicolor. The couch had a card stuck into the back: Store. The coffee table said: Giada. As did the rickety TV stand.

He was moving.

Luke was slow in the shower, so she had time to think about it. It wasn't across town. He hadn't used the lottery money for a down payment on a house. She'd been there, he likely didn't even have the money yet. If it was just a new apartment, he wouldn't store his couch, his TV, his kitchen. He wouldn't give away the coffee table.

By the time he came out, dressed and ready, she was a ball of nerves. Luke's smile faded as he saw her, "What's wrong?"

She held her hand out toward his boxes, the categories that didn't make sense any other way. "Where are you going?"

"Oh!" He smiled, further twisting her heart. "Quantico!"

That didn't mean much to her. She'd heard of it, of course. "Virginia? You're moving across the country?"

This time his smile fell away, too. "Yes, but . . ."

Her chest froze, her lungs constricted and her vision clouded. She'd just gotten him. Flashes of thought of following him to the other side of the continent raced through her brain, but she knew she couldn't do it. She worked hard to build her own life here. But this life was turning out to be cruel. Finding out that Luke was the real deal, only to have him snatched away from her at the last minute was too much to take in.

Her feet started moving toward the door. She had to get out of here. She couldn't breathe.

Luke couldn't chase her but he tried. She could feel the bolts of pain shooting up his leg as he moved faster than he was supposed to.

But she figured if she could get far enough away from him she wouldn't have to feel it. She started a list as she was turning the doorknob. She had to feed the kittens. Clean the kitchen. She was out of cereal. She needed to call Shori and check on the girls. Why wouldn't the door open?!

The bolt!

That silly bolt over head where no one would think to look, including her, trying to get away. She was reaching up when he practically tackled her from the side. "It's just training. Don't go."

"How long?" Her heart was racing, afraid it was all over before it even started.

He sounded resigned. "Six months."

Her breath sucked in. "It's so long."

Luke's hand covered hers, and she caught a glimpse of orange track pants and a yellow shirt. Yasmin almost laughed in spite of herself. He turned her, pushed her into the corner where he could pin her stay balanced on his good leg. She didn't fight. She didn't have it in her.

"I don't leave for another two months. They postponed my entry so I could heal up and be ready for the physical tests."

Two months. That was good.

He was breathing hard too. In two months he had to be able to bound across the room (and do a lot more) with no pain—at least without any visible twinges. He would do it.

But she didn't have time to think about that, he was kissing her, killing her with the thought of losing him. When he finally pulled back, he rested his forehead against hers. "Are you in?"

"In?"

"Us? Are we a thing?" His eyes searched hers. "You said last night that you loved me. I love you. Are you in?"

She nodded fiercely. "Yes." Yasmin had no idea what she was agreeing to, but she agreed. The chance to have Luke was worth it.

"I haven't officially resigned LAPD yet. If you want, I won't go."

Holy shit.

Her eyes widened and she just stared. One night and he was offering to stay?

But it hadn't been one night. It was a lot more and she felt it. She'd cast for her true love thinking it was Tristan and she'd caught Luke. Here he was, offering to give up a chance at his dream, proving that she'd caught the right guy. "No. You go. We'll work it out."

"I don't know where I'll get stationed. But I already requested this area, and I know it well." He shook his head, "It's no guarantee."

She kissed him, her heart thawing, her breath unlocking. "Nothing is."

Luke laughed at her. "Me. I'm a guarantee. I wanted you from the moment I saw you. And it all went to shit pretty fast. But today I have everything."

Pushing up on her toes, she kissed him again holding his face to hers, feeling the length of him against her, reveling in the comfort and safety of his touch. "I can't follow you to Quantico—"

"I don't expect you to. I'll be in training long days, I'd have to free time for you. But we get chances to come home. Take breaks. I'm hoping to let go of the apartment. . . .could I stay with you when I—"

"Yes!" Her smile was genuine and reached her fingertips and toes. "And when you get assigned. If you still want to, I could follow you then." Her smile faded. Who knew where they'd be in another eight months. Many relationships didn't last that long.

But his voice was almost chiding. "I'll still want to. I'm all in."

CHAPTER 25

Yasmin told him she loved him and hung up the phone. She was proud. Luke was following his dreams, earning good marks in DEA training and enthusiastic about what he was learning.

He'd called midday—unusual for him—because he'd gotten his assignment. Calabasas. Not that close, but not far. He could commute. Or they could move a little further out and she could. He'd called again before bed which was more the norm while he was away.

Yasmin didn't realize she'd been holding her breath, afraid they would wind up in Nebraska or Alabama. But she was resting easier, a weight lifted, tonight. She assured Luke that she had talked to his mother. The woman had spent a happy half hour excited that her baby boy was coming back home. Yasmin had listened.

They were doing well. Really well, despite the distance.

So she followed her usual routine: invited her growing kittens up on the bed with her, read for a little bit and turned off the light around midnight. Her eyes drifted shut and she fell deep asleep only to feel the mattress dip beside her a few moments later.

She reached out and found Luke, reaching out for her.

Thank you for reading! I love romances with real love and believable characters, and I hope you found all that in these pages. I want to fall in love right along with the characters, and I do, while I'm writing it.

About Savannah

I started writing when I was eight--I hand wrote an 80-page novella that I believed to be (adult) romantic suspense. I'm proud to say, I've gotten a lot better since then. I've grown up to be a nerd at heart! I love neuroscience and people watching, and if you look, you'll find some of that in each Savannah Kade book. Most days you'll find me in my office, looking out my window at a handful of the neighbor's cows, or watching my dogs or my cat roam the backyard.

Follow me, find me, ask me questions! I would love to hear from you.

www.SavannahKade.com
Savannah@SavannahKade.com

www.ingramcontent.com/pod-product-compliance
Lightning Source LLC
LaVergne TN
LVHW091032080826
845145LV00002B/457